DEMONS

DEVIL'S REACH, BOOK TWO

J.L. Drake

DEMONS

Limitless Publishing, LLC
Kailua, HI 96734
www.limitlesspublishing.com

Formatting: Limitless Publishing

ISBN-13: 978-1-64034-917-9

DEDICATION

To my light side. We had a good run. I'm sorry.

PROLOGUE

I squeezed the clutch, rolled the throttle toward me, and switched into fifth gear. The wheels screamed as they tore at the pavement, blurring the colors around me.

I was pissed. They knew better than to pull this shit on my territory.

Traffic was heavy for midnight, but I managed to take the back roads and alleys most of the way.

The fire was high, which meant the match would soon be over, and my blood burned through my ears when I came up over the dusty hill. I'd been more than fair with these guys, but since they disobeyed a direct order, blood would be shed.

As soon as my engine was heard over the screams, the massive crowd jumped out of the way and let me swing my bike into the center of the commotion.

Both men pulled the savage dogs apart and dropped them at their feet.

I rested my bike on the kickstand and removed my helmet. A few people ran away, and others tried to see who I was.

I pointed right at the local drug runner, who mostly sold shitty weed, and waited for him to sweat it out.

"Trigger, man, I know what you said, but…"

I tuned him out and looked down at the pit bull. His throat was mangled, and he struggled to breathe and let out the tiniest whimper. A plea to end this shit.

He never asked for this life, never asked to fight to his death for a few hundred bucks.

I couldn't help but see my own reflection in his eyes. See the hate rooted deep, entangled to his core. No peace, only darkness.

"I needed the cash, man. My sister is in trouble, and my ma is strung out." The drug dealer tried a different angle.

I raised my gun and pointed it at the junkie while I whistled for Brick and Rail to remove the dog to a safer place. At least he could die somewhere peaceful, if only for a moment.

"What the fuck, man? He had another fight left in him."

I swung around and punched him so hard he blew back off his feet and landed next to the winning dog, who was foaming at the mouth.

The owner looked around while he fought to hold back the hungry dog.

"I said no dog fights." My voice boomed over the crowd. "Not on my territory."

No one said a word as I took the rope and pushed the owner next to the drug dealer. I leaned down and stroked the dog's back. He started to bark and whip around at my touch. Something I understood all too well.

"Go," I said simply and let the rope race through my fingers.

The crowd went still as the dog ripped apart the two men limb by limb. Blood covered his head, and screams flooded into the night.

CHAPTER ONE

Tess

"What's your name, sweetheart?"

I glanced up from my book and saw the man again. I had noticed him at least a couple of times over the last few days. He moved closer. He wore a suit and tie, but he pulled at his collar as if he were uncomfortable in it.

He sat forward on his stool and shifted it closer, and his Hershey-brown gaze held mine. He pushed up the spine of the book, and his brows rose.

"Nora Roberts? Isn't that a little old for a...?" He waited for me to answer.

"Ten, and no." I glanced around the room. "When you grow up here, mister, nothing is left to the imagination."

He smiled, and his mouth rose higher on one side. His hair was a little longer than most of the men in here, but it was styled as if each strand had its own place. "Fair enough."

I waited for him to leave, but he unbuttoned his

jacket and made himself comfortable. I went back to reading then felt his eyes on me again. I looked up to find him smiling, as if waiting for me to answer something I missed.

"What?"

"You never answered my question."

Huh?

"What's your name?"

I studied him for a beat before I finally let my guard down. "Tess."

"Nice to meet you, Tess. I'm Clark."

"You wearin' Spandex under your suit?"

He paused before he broke into a husky laugh, which immediately put me more at ease. "Yes. Is it showing?"

"You may want to fix your collar."

He tugged at it dramatically. "Better?"

"It'll do."

"Clark Anderson?" Rachel, the receptionist, called in our direction. "We're ready for you."

My stomach sank and reality came crashing down when I remembered he had an appointment at the house. He must have picked up on my mood, because he frowned before he rose and fastened his coat.

"Have a nice day, Tess."

"Yeah." I broke open my book and sank back into a fantasy world where everything was okay.

The door opened, and there he stood, handsome as ever. He smiled at me and leaned against the doorframe. I never thought I'd be back in this position again.

"Clark."

"Welcome home, Tessa."

His smirk rose on the one side as his gaze dragged down my front then snapped back up to my face. He looked smug, as always.

"Guess I won the bet." He opened the door for me to walk through. His chest was a little smaller than I remembered, and his arms had lost a little of their sexy curve. "About time you finally listened to me."

I rolled my eyes and shifted the heavy bag over my shoulder. "I'm not staying for long."

"You're not leaving again." He grabbed my wrist and turned me to face him. His expression darkened. "I'll make this work."

My insides twisted. There was a time when I would have sold my soul for him to utter those words to me, but now...

"I've heard your empty promises before." I eyed his hand, and after a beat, he let go. "You made your choice."

"It's not like that..." His voice trailed off when he saw a woman move forward to block me. "Felicia, look who came home."

My mother's face contorted with hate, as it did whenever we were in the same room. Her hands landed on her slim waist wrapped in a velvet corset and a gray silk robe that flowed about her with feather-like softness as she walked. This was the expected dress in the house—lingerie and heels. My mother was stunning and knew it. Everyone said we were sisters, and she'd reply, "She's older."

"You need money?"

There's my loving mother.

"Felicia." Clark cleared his throat and nodded at two men who stood within earshot.

I saw her pull her mask down, and her tone came out a little less harsh.

"If you're back, you work as one of the girls. I already have a shitty receptionist, and I don't need another."

I hid my sudden nerves. I once worked the front desk but was soon pulled onto the stage. Whenever there was talk about me working as "one of the girls," I nearly flipped the fuck out. I promised I'd never lower myself to my mother's level. No one was allowed to touch me on stage, and I felt safe, so now...my hand flew to my stomach as it took a dive.

When I started to speak, she shot me a look, and I swallowed my words. Now wasn't the time for this. Besides, the men were approaching us.

"Work or leave. Your choice, Tessa."

I cringed whenever she used my full name, but at this point, I had thirty-five cents and maybe some lint in my pocket. What was I supposed to do? Plus, I needed to know what Clark had on Trigger.

"Fine," I hissed, and Clark flinched. "I'm going to shower."

My mother dismissed me when she greeted the men, linking her arms with theirs to steer them away from me. Clark made a move to get in front of me, but I dodged and left him to deal with his new clients.

I was shocked to find my room was the same as I had left it, empty and over the top like the rest of the house. The walls were swathed in red velvet that matched the drapes and canopy. The black bedspread was satin and had fancy buttons that dimpled the fabric to give it a pillow-like effect. A shag rug lay at the foot of the bed where I stood feeling unbelievably lonely.

I dropped my bag and sat on the edge of the mattress. The idea of going backward in my life scared the shit out of me, but there I was, standing in the very spot I promised I wouldn't be again. This place had broken me more than once. I could only imagine what it would do this time around.

Laughter drew me out to the balcony. I saw Clark with his arm around my mother's waist as they showed the guests the pool, and then they moved off to where I knew there were underground personal hot tubs reserved for the VIPs.

I rested my arms on the marble rail and let my mind wander.

It all started out with warm smiles and conversations that made me incredibly happy and sometimes made me blush. He often came into my room after dark. He would close the door and sit on the edge of my bed and pay me compliments. He was such a gentleman then.

"You have such pretty eyes, Tessa. They're like little gumdrops with a sugar coating." His hand would gently brush over mine. He would talk to me about TV shows or music. He would ask questions and listen to my replies like he was really interested in what I had to say. He usually stayed about an hour, and as he left, he would always turn and

repeat the same words as he went out the door. "I love that we have secrets, Tessa. Secrets mean we're close, and I want to stay close to you."

I craved attention from him, and maybe I knew deep down inside that it wasn't right to have a much older man as a friend, but I didn't care. The world I lived in was all about sex, and had been from day one. I knew a lot for my age, and I wasn't stupid, but he wasn't like the rest of the people here.

I wasn't wrong at the beginning. I never thought how it might look. All I cared about was that this man was paying attention to me. Finally, for once in my life, someone cared about me.

When I focused on my surroundings again, I caught Clark staring at me. I shook my head to clear my thoughts and turned to leave when I heard my mother snicker at him to focus on her.

He made his choice a long time ago. I was just too stupid to see it.

The hot water pounded against my skin as I washed away the grime from the Greyhound bus. Desert dirt swirled around my feet before it flowed into the drain, leaving me behind. I moved my fingers around my ribs and felt how sore they were, then probed my lower stomach, which hurt like crazy too. Blue and yellow still marred my flesh, and I wondered how long it would take for it to go away. Everything was so fucked up...what the hell happened? My throat constricted, and my eyes prickled.

"No." I pressed my hands against the cool tile and forced my head anywhere but there. Trigger's wild eyes flashed in front of me, and my guts twisted.

"Stop." I breathed through the tears to control my emotions.

Just as I was about to open the door to my bedroom, I heard another door shut.

"Hello?" I tightened the towel around my chest. "Mom? Rachel?"

Nothing.

I stepped into the room and glanced around. It appeared to be empty. I needed to remember the number one rule of the house. If you weren't entertaining, you locked the door to your bedroom.

With the remote in my hand, I turned on some music to help drown out my thoughts. Chris Stapleton's "Fire Away" softly flowed throughout the room, easing the nerves that had attacked my stomach.

Suddenly, I honed in on a dark blue corset with black ribbon and lace that was laid out on my bed along with a pair of heels. So, I *had* heard an intruder.

"Shit." I ran my hand along the garter clips then noticed my jeans and tank top were missing. I whirled around to see my Chuck Taylors were gone too. "No!" I swiped my bare foot under my bed and caught the strap to my bag that I had slipped under there earlier. Tugging it free, I clung to it as I searched for a safe place to keep it. My hand cupped the heavy grip through the fabric, and I hoped to God the safety was on. I pulled on the armoire and freed it from the wall and peeled back the paneling. My secret place. When I was younger,

I found this little space when the painters were working on my room. I used to hide all my books and cash there. My bag fit perfectly inside, along with my beloved camera.

I hated this place.

I glanced in the mirror one last time and recognized my worst nightmare. I had become my mother. I cringed and closed my eyes. This was only temporary. I tried to use my fingers to soothe the achy spots, but the bone inlay of the corset didn't help.

Draping the cool silk robe along my arms, it rested around mid-thigh and flowed around me like a cape. I knew it was only a matter of time before someone came looking for me. Better to save face now than look like I was hiding.

I shook off my nerves and headed downstairs.

***

Trigger

Two weeks later

Radiohead pounded through the slaughter room. The beat vibrated through the bottoms of my feet, up my legs, and filled the dark space inside my chest.

The three men who sat across from me had been stripped of their clothes and sat naked in a line. Sweat dripped from their foreheads and settled along their brows.

"Choose." The word eased off my lips.

11

The first man shook as he glanced at his options. His skinny fingers skimmed over the lineup of weapons.

In front of them were a hunting knife, pliers, bleach, a gun, and a pair of brass knuckles.

He tapped the gun and closed his eyes.

I raised the pistol and blew a hole in the center of his face.

One down.

The second started to cry. His chest pumped in fear, and his hand rubbed the side of his head.

"You had your chance to leave, but you didn't." I placed the gun back in the lineup and sat back, waiting to see what he wanted. I couldn't care less. I was bored and wanted to feel something, but like the last few weeks, I felt nothing. "Choose."

"And if I don't?" he challenged as his bloodshot eyes searched the room for a way out.

"Then I do."

He knew better and looked over at his friend, who was in total shock.

"Fuck! Gun, the gun!"

I rolled my eyes and wished Brick hadn't suggested it at the last minute. I slid the weapon over in front of him. He looked up at me, confused.

"You do it."

"Me?"

"Five, four…" I started to count.

"This shit for real?" He looked at Brick, then Morgan, who both were behind me.

"Three, two, one." I snatched the gun away. "Now I choose."

With a flick of my wrist, I flung the gun off the

table and rammed the knife into his neck. I turned and used my momentum to kick the last guy's hand away from the brass knuckles. He screamed but stayed put as Brick held his gun to his cheek.

I twisted the blade into his jugular and felt it tear. He slumped in his seat, and I released him and turned back to the last pathetic excuse for a man.

I shoved the table out from between us and leaned down with my hands on the armrests. Hovering just above his shaky head, I waited for him to look me in the eye.

"Where's Mateo?"

His eyes closed as he mumbled a prayer.

Enough of this shit!

I snatched Brick's gun and shot the asshole in the thigh. He screamed, and I grabbed his sweaty head and yanked it back to look at me.

"Where's Mateo?"

"Ah!" he shouted, but I saw he was close to the edge.

"Matching set it is, then." I shot the other thigh.

He bucked and tried to slide off his seat, but my fingers found the gaping hole and dug deep.

"You like to fuck with me? Allow me to repay the favor." I fished around and felt bone fragments.

"Him and Tiago!" He huffed between screams. "They are hiding up north somewhere."

"Where?"

"I don't know!" He stared up at me, the skin around his mouth growing paler as the seconds ticked by. His eyes became dull, and I saw his soul packing up its shit to leave.

Fuck.

"Why did you stay behind?"

He squinted as he tried to form a thought. "They're not done with her yet."

I heard Brick shift his weight at the mention of *her*.

"Fine." I rose to my feet then pointed the gun at his head and shot him in the mouth. Blood drained from another hole in his body.

Silence fell. The only things screaming were the demons inside my head. My anger rose rapidly.

"Jace!" I barked. "Clean this shit up."

He and the newest prospect, Rich, started to push the human waste down the industrial drain with a shovel.

Blood dripped from the tips of my hair and ran down my face. I grabbed the razor we used to skin the heads and moved over to the mirror. I gathered the hair in the center of my head and lifted it up then buzzed the sides. I left the mohawk long.

Better.

I flipped my hair out of my face and spun around to face my men. They seemed unsure what to think.

"Like the new look." Rail said, trying to break the tension.

Gus nodded in agreement, but I caught him glance to where Morgan stood off to his side.

"Fuck, I would give my left nut to have Tess back," Rail muttered to Brick.

Brick remained silent, which was good, as I was moments from flipping my fuck switch.

I grabbed a bottle of whiskey on my way out and stuck it in my saddlebag before I kicked my bike to start the engine. The air was cold and whipped through my hoodie as the smell of the rain to come made memories come thick and fast about the last time it poured.

Her lips shivered, but her eyes told me she had a lot more fight in her.
"You're cold.
"I'm fine." She pulled the joint from my lips.

I shook that thought from my head and turned down a side street. I cut the engine and found Mud outside his surf shop.

"Evening." He grinned when he saw the bottle dangling from my fingers. "You want to keep going?"

I nodded and removed my hoodie and tossed it on the table, but carefully laid my cut on the leather couch away from the mess.

He motioned for me to take the chair. I flopped back and looked up at the naked posters that littered the ceiling.

Mud lit a joint before he spoke. "This new?" He pointed at his head.

I nodded.

"You want a glass?"

I wiggled the cap off with one hand and drank the neck before I set it aside. Mud huffed with a grin, and smoke poured out of the corners of his mouth. He tapped his phone, and The Black Keys' "Lonely Boy" played through shitty speakers. I eyed him, curious if it was meant for me, but he just clicked the machine on and went to work on my pec.

I focused all my energy on the needle that drilled tiny pinpricks into my flesh, but sadly, it didn't last long. The pain subsided, and I was left with my demons gnawing on my memories.

Nolan was nowhere to be found.

CHAPTER TWO

Tess

"Sorry, Tess." Venna, the only trustworthy friend I had left in this house, gave me a grim frown. She turned the computer around and showed me I had a four p.m. client this afternoon. I broke out in a sweat.

Somehow, I had managed to avoid being booked by complaining about the pain I was in from my stomach, and threw in being on that time of the month. Plus, Rachel still worked the front desk, and when I showed her my bruises, she felt bad for me. Of course, I kept the truth of what really happened quiet and only gave a vague story, which seemed to work better. Everyone loved a little mystery.

"You see who booked it?" She tapped the screen, her expression pissed off. "Seems kinda fucked up, if you ask me."

I glared at my mother's name. "She never thought of me as her daughter, anyway, so this doesn't shock me. All I am to her is someone she can pimp out to make money."

Venna's hand landed on mine. "Least you're getting booked. Felicia has me on probation for leaving."

"This is my punishment for coming back."

She bit the inside of her lip, thinking about something. Before she could say it, she stood a little straighter and tapped the keyboard to make the schedule disappear.

"Clark," she greeted him before she checked her phone.

"Ven, you look lovely today."

She blushed.

"That's right, you're a fan of red." Her fingers brushed down the front of her red corset. "I really need a new one. This is getting old."

"I'm sure that can be arranged." He glanced over at me. "I see you picked the blue one. Nice choice."

Internally, I rolled my eyes, but decided to treat him as I would any other man here. "Well, let's hope my four p.m. agrees."

His brows pinched together as he swung the computer screen to face him and hit the keyboard.

"Felicia booked it." I pushed away from the desk. "Time to pop the house cherry." I snickered as I left the two of them alone.

I heard him whisper, "That's not entirely true."

It took everything in me not to waver my step.

Wow.

Back in my room, my hands shook, and my heart beat to an unknown rhythm as I watched the time tick by. I didn't think I could do this. My stomach ached, and my ribs were on fire.

"Tess?" Venna slipped in and closed the door behind her. "How hard would it be to convince you to let me take your spot, and you can dance tonight?"

I nearly fell forward as I grabbed the post at the end of my bed.

Someone is looking out for me somewhere.

She came closer and noticed my pale face. "You okay?"

"Ven, I'll take any spot you want to trade with me."

"I need the money, Tess. I need to get the fuck out of here."

I so wanted to repeat her words back at her, but I would rather take a little more time making the money dancing than have someone stick their pencil dick in me.

"The appointment is all yours."

Her face lit up, and a sense of relief spread through me. "Just keep it quiet, okay?"

"Trust me." I waved her off and eased back on the mattress. "If my mother thinks I'm working here the way she wants, she'll leave me alone. My lips are sealed."

A knock at the door brought us both to our feet. Venna grabbed my hand and pulled me closer. "Get him set up, and once he's ready, I'll step in."

I nodded, and she disappeared into my bathroom. I walked on shaky legs to meet my client.

My fingers brushed my bracelets to remind myself to stay strong, and I took a deep breath and opened the door.

"You have no idea how long I have been waiting

for this moment, Tessa." Bret flashed his million-dollar smile at me then reached out and fingered the lace between my breasts. It was difficult to hold my tongue, but somehow, I managed. "Let's see if you're anything like your mother."

I want to puke.

Bret had been a member of the house for seven years, and had his eye on me for the last five. Of course, his wife and three children had no clue their daddy wasn't at the office. Bret loved the chase, and he continued to chase me because I sure as hell would not let that man poke me with anything.

I stepped back and motioned for him to enter. He slapped my ass as he strolled in and removed his jacket and tie.

"Top or bottom?"

My mouth went dry, but I managed to speak as I moved to my dresser and pulled out a blindfold. "I had something else in mind."

He reached out and hooked my waist, pulling me to him.

Don't slap him, don't slap him.

His long, bony fingers dug into my hips, bordering on painful rather than sexy.

"The kinkier the better."

I pushed out of his hold and patted the mattress. He complied willingly and obeyed my instructions.

Yuck. I hated a man who wanted to be told what to do. I wanted to be thrown up against the wall for passionate, animal sex. Trigger's face flashed in front of me, and I tried to shake the memory away.

He doesn't want you, Tess.

The cuffs snapped over his wrists, and satin ties

held his ankles in place. I straddled his waist while I slipped the blindfold over his hungry gaze. Turning up the music, I whispered, "Let me grab the oil."

He thrust his hips to grind his erection into my leg. I hopped off and hurried into the bathroom where Venna was prepping herself. Thankfully, we had the same length hair and were pretty much the same body shape.

"He's all yours."

"Is he big or small?"

I shrugged. "Depends on what you call big. Just be sure if he's in or not before you fake anything."

She laughed then headed out to the room, and I sank to the cool floor with a disgusted huff. It wouldn't always be that easy to avoid clients. I inched toward the counter and grabbed the phone Brick had given me. It was turned to airplane mode so it couldn't be tracked. My finger hovered over the photo app, and after a moment, I tapped the screen, and a ton of pictures flashed in front of me. I scrolled through and stopped at my favorite, Trigger standing next to his bike, reading something off his phone. I took it one morning as I rounded the corner to the clubhouse. He looked so real at that moment. The darkness that normally surrounded him wasn't there. He was just a man leaning against his bike before he started the day. Hell, I missed him. I closed my eyes as the pain lashed at my raw memories.

After I got Bret out of my room and had wiped his long kiss goodbye off my mouth, I hurried down to the back yard. I raced through the maze of high shrubs, down the little hill to the building where the strip club was nestled in a sea of greenery.

Dirty Promises was built twenty years ago and was one of the most prestigious strip clubs in Vegas. The membership alone cost more than most homes there.

I wiggled a pebble out of my shoe as I knocked twice on the big industrial door. Music, cigar smoke, and booze blasted me like a gust of wind as it opened in a hurry.

"Oh, shit, look who came back." Jarmon, the doorman, laughed and gave me a hug. "They always come back to the pole."

"Thanks, Jarmon," I muttered but surrendered to his hug. He was a good guy and always had our backs.

"Are you filling in for someone?"

"Yup, Venna."

He didn't ask any questions, simply pointed to her locker and told me to help myself.

The perks of having Mommy own the place.

I opened the door to her locker and sighed. "Really, Ven?" I grabbed the outfit and reached for the hook in the back of my corset when I felt someone bat my fingers away.

My gaze flashed to the mirror, and I yelped.

"You look like you saw a ghost, sweetheart."

Squinting to be sure I was right, I slowly lowered my arms. "Sean?"

"It's Shantee now." He—or rather, *she*—made duck lips in the mirror, admiring herself. She was stuffed into a shiny gold dress with a rack that would make Pamela Anderson self-conscious. A straight brown bob lined her jaw and made her silicone-plumped lips pop. Sean was never small as a man, and now that she had transitioned, she had lost some weight. I had to say she was now quite stunning. "Turns out Felicia has quite the homosexual client list. So, naturally, I stepped up and took one for the team."

"I'm impressed."

"Not shocked. You always were good with weird." She pulled my zipper down, freeing my ribs. I heaved forward with a wince.

"You okay, sweetheart?"

"Yeah." I felt around, curious to know if I did any more damage to them.

She pushed my hands away again and leaned down to examine the injury. Her drawn-on eyebrows rose in speculation.

Just when I thought I was going to be drilled with questions, she leaned back, grabbed her designer purse, and handed me a pill bottle.

"Take two now, two at bedtime."

"What are they?"

We both went quiet when I was paged that I was up next.

"Does it matter?" She snatched them out of my hold, dropped two in my hand, and gave me the glass of gin and tonic she had been nursing.

"Thanks." I tossed them back and pulled on the ridiculous outfit.

"Tess," she called out when I hit the first step to the stage. "I hope whoever did that to you got his ass handed to him."

I tried to force a smile. I pictured those green eyes staring at me from his cut. "He will."

"Glad you're back."

That comment had my stomach in knots. I didn't want to be back.

Dressed in a skimpy business suit and tie, I stood behind the curtain and waited for Justin Timberlake's "Drink You Away" to pound through the curtains.

I couldn't help but scan the crowd for his face, but he wasn't there. Of course, he wasn't. Trigger didn't even know where I was.

***

Trigger

I flipped the joint back and forth through my fingers like a drummer would his stick. My skin ached, and it aggravated my nerves. The smallest thing would set me off. I needed a reason to hurt someone.

Brick finally joined us in the meeting room. He mumbled something about not getting enough sleep. Gus glanced at me, and I knew what he was thinking. We needed to get past this shit if the club was going to continue to run smoothly.

"Anything?" I barked out at the guys. They all leaned back in their seats and looked around the room.

"My guess would be back in Vegas," Brick finally said, but he wouldn't look at me.

"I was referring to the asshole who rose from the grave," I shot back.

His head came up, and he held up his phone. "I

24

need to make a call."

I nodded for him to leave, but it was a shit excuse.

"It's like he dropped right off the grid again." Morgan tugged at his beard as he thought. "You think you can get some help from Blackstone?"

I was debt clean with the Blackstone guys, but given the situation, I might consider the idea.

"Gus," I turned my attention to him, "spread the word to the VPs. I want all the eyes I can get."

"Okay." He left with the phone to his ear.

"What about Fox? Are we all still lookin' for him too?" Jace spun his paper cup between his fingers.

I wanted Fox's head mounted above my office door for what he did to Tess in the desert. It took some digging, but the jackass was runnin' his mouth at a bar about how he beat up Tess. Once the word was out, I knew he'd disappear. Coward.

"Yeah, but I better be the last fucking face he sees."

"Got it."

Twenty minutes later, I shut down the meeting, not wanting to hear petty shit about Tammy being back. I'd deal with her myself when I saw her.

"Trigger," Jace stayed behind as the rest filtered out, "can I steal you for a moment?"

I lit my joint and swiveled my chair to face him. The smoke hugged my lungs while the THC absorbed into my system. I welcomed the hit as it momentarily tamed the demons. My mind played with the image of them as they hunkered down at the door of their cages, eyes wary.

"I know I'm overstepping here, but I want to look for Tess."

I sucked in a tight breath that came with the mention of her name.

He lifted his hands when he sensed my mood change. "Look, that girl was there for me when others didn't see me slippin'. Let me do the same for her."

Fuck. I rubbed my brow, more out of sexual frustration than anything else. I would give my left nut to have that chick back, but with my father back in the picture, it was a whole new level of dark.

"Trigger," he stepped closer, but I could tell he was scared shitless, "just let me make sure she's all right until you decide whatever it is you're doing or not doing with her." His gaze moved away from mine. "She's my friend too. I just wanna know she's okay."

I closed my eyes and inhaled deeply to take a moment to think this shit through. I wanted her here, next to me, safe. However, history had proved itself to be a bitch, and when I was near anyone I remotely cared for, they became a target.

"Jace—"

"Please." His shoulders tensed when he realized he blurted that out, but he went on. "Just let me see if she's okay."

I swallowed back the lash of words for interrupting me. I could see he was genuinely concerned for her.

I gave a slight nod, and that was all he needed before he broke out in a boyish grin and bolted from the meeting room.

26

Fuck me. I hoped that didn't backfire. I would be annoyed if I had to kill Jace too.

***

Sweat poured down my face, my hands ached, and my knees were like rubber by the time I finished my workout on the rooftop. I popped off the cap and downed my third beer and leaned over the edge to where Tess's old apartment was.

"Hey, man." Brick stopped me at my bike. "You know how Tess is coming in next week?"

I shrugged and clipped the buckle to my shell cap helmet.

"Look, I think she should have her own place. I wanted to rent out the room across from your building. You know, more eyes on her and shit."

"Yeah, fine." I started my bike, not thinking more of it.

"I think you'll like her."

"I don't really like anyone." I tossed the bike into gear and roared down the open road.

I dropped my bottle and watched how it shook from the wind and exploded in the garbage bin below. I wanted to know what she was up to, but at the same time, I didn't.

During the ride home, I couldn't get Tess off my mind. Jace's absence didn't help me keep my head on straight. I noticed his bike was gone when I arrived at the club. Just as I backed in, Big Joe was at my side with his phone out. He handed it to me and stepped back.

I hated that my body jerked with amusement when I scanned the encrypted email. To anyone else, it would look like a jumbled mess of codes, but to me, it was a second language.

First prize—a hundred grand
Second prize—fifty grand
First and second place winners
will move on to the semifinals.
Location revealed when winners are
announced.

I was intrigued, but fucking irritated he would hand me the one thing I promised I'd never do again.

"What, you think we need the money?"

"Nah, boss, I think you need the outlet."

Fuck!

I jammed the phone in his hand and went inside. Morgan had a full bar, and it was only eight p.m. Nice to see the business was picking up.

"Brick?" I shouted when I came behind the bar for a water.

"Out back in the gym."

Minnie blocked my path.

"What?" She had fire, but not the kind I liked.

Her arms folded over her chest, and she cocked out her hip. "When are you going to fix whatever the shit is between you and B?"

"Not now, Minnie."

"Yes, now. And go get Tess so you can get laid again, because honestly, you're a huge asshole

28

without her. And why the fuck is Tammy back? She could be the damn mole, for shit's sake."

Closing my eyes, I tried to calm my temper, which proved harder than I thought. When I opened them, I saw she had walked away.

Good.

The gym was stuffy and hot. We hated to use the AC when we worked out. Living in the desert, you needed to have stamina when it came to the heat. Couldn't fight if you went lightheaded. Shit happened, and you died.

Brick was bouncing around in the ring with Rail, who looked to have gotten hit in the face a few times. It wasn't a fair fight. Brick was stronger and leaner.

"Rail," I called out. He dropped his arms and ducked under the ropes.

I hopped in and raised my fists to spar.

"No." Brick sighed.

"Didn't ask." I smacked his shoulder and then his cheek.

"Why?" He flinched when I punched his arm.

"Fight back."

He rolled his eyes and took a punch at my face, but I ducked and kicked his knee. He yelped, but it fed his fire.

About fucking time.

He swung again, and I let him smoke my face. He saw through me and cursed. Physical pain was my drug.

"I hate that you made her leave."

"Wasn't my intention," I grunted. Dodging his hit, I sent a blow to his chest.

"You tossed me under the bus." He kicked my ribs hard.

"I did, but it was either that or have my father sink his claws into her." It was hard to hold back when I nailed him in the jaw with my foot.

He stepped back and spat blood from his split lip. He pointed his taped-up hand at me. "You know she loved you, and you fed her to the wolves like just another pussy that got too close."

I lunged and grabbed him around the neck, slamming him into the corner of the ring. A few of the guys rose, but Rail raised his hand to tell them to back the fuck off.

My fingers curled into stone as I drew my hand back. My heart pumped at a dangerous rate, and my vison clouded. My switch begged to be flipped, but I held it down. What he said sank in, and he closed his eyes with a frustrated sigh. I waited a beat before I let go and dropped my arms heavily to my sides. The demons screamed at me to rip his head off. Fucking animals wouldn't let up.

"She *is* at the house," Brick muttered, which made me whip around. "I just got a call from a friend who still lives there. You were out, and I needed to process it." He waved around the ring.

Jesus Christ.

"Tell Jace."

"He knows. He was there when he called."

I turned to leave when Brick stopped me.

"It's not as easy as going in there and getting her back. If she went home, it means she went back to *him*."

"You ready to tell me who *him* is now?"

30

DEMONS

***

Allen

My hands flexed over the sides of the pulpit as I felt the connection with those below me. Power traveled through the soles of my feet. I envisioned myself like a tree, absorbing it through my roots, and the heat of it flooded through my soul. I inhaled deeply with my eyes closed.

Slowly, my eyes opened, and I gazed down at the twenty pairs of ears waiting for me to speak.

"Today, we talk about sacrifice and how the Lord wants you to do him justice."

Two hours later, I packed up my things and shook many hands before I loosened my collar and downed a bottle of Jack from under the dusty organ. This gig was pretty damn good. I could really get off on this whole preacher in the pulpit thing. It suited me.

"Alle—" Zay, one of the oldest members of my *family,* cleared his throat when I glared at him. "Father, we have a new development."

"Which is?" I cleaned the dried blood off the ridges of my knife with my jacket. The edge of excitement I had experienced earlier after disposing of a local was only now beginning to dull.

"We found the girl."

That piqued my interest. Trigger had never given a shit about anyone before, but for whatever reason, he cared enough to make that blonde woman leave. I couldn't get my head around it. Far as I could see, broads like her were a dime a dozen, nothing more

31

than a warm, wet hole. Love was a conspiracy that was beaten into our brains by society, like we needed an old lady to make us feel complete. I snorted out loud at the thought. All you would be left with was a bitch to nag you and suck away all your money. If the common man could step back and look at our history, they would see that feelings like love were nothing more than lust. A few hip thrusts and a spent dick, and that was it.

Like that old saying goes, fuck and chuck.

"Where is she?" He looked over his shoulder and handed me a folded piece of paper. That was why I kept Zay around. He was loyal, discreet, and could find anyone. He was, after all, the one who came up with the idea to win over the Stripe Backs.

I glanced at the address and smiled. "Put fifty on blackjack for me."

He nodded. "I'll report in tonight." With that, he left.

The rest of the men started to bring in the shipment of guns that arrived last night. I moved to the table and relished the smell.

"What do we have here, Father?" My potential buyer was practically salivating.

I pointed to the far end of the table. "AK-47, ML 18 inch 5.56, and this." I picked up the sexy, sleek weapon and looked through the scope. "This is the Black Mamba."

"Which is what, exactly?" He eyed the rifle and ran his tongue over his lips. I slipped it back into the soft velvet case.

"Custom made. It's a cross between both of those weapons. Sniper approved."

32

His eyebrows rose and he shook his head, clearly not interested in my specialty. "I won't lie. I was surprised to hear you were dealing weapons."

I flipped a bullet between my fingers. "Actually, I'm not looking to sell. I'm looking to build an army."

His face fell, and he flexed his jaw. "Army? Who exactly are you fighting?"

"Devil's Reach," I said bluntly as I eased into a chair.

He stepped back and held his hands in the air. "Fuck, man, I don't know why you'd go up against someone as crazy as Trigger, but I want no part in it."

"Scared?" I taunted.

His fingers ran along the Black Mamba before his gaze flickered over to mine. "I watched him screw up my nephew's eyeballs with a fork because he caught him skimmin'. Then he tore out my uncle's fuckin' kidneys because he defended him. I lived, but those images are burned in my brain." He rubbed his head. "I don't know what was worse, watching that or living with it." He closed the lid on the gun. "I was fine with buying guns from you, Father, but if you're looking for an army, my men would rather off themselves than go up against Trigger."

I hated that my son had such a reputation. If I hadn't gone into hiding, I'd be more feared than he was by now.

"Suit yourself."

He looked away, his face growing paler by the moment. Fucking pussy. "When are you planning to move on him?"

I tilted my head as I studied his face. I wondered what his motive was. "Why?"

He shoved his hands into his pockets. "Because I want to be as far away from you as possible when it happens."

I grinned, excited to know the war would be epic.

CHAPTER THREE

Tess

For three days, Venna and I played every client. All it took was some acting, a blindfold, and some music to drown the voices. I hated every moment of it. I felt dirty and used, more by my mother than by the clients. I may not have been sleeping with the men, but more than half the time they would stick their tongues down my throat or slip their fingers into my panties every chance they got, but at least they weren't hiding who they were.

The only time I felt all right was when I was dancing. They weren't allowed to touch me then. Venna was making a fortune, and I wasn't too far behind. Half my money was going somewhere else, so it would take me a little longer to get out of here. It was a hard pill to swallow, but I still needed to find out what Clark had on Trigger and the club.

I spun once more on the pole then started to feel ill. My ribs were on fire, and my stomach rolled. Feeling like the world was about to fly off its rocker, I danced around and waited until the lights flickered off.

I nearly fell down the stairs as I descended and crashed heavily into someone who broke my fall.

"What's wrong, Tess?" Clark bent down to my eye level.

"Nothing." I pushed him away, but he wouldn't have it. He half carried me to the private dressing room and sat me on a chair before he handed me a bottle of water.

"You're white as a ghost. Have you eaten today?" He felt my forehead, but I pushed his hand away.

"Yes, and stop touching me." Even the water made me want to vomit.

"You're not fucking pregnant, are you?"

My eyes stung as I glared at the asshole in front of me. "If I was?"

He rubbed his face, then his neck. His expression darkened, and I could see where his head went. *He thought it was Trigger's.*

I slowly rose out of the chair and turned toward the door before he jammed himself between me and it.

"Are you?"

"Move." I breathed through my nose to try to calm the storm inside.

He bit his lip but lost the asshole behavior. He brushed my hair away like he used to, and he carefully lifted my chin so I'd look at him. "Despite your anger toward me, sweetheart, I really care about you and your wellbeing." His fingers dragged across my bottom lip, and for a moment, I gave in to it. It felt good, like I was home again. He leaned in and brushed his lips across mine, and I nearly broke. "I missed this." When I started to speak, he sealed his mouth over mine and kissed me sweetly. His kisses had always seemed tender and caring, but really, they were a mind fuck. "Tess," he whispered against my wet skin. "I just want to know if you're okay."

It was as if someone sucker punched my heart. I stepped back, wiping my lips dry.

"Don't." I wanted to cry with how much his words made me miss Trigger.

"Don't what?" He moved closer. "Don't do this?" He again pushed himself on me, but in a gentle manner. It felt wrong. I was so fucked up and twisted inside, any sweetness during intimacy made me feel gross.

He did that to me.

His arms wrapped around my back and pulled at the string holding my top on. "Remind me of how sweet your breasts are."

Jesus.

Tears prickled my eyes, and that annoying lump returned to the center of my throat. I ripped the string out of his hold and wiggled away with my hand over my breasts.

"Clark, *enough*," I bit out and tried to make sense of my million and one mixed emotions.

"Sorry." He held up his hands. "Just hard when I haven't seen you in a while. You know what you do to me."

"I need to go."

"Okay." He got the hint but still waited a beat

before he opened the door for me.

Once I was alone in the hallway in the back corridor of the house, I slid to the floor and held on to my knees for something to stabilize me. Clark stirred up so many dormant feelings that I'd finally managed to chase away. He wasn't good for me, but shit, that kiss clouded my head.

Later that night, my ribs got worse. Or was it my stomach? I couldn't really tell. Taking the pills Sean—or *Shantee*—had given me, I slipped off to a very uncomfortable sleep.

The next day I spent in my room trying to take it easy. My mother was pissed she had to reschedule my appointments, but Clark helped convince her. I stayed in bed, hoping time and rest would help. Sadly, by three p.m. the next day, that wasn't the case.

***

The lady behind the desk kept her eye on me while I waited for the doctor, who was running behind. I could have seen the house doctor, but the last time I did, it had severely scarred me. Literally.

"Tessa Marin, come on back." The doctor smiled at me from behind her red-framed glasses. Her office was just as funky as her outfit that peeked out from her white coat. She had taken a sponge to her walls and had made a neat mural of the park across the street.

"So, you're new to me." She grinned at me as she propped up her laptop. "Why are you here today? Tell me a little bit about yourself."

Where to begin?

"To make a long story short, I was in the wrong place at the wrong time and got jumped. My ribs took the majority of the beating."

"Okay." Her tone immediately changed to a more serious one. "Did you see a doctor when it happened?"

"Kind of." I made a face that told her my story had some holes. "He didn't see any problems that would lead me to think I should go to the hospital."

She squinted before she typed something in her laptop.

"I'm having some pain here." I pointed to my lower abdomen, and her eyes followed my hands. "Not really sure if it's connected to what happened, but it doesn't seem to be getting any better."

She placed her laptop on the desk and started to warm her hands by rubbing them together.

"Lean back and let me take a look."

Easing back on the bed, I lifted my shirt and watched her facial expressions. Her cool hands felt around, and I nearly hit the roof when she applied pressure to my left side.

"Your bruises are yellow, so to be having that kind of pain, I would think there may be more going on. Maybe a cracked rib as well." She glanced at my file before adjusting her glasses as she looked me over. "I would feel more comfortable if we did some x-rays."

"Now?" I needed to get back.

"Yes."

"I can't. I have to get back to work."

"I'll squeeze you in."

Fuck.

"Okay."

She sank back in her seat and scrolled through her laptop. "Okay, let's go."

Twenty minutes later, I quickly dressed and promised the doctor I'd come back for the results.

I gathered my things and plastered a smile on face. "I'll be waiting for your call."

She stood as I handed her the very lengthy questionnaire she made me fill out. She immediately flipped to the third page and frowned. "Here." She handed me a prescription. "I have a theory on what's going on, but until I'm sure, please take these. If they don't help, come back, and I'll try something else. In the meantime, take it easy, okay?"

"I'll try."

"Tess?"

I opened the door and stood in the doorway as if to ask, *what*?

"Whoever did that to you, were they caught?"

Trigger's face broke through my walls and made me smile. "One did, and the other will get his day."

She nodded then reminded me once again to keep my word to return for the results.

I didn't even get outside before my phone lit up. I tossed back two of the pills she gave me and opened my messages.

Ven: I'm stuck at the club and your mother is on a rampage. Call Rachel asap!

Tess: Not a good time.

Not even ten seconds later, I felt her reply.

Ven: Call her NOW!

Shit.

"Where the hell are you?" Rachel, the house admin, screamed at me.

"I had an appointment."

"Not from what I see. You know the rules better than anyone here, Tessa. You always block out the times you're not here."

"Sorry. I wasn't thinking."

"Yeah, well, you better, because there's a new client here insisting he has an appointment with you."

Come on, not today!

"Can you rebook him?"

"Girl, he's sitting in the waiting area saying he'll wait until you arrive. When your mother stepped in to try to get him to take someone else, he said no, but that he'd triple the normal rate for you."

Who the hell was this guy?

"I'm fifteen minutes away."

"Make it five." She hung up.

I quickly called Ven and told her what was going on. She told me she'd wait in the lobby, and we'd go from there.

I skipped on the Uber and nearly ran all the way back. I managed to get there in under ten. Thankfully, the sidewalk was clear, and the atmosphere was heavy with upcoming rain. Autumn in Vegas was the best.

"You look like shit," Rachel muttered as she

tried to smooth my wild hair. "Go over there and get changed." She pointed me toward a small changing room we rarely used, but it was good for times like this. "I'll get him to your room."

"Wait." I caught the door before she left. "Where's Ven?"

"Felicia needed her for something. She just rushed her away about three minutes ago."

What?

I pulled my phone free, and sure as shit, there was a text.

Ven: Your f'ing mother needed me to take care of her client. Not sure if she is on to us.

The blood drained from my face and pounded in my chest.

No.

I can't.

I won't.

My hands shook as I did up the zipper on my corset. I flinched at the pain but quickly masked it as I tried to figure out what was about to happen.

"Tess!" my mother barked from the other side of the door. "Move it!"

I opened the door, and her cruel expression lashed through me.

"You look like shit. This man has a ton of money. You better not screw this up for me." She pinched my cheeks painfully and rolled her eyes at the rest of me. "Why he wants you is beyond me. Go!"

"Your encouragement always does wonders,

Mother."

She snickered at my sass before she walked away.

Each step took a tremendous amount of energy and willpower. I shook like a leaf as I opened the door. He was standing in front of the window looking out at the pool area.

Kill me now.

He turned to look at me, and I nearly fell over.

***

Trigger

Brick downed the neck of the whiskey before he clinked my bottle. We were in the back of my pickup truck by the pool. We had just gotten back from dealing with my North Carolina crew and needed a breather.

"You have to understand that you come after Tess. You know I'm all about loyalty, and I have always had your back. But Tess always comes first."

"Okay." I understood that. Loyalty was earned over time and proven in the worst situations. Based on what I did know about Brick and Tess's past, they had a tight bond. Still, it was time to hear the truth.

He sighed and tossed a beer bottle into the trash bin a few feet away. "Clark weaseled himself into her life when she was ten, and not the way a father would."

My grip tightened around the neck of the bottle

as his words burned my stomach lining.

"Clark is eleven years older. He saw an opportunity and took it."

Fuck. He was only twenty-one when he met her. To be so twisted at that age was something else.

"Why?" My throat quickly became dry.

He chuckled darkly then rubbed his free hand over his jeans. "Because Tess was vulnerable and needy, but mostly because she comes from a lot of money, not that she's seen a dime of it."

My chest ached when I remembered all the times I'd given her shit over being a spoiled princess running from Mommy.

"Did they ever..." I cracked my neck to relieve some tension.

Brick stuck his thumb over the mouth of the bottle then looked at me with the most haunted look I'd ever seen on his face.

"Don't make me answer questions that will flip that switch of yours, dude."

I hated to be denied an answer to something I wanted to know, and my dark expression made it clear to him he should go on.

"Come on, Trigger."

"Brick," I warned.

He huffed through a sigh. "They didn't have sex until she was eighteen."

"Least he waited until she was legal."

"Yeah, for sex." My head whipped over to find his jaw locked in place. "I'm telling you, Clark sank his claws into her at an early age."

"Then, what?" I needed to know everything now, so I could deal with it.

44

"It's not a matter of *what*. It's that he won over her trust, messed around with her, made her fall in love with him, then saw an opportunity to secure himself in the house and married her mother. He ripped her world out from underneath her and betrayed her."

Wait, what?

"How old was she when he married her mother?"

Brick nodded. "Eleven."

That's when she tried to kill herself.

"I know Clark loves Tess in his own sick way, but he loves money just as much. That way, he got both. Only took him a few years to brainwash Tess back into submission after the wedding. Hence them sleeping together on her eighteenth birthday."

Jesus Christ.

"Clark is the only man who paid any attention to her. Her father wasn't around, and her mother looks right through her like she doesn't exist. Clark stole any innocence she had. You can see why she was his target. She's pretty, smart-mouthed, and underneath her armor, she has the biggest heart, and he fucking destroyed her."

"So, why did she come here then run back to him?"

Brick lowered his voice when Rail brought a girl to the edge of the pool and dove in.

"Something changed six years ago, and she decided she wanted to go back to the house when I wanted to leave town. No matter how many times I begged her to come, she wouldn't budge. Whatever it was, it was important enough to keep her there, so whatever happened after that to make her leave to

45

come to me must have been big. She lived on the streets before we met, and I know she must be lost if she went back there. Tess has a lot of demons she keeps locked up because of that house."

The girl with Rail screamed when he grabbed her from behind and tossed her in. I spotted Peggy watching us from across the property, and when I caught her eye, she licked her fingers and motioned for me to come over. I looked away then downed my whiskey.

"What was Tess like on the streets?"

Brick chuckled then leaned back, clearly at ease with this topic.

"She was guarded and sassy, but I earned her trust. Doesn't take long for a girl who looks like Tess to find trouble on the streets. Every guy wanted a piece of her, and every girl wanted to hate her. You can imagine how much sleep she got."

I shuddered at the thought.

"Did she ever take you to the house?"

He folded his arms and sighed.

"Once, she tried, but we never got through the gates. She had a full-blown panic attack, and I told her it wasn't worth it." He glanced at me. "I'm telling you, that is not the place for her to be."

"Trigger?" Morgan suddenly appeared next to me. "We should talk."

Once inside, I closed the door behind Morgan and sank into my seat at the head of the table. Morgan pulled out his phone.

"You remember Harmos?"

I thought for a moment until I placed the memory.

"Yeah, nephew skimmed off the Vegas drop, and the uncle had a hand in it?"

"Yup. Well, you remember how we let the other uncle go?"

I nodded, wondering where the fuck he was going with this.

"Well, that uncle just ran his mouth to Cray. Turns out he crossed paths with your father."

My hands drew into fists, and I steadied myself for what was next.

"Seems your father is looking to build an army and wanted him to join."

"That so?" I bit out. "And did he?"

"Nope, said he wasn't going up against you. Not worth it."

"Smart man," I muttered and thought about what my next move would be. "Any lead on his location?"

"He wouldn't say anything much, but that he was still posing as a priest, seems to like being called Father." He looked at me for a reaction to that, but as ironic as it was, I let it pass. "Puts up like he's all about selling guns, but really he's drawing in men to recruit."

I let the information absorb without comment then drew a heavy breath.

"Who do we have right now?"

Morgan pulled out a seat and thought for a moment. "I mean, we got Ty's replacement."

"I want Rich here, especially while Jace is gone. Send Cooper."

"Your father knows our men. Why not send in Peggy?"

"For what, a handy? She's useless. Send Moe."

"On it."

I leaned back and tried to piece together what the fuck my father was up to. Was he building a club? Or was it a trap?

"The first key to succeeding, boy, is making others think you're doing one thing when really you're doing another," he barked at me from the corner of the ring. *"People are expendable, and the sooner you realize that, the better off you'll be."*

Langley stepped in front of me and rested his hand on my shoulder. I jerked back, but his hand stayed in place.

"Clear your mind, Trigger. The longer you keep him inside your head, the harder the fight will be. Focus on me, and me only."

I nodded but eyed my father, who watched us. He was threatened by Langley, but needed him more. He was, after all, the only one who kept me in line when Gus couldn't.

"Like I said," my father slammed Langley hard on the back, *"everyone is expendable."*

CHAPTER FOUR

Tess

My hands flew to my mouth as the tears flowed from my eyes.

"Hey there, Tess." Jace beamed at me in a three-piece suit. He opened his jacket like he was impressed at how he cleaned up. "I look fucking fetchin', right?"

I laughed at his words. How he got in here was beyond me.

"I know I'm not Brick, but can I still get a hug?"

I hurried over and wrapped my arms around his midsection. He smelled like the club, and the walls I had been carefully building started to buckle under the pressure.

I flinched when his arms tightened.

"Oh, you okay?"

I nodded while I stepped back and willed the tears away. "Just still a little sore from—" I shook off the memory. "How did you get here? They run a detailed background check on everyone. You'd have to have at least a hundred grand in your account, or they wouldn't even consider you."

He smiled as he sat on the edge of my dresser. He looked so different and so much more grown up. Well, until he opened his mouth.

"You're forgetting Trigger's rich, and he knows a lot of people."

The very mention of Trigger's name in such a casual way nearly tore me down. I reached behind me for the mattress and eased back to help with the heaviness.

"I suppose that's true." My mouth became dry.

"This room is bomb, Tess, and that bathroom! Shit, your tub is the size of my bed." I welcomed Jace's lack of attention to my emotional state. "No wonder Brick got you an apartment and didn't make you slum it at the clubhouse right away."

Trigger.

Brick.

Clubhouse.

All the words I hadn't dared to utter since I left three and a half weeks ago. Damn, it felt so much longer, but with Jace here, it felt like yesterday. I rubbed my chest where my heart was determined to make an imprint.

I yelped when he jumped onto my bed like a seven-year-old, landing on his back. His arms went behind his head as he sighed. "I slept in Rail's garage for a month before I got a spot in the clubhouse. I thought that was nice." He chuckled as he wiggled into the comforter. "Now I can see why you came back here."

I hated that he didn't see how dark this place was

for me. How much I'd died inside the past few weeks. My insides coiled, and I wanted to scream. I closed my eyes and tried to calm down, but it was hard because he kept rambling. "Why are you here?" I blurted, harsher than I intended.

He sat up and tugged at his tie, and his mood changed.

"Trigger needed to know where you were."

My body tingled in an alarming way. There was more to this.

"Why?"

"Someone showed up and caused problems." He wouldn't look at me, and I wanted to question why. "Trigger just needed to know you were all right."

Oh.

"Well," I cleared my throat and rubbed my wrist, "as you can see, I'm fine."

"Yeah, I can see that." He grinned, but it fell when I didn't match it. "You sure you are Tess?"

My phone vibrated, and I pulled it from my purse.

Ven: The Wicked Witch is finally busy. You need me?

Tess: I got this one.

Ven: Okay...just text me when you're done, okay?

Tess: K.

"How's Brick?" I diverted the attention off me.

"Pissy."

I felt my lips go up without thinking. Brick could be wicked at shutting people out when he was digesting something heavy.

"Give him a chocolate milk drink box."

Jace looked at me oddly. He folded his arms and nodded for me to elaborate.

"Just something from when we were younger."

"I'll stop on my way home."

Home. Ugh.

"Any tricks for Trigger?"

His words were like a physical punch to the gut.

"You should see the slaughter room. It's permanently stained red."

Shit.

He stood and straightened his tie in the mirror. "Even Tammy can't get near him." He grinned at me and missed my mood change yet again. "Well, I've seen you, and you look fucking sexy. I'll report back you're great."

"Jace." I huffed in disbelief that this was happening.

A knock at the door sent a jolt through me.

Oh, no!

"Jace, lose the jacket and look like you're buttoning up your shirt."

"What?"

"Play along, okay?" I tugged off his jacket and pushed him on the bed. Just as I settled in on his lap, the door slowly opened.

"Tessa—oh, forgive me." Clark's eyes narrowed in on Jace's shocked expression. "I didn't realize you were working."

Like hell. The blood pumped to my face, and I hid behind my hair. My hands trembled as I pressed them into Jace's chest.

"Close the damn door, asshole." Jace covered my hands to hide my nerves and glared at Clark.

Clark ran his tongue across his lips as he stared at Jace, and then he looked back at me.

"Tessa, please find me when you're finished here."

I gave a slight nod and waited for the click of the door. I let out a long, deep breath to calm my nerves.

"Thanks for that, Jace." I couldn't look him in the eye.

"Shit, so you *are* a—an escort."

No wonder Trigger sent him. To confirm his ex was a tramp.

My eyes welled up. This wasn't something I chose, it was something I was born into. I had never slept with any of the men here except Clark, but that was different.

"No wonder Trigger flipped the fuck out after you left the church."

I shifted back and covered myself up with my pathetic excuse for a robe. I shoved hard against his chest. "How dare you judge me? It's none of your fucking business, or Trigger's. Get the hell out, Jace, and tell him I'm just fine."

Jace shifted on the bed and pulled his phone free.

"I gotta go." He shrugged on his jacket and mumbled about missing his bike. "I miss having you around, Tess. I wish you hadn't left."

"Well, I did, so…"

"Okay, well, I gotta run."

I tucked my hair behind my ear and nodded. I wished it was Morgan who came instead of Jace. He would have heard me.

I barely registered his hug and turned away as he left. I felt raw and exposed, and I had to get a grip on my emotions.

I locked the door, turned off the lights, closed the curtains, and curled up in a tiny ball on the blanket in the center of my bed.

Maybe I wasn't a whore, but I sure felt like one now.

***

The next morning, Clark paced his office like a panther, while I stood like stone, curious what he had to say. I was *sure* it was something important.

"Are you enjoying working here?"

I felt my back go up. Seriously?

"If I did?"

"Clients are asking for you specifically now?"

"Clark," my voice carried a warning, "I never asked to work in the house. I wanted to go back to the stage. If you want to change that, I welcome it. You made your choice, so keep your jealousy out of it."

He thought for a moment before he came around the desk and towered over me, just like Trigger used to. His soap was different, though, and it brought back so many memories of feeling loved and cherished by him. I had to shake myself and remember the truth, that there had been an undertone of deceit the whole time, and I would do well to not forget. I took a step back. He clouded my head and confused me.

"Tessa," he whispered and brushed my hair off my shoulder. "God, I have missed the heat from your skin."

I closed my eyes and tried to concentrate, and I pulled hard from a deep place. His lips brushed my earlobe, and I turned my chin away.

"Don't."

"You used to love it when I kissed you here." He pressed on the side of my neck, and Trigger flashed before my eyes.

"Stop."

"Your body doesn't agree with your words, sweet girl."

I pushed at his shoulders and shoved him away before I turned on my heel and hurried to the door. It opened as I touched the handle.

My mother's evil glance tore a hole through me. Her eyes honed in on my neck, and I felt she could see his kiss.

"Clark, honey," she said over my head, "come to bed."

I sighed as I moved around her. My mother's hand snapped to my upper arm. She glared inches from my face. "Give me a reason to kick you out *again,* Tess. Just one."

"Felicia." Clark's tone told me he knew what she was referring to. "Enough."

Her words lashed at the deep wound. Just as she was about to let go, her hand slid down and fingered my scar.

"Sometimes you *do* have good ideas. Shame you can't follow through with them."

The air was sucked from my lungs as she slammed his door in my face.

***

Trigger

"Where?" I rolled out the map in front of Cray, the VP of the Arizona crew. Morgan leaned over the table with Gus. Brick closed the door behind him after he sidetracked Peggy, who wouldn't take *get lost* for an answer.

"Here and here." Morgan pointed to two spots that ran over Twenty-Third and Ocean Park Boulevard.

I glanced at Gus. He knew southern California like the back of his hand.

"Just an old drive-in theater. There's a building in the back. Maybe he's squatting there?"

I popped my neck, weighing the odds of whether this was a trap.

"Look, I have eyes everywhere. If they said they saw him, I believe them." Morgan stood while we all sat. I knew he trusted his men, but I didn't. I caught Brick's eye, and he shrugged, but I could tell he wanted to follow this lead.

"Vote," I ordered.

"Aye." Morgan started us off and raised his hand.

"Aye." Cray nodded.

Gus started to cough from his joint but managed

to squeak out, "Aye."

"Aye. This shit needs to end." Brick checked his phone before he tucked it away.

My eyes hurt as the demons within weighed in their vote.

"Just us, and bring the rifles. We leave at dark."

Morgan waited until the rest of the guys left before he rolled the map and put it away.

"I need Peggy out from behind the bar," he muttered as he turned to look at me. "She can't pour for shit, she's leaving to fuck whoever during her shift, and God forbid she counts to twenty."

I leaned back, not needing that right now, but I knew his frustrations were legit. Peggy was a fucking train wreck.

"Who do you want?"

"Tess," he blurted and sucked his lips inward.

A burn ripped over my skin, and I relished it. Pain was good for the body, kept you sharp. What her name did to my head was a different story.

"I have someone I can bring in for a while," he said, not fazed by my look. "My friend's cousin used to work in that shithole by the beach. If he could work there, he could work here."

"Fuck Tess. She's gone. No outsiders. Speak to Cray, see who he can send over." I was pissed. I had never needed a damn bitch to care about, and now look what the hell it was doing to my head. Just the sound of her name set me on fire.

He nodded, but I could tell he wasn't happy about it.

The nights were cooler, and the days were shorter now that it was November. Our hoodies covered our skin, the rags hid our faces, and the reaper rode bitch on our backs.

I tapped the button on my helmet and filled the dead night with "Psychosocial" by Slipknot. I needed something to calm the chatter.

A thick thrill seemed to hover in the air. It sent tiny shocks into my skin that absorbed into my bloodstream and set my senses to overdrive.

I pointed to the turnoff, and our headlights lit the driveway as we swung in off the main road. We stopped a few yards back behind an old bus.

We moved swiftly in pairs across the property to the only door on our side.

"This feels a little too familiar." Next to me, Brick checked the clip of his 9mm. "Ready?"

I scanned the guys to make sure we were good to go. Big Joe was further back and would stay outside to text if we got company. I opened the door with my flashlight and stepped into the blacked-out warehouse.

The moment my boot landed and I felt the texture, I didn't need to look down to know what it was. The smell hit second. Rotting flesh was something you only needed to experience once to have it permanently burned into your memory.

Rail gagged behind me but kept it together. Brick snickered something, and he shut up.

"What's the noise?" Morgan whispered as he came up to my side. "Pipe leaking?"

I tuned out the guys and moved forward, my light scanning at waist height so as not to miss anything. There was a door ahead, partly open. I nodded to the guys that I was heading over, and they followed. I turned back once to count to make sure they were all with me. I didn't trust this place, and the mole was playin' hard on my mind. If one was going to show themselves, now would be the time.

The slime grew thicker as we approached. Our boots squashed with each step, alerting anyone around that we were there. All things my father would think of.

I pushed the door open, and my light played over the walls. I felt a deep chill enter the room.

"No," Gus hissed when he saw one of his oldest friends hanging from the ceiling with barbed wire wrapped several times around his neck. The blood had drained from his body in sticky puddles. His hands were torn up, and a bone from his thumb was sticking out—all signs of a fight to the death.

A heavy wave of grief ran over us when we saw more of our San Diego crew strung up across the room like holiday lights. One, two, three, four, five, six, seven. I stopped when I saw the seventh was different than the rest. I stepped closer and saw the tattoos.

Gator.

His lips were sewn shut with wire in an X, meaning he ran his mouth. Gator had brought the drugs to Palm Springs to test the zig-zagged product, and the result was Ty, my prospect, meeting the same fate. A brutal death. I shook my head, and rage started to take over my body.

"Seven," I hissed at the men when they joined me.

"Eight," Gus corrected. "They got the other

runner too."

My fingers were buzzing. The blood pumped to my arms, and the veins grew big and thick with it as the pressure increased under my skin.

He touched my family.

My phone lit up my pocket just as a door in the far corner opened and slammed shut.

Holy shit, we're not alone.

Rail was the first to step forward when we heard three shots from outside.

"What the hell?" Morgan quickly raised his weapon to scan above us.

I turned my phone over to read what I thought was Big Joe's warning.

Jace: I found Tess.

Suddenly, the lights flickered on, and there were at least thirty cops with laser beams pointed at our chests.

"Drop your weapons!"

Fuck me!

***

Everyone was separated and taken to the station in handcuffs. Big Joe had fled the scene before anyone saw him. He called our lawyer, who was now next to me and had just given me the same old speech about keeping my mouth shut. I had been through this enough times to know what to do—and what not to.

We sat in a room for four hours before we saw

anyone else. The loss of my men sat heavy on me, but that three-word text from Jace hounded me the most. Was she okay?

"Sam." I kept my head down. I knew we were being recorded. "I need my…" I made a gesture for my phone under the table.

That he was nervous around me had been made clear a few times before. I punched him in a bar once for mentioning information in front of a prospect. Sam was good, which was why he was still employed. "I can't. They have it."

"Get hold of Jace for me."

He nodded and pulled out his phone and started to text. Just then, the door swung open, and in walked one of the biggest dicks I knew.

"Officer Doyle." I leaned back in my chair and examined the douche-bag kid I grew up with. His sister was decent in bed, but she wanted more, and I didn't. I thought Doyle was more upset about that than we were. "I hear you've been working a side job."

His smile confirmed what I'd hoped was a lie.

"Well, now," he pulled the chair out and held his tie back as he eased into the seat, "always fun seeing you with bracelets on."

"Not for long."

"We'll see." He opened the file in front of him and ran his finger along my rap sheet.

"My client didn't do this," Sam started. "There was no evidence that would suggest they were there during the actual murders, and let's be frank, this is his crew. No reason to kill his own."

"There's always a reason when Trigger's

involved," Doyle answered while still reading.

The door opened, and there was Sam's hot assistant. She gave me a shy glance before she handed him an envelope.

Sam smiled as he pulled the photo out and slid it across the table. "As you can see, my clients were caught on camera coming out of the bike shop at the time of the murders." He tapped the time stamp. "Now," he stood and motioned for me to do the same, "we are done here."

"Actually," Doyle squinted, "there is still a little problem with the shooting that happened only two minutes before we turned the lights on. Sit back down, Trigger. You're in for a long night."

"You don't think my client shot that guy and raced back inside in time."

"I don't know anything at this point." Doyle's tone dropped. "So, sit back down until we do."

I folded my arms. "Must feel good to finally have a little power in your life."

"Trigger," Sam warned as he settled into his seat again.

"You know what? It kind of does." He smirked.

I calmed myself then glanced at the clock and wondered if Jace made it home yet.

"I want my phone call."

CHAPTER FIVE

Tess

There were pros and cons to living in a house that never slept. There were always enough people to blend in with, but there were always people around. I waited for Rachel to be pulled away by my mother before I tapped on the keyboard to bring up my schedule. I was curious to know if Jace had booked any more sessions with me. I hit the arrow to slide through the month, only to find I was booked at least five times a week, but not with Jace. Disappointment rippled through me, but it only proved I needed to get the hell out of here fast. At least Venna was still booked for the stage, which meant I was.

I heard my mother's voice and had just enough time to click out and turn down the hallway. I pressed my back against the valet wall and listened to learn if they noticed I was there.

"Take her off the books," my mother snapped. "She's a train wreck. We don't need another Mags."

My heart sped up. I hadn't heard my best friend's name mentioned in this house for so long. I inched closer to the corner.

"Do I pay her for the week?"

"She almost cost me our biggest client. I should be taking her pay." She slammed her hand down on the desk. "Clear out her room, toss her shit in a cab, and get her off my property within the next six hours, or you'll be looking for another job."

"Yes, ma'am." Rachel started to type away on the keyboard.

"Where's Clark?" I turned myself carefully so I could just barely peek around the corner.

"Um," Rachel clicked on the cameras and studied each one, "he's in the pool with Summer and Angela."

"Of course he is." She snickered and stormed off.

Damn, I hate that woman.

"Girl, are you asking for trouble?" Rachel was typing again, but I knew she was speaking to me.

I shamefully came around the corner with a shrug.

"You're lucky I saw you on the feed before your mother did. Why are you creepin' around?"

I ran my hand through my hair and wondered how safe it was to share with Rachel. I'd known her almost my whole life, but that wouldn't mean much in this house.

"Just wanted to know who was being canned."

"Dezzy. She took too much coke before her client came and nearly overdosed during a BJ. Dude almost lost his twig."

Shit.

Her dark eyes narrowed in on me. "Why are you really here? Don't lie to me. No one would have come back after what happened to you last time."

"Money." That was a fucking lie, but I wasn't going to go there.

"Umm hmm," she muttered. "I heard you were tangled up in some biker gang. That true?"

"What do you know about it?"

"I know Clark had some real shit-looking cops here dressed in plain clothes. They flashed their badges to get in. Once they got inside, Clark nearly took their heads off for coming to the house. Something about you and a biker gang. Once they talked to him for a bit, though, he cooled off, and they went into the bar. Right as they were leaving, they handed him something that looked like a computer stick, you know, one of those USB thingies. Then he went right into his office."

"You hear a lot for working the desk, Rach."

"You be surprised what goes down in this house, Tessa." She gave me a strange look and went back to typing.

"Good to know," I whispered then headed upstairs, but instead of going to my room, I went to Clark's office. Now that I knew he was given something, I needed to find it and deal with this shit. I wouldn't last much longer.

His office was locked, but I had picked up a few tricks while living on the streets. I used my keycard that allowed access to the viewing rooms and wiggled it past his sorry excuse for a lock. It only took a couple tries to get it open. With a look over my shoulder, I slipped inside and gently closed the door behind me.

I never liked his office. It had white walls with white furniture. How fucking bland could you get? I headed for the file cabinet first and thumbed through the tabs, but nothing really stood out. I did pull my file and placed it aside while I opened the next drawer.

"Come on!" I flipped through everyone who ever worked here since the nineties. For someone who had such a modern office, he certainly had an old-school filing system.

My stomach jerked when I saw her name written in red pen across the tab.

Mags Hurtle.

I flipped it open and leafed through her paperwork. Her family's info, her health report, details of her pregnancy with Lily, the asshole baby-daddy's info. I stopped when I came to the police report. A lot of it was blacked out, which was odd but not surprising. I shifted to lean against the desk when a DVD dropped to the floor and slid under his bookshelf.

Fuck.

Just as I bent to grab it, Clark's phone rang. I jumped, shoving the file back into place.

"Jesus." I tried to calm my nerves as I fingered the DVD out from underneath the bookshelf. I jammed it into the back of my corset.

With a frustrated sigh, I moved to his desk again. It was a simple desk with no drawers, just a table with four legs. I clicked on the keyboard, and his Mac screen flickered on. I closed my eyes, wondering how the shit I was going to navigate through this. I was used to Microsoft technology.

After four failed attempts at the password, I turned off the screen and looked elsewhere. If they handed him something, the proof should be here. I checked inside the few little containers on the desktop for a small USB, but had no luck.

Dumb yourself down, Tess, and think like Clark.
Think.
Think.
Think.

I saw his Monet panting on the wall and wondered if maybe he was that much of a cliché to hide a safe behind it. The frame was about an inch from the wall. My fingers moved along the bottom and tugged, but nothing.

Hmm.

Then I spotted a display box for his beloved rocks on the table under his bar shelf. I was five feet from it when I heard the familiar footsteps. I scanned the room, desperate to find a place to hide. His shit furniture provided zero cover, so I slipped into house mode.

"Tess?" Clark stopped when he saw me sitting in his chair in front of his desk. "What?" He looked over his shoulder then closed the door behind him. "What are you doing here? How the hell did you get in?"

I crossed my legs, which typically drew his gaze to my upper thigh. I dragged my fingers from my stomach, lingered at my chest, across my collarbone, and up to my ear to play with my earring. Clark was incredibly predictable when it came to the female body, so I used what I had.

"I want to ask you to talk to my mother about my schedule."

He pulled the chair next to me around so he could face me head on. *Crap.* I noticed I hadn't moved my own folder that I had pulled.

Mother of fucking Christ, Tess!

"You know that would be easier said than done with our history." His hand fell on mine, and I felt like my skin was on fire. The urge to pull away was overwhelming. "Have you spoken to her about it at all?"

I saw my opportunity and used it.

"Yes, I just tried, which is why I was in here." I waved my hand around but made sure to stop at the file. "Why I ever thought she'd listen is beyond me." I slowed my breathing to make my point. My free hand landed on his. "Clark, I can't do this. It's not who I am. I'll dance, but to be a madam…I just can't. Please."

"Tessa," he leaned closer, and I responded and leaned into him, "just let me have a taste, and I'll see what I can do."

Trigger's face popped up in front of me, and I had to force myself not to pull away.

As Clark's lips pressed to mine, so much resentment filled me I wondered at my ability to control myself. I thought hard about why I was here, forcing away the belief that it felt like cheating. God, I didn't even know if I was really with Trigger.

"Clark," I whispered and dropped my head.

"What?" He trapped my legs between his. "Just

give in to me, Tessa."

I jerked back and felt the fire lick through my veins. I shoved him away, jumped up, and darted to the door, but before I opened it, I turned to him as he stood.

"If you ever loved me at all, you will get me back on the stage, Clark."

"I do love you, Tessa."

"No." I cut him off. "If you did, you would have let me go years ago, not played mind games with me, not hunted me down, and not destroyed lives along the way."

His face dropped, and I could see he was conflicted but didn't really get what I was saying.

"Tessa! What the hell?"

I slammed the door. Clark was so embedded under my skin it was hard on my emotions. He twisted them up and confused me. It was no wonder I was such a mess.

I heard footsteps and wondered if Rachel saw me on the camera and let my mother know I was here. I tried the door across the hall, but it was locked. *Shit*, I didn't have time to pick it. I moved to the other, and thankfully, it opened. Closing the door to a small slit, I saw my mother swing open his door.

"Where is she?" she hissed at him. "Rachel said she saw her up here."

"Calm down, calm down. She was here. She just wanted to discuss being put back on stage, and you know what, Felicia, I have to agree. It's strange you'd even allow her to be a call girl. She's your own daughter."

"Please spare me your concern for little miss

perfect. She's been a pain in my ass since the day she was born. I'm just making her work in the house so she'll leave. She's like an alley cat. You feed it once, and you can't get rid of it."

"Wow," Clark muttered. I wanted to take her head off but stayed where I was.

"Don't make me remind you, Clark, I know your secrets too." I heard her heels click on the wooden floor before she spoke again. "Ones that could destroy her."

"We had a deal."

"Yes, we did, and a deal works both ways, so keep your dick in your pants."

***

Trigger

After sixteen hours, I slipped into off mode on the outside but gave in to the chaos happening inside. That was what they wanted, after all—for me to sweat. Thing was, there was no way they could pin that murder on me. There wasn't enough time for one of us to have done it. It was just a waiting game on their turf.

The mirror that faced me rattled slightly, more than likely from a door being shut. I waited for a moment and slowly let my lips part into a smile. The same smile I used whenever Doyle brought up his sister. It rattled again before the door opened, and there stood Doyle and Sam.

Sam tapped his side, which signaled me they had to let me go since there was no evidence.

Doyle's pissed-off face was the icing on the fucked-up cake. I stood and reached for my phone Sam held out before I towered over Doyle.

"The next time you think about arresting me and my men, you better have some goddamn good evidence. Now, move."

His face twitched, and he cleared his throat and stepped aside so I could pass.

"Where are the guys?" I grunted at Sam as he raced to catch up.

"Waiting in the car. You were harder to get released." He raised a hand and scrambled to get in front of me. I stopped and looked up from my phone. "Trigger, I need you to know this looks like a setup."

"I know."

He fixed his glasses and shifted his files from one hand to the other. Sam was a plump little man who looked like an inmate's bitch. His clothes were wrinkled, and his face was always beet red. But he was smart and had my back, even at the times I didn't think he had. Besides, he wouldn't fuck me over. He knew what I was capable of, and he had a family to lose. I had made it a point to meet the wife and kids when we first hooked up.

"You want to share anything with me? I need to be kept in the loop."

I rubbed my head. "My father is still alive." I let that sink in. "And, apparently, he is determined to get me six feet under, or behind bars, at least."

"Jesus Christ."

"Not even close." I stepped around him and scanned my text messages. Nothing else from Jace.

"Trigger, we need to discuss this."

I tapped Jace's contact info to start a call and turned to Sam. "We just did."

Cooper was at the curb in his 1966 Lincoln Continental convertible. Way flashy for my taste, but the guys had picked up our bikes, so it would have to do.

I slipped into the front seat and motioned for him to leave.

Jace finally answered on the sixth ring. "You're out?"

"You found Tess."

"I did. She's in Vegas."

I glanced away from the side mirror and closed my eyes. At least she was okay.

"Trigger, you need to know something."

"What?" *Fucking spit it out.*

"She is working as a prostitute."

I glanced back at Brick, who apparently heard Jace. He muttered something and looked out the window.

"You sure?"

"Yeah, and that Clark guy is a real dick."

"You met him?"

"He came in her room. He thought we were done." I pushed away the murderous thought of the two of them in bed together. "He wasn't happy. He wanted to see her after."

"And besides that?"

He took a moment to answer, and I wasn't sure why.

"Sad, man. She seemed just…sad. But you know Tess. She turned it to mad."

I rested my elbow on the open window and covered my eyes with my free hand.

"I don't wanna overstep here, but—"

I hung up and tossed my phone on the dash.

We all remained silent as I mulled over Jace's words.

What the fuck is she doing? And who *the fuck is she doing?*

"Hey, Trigger." Morgan stopped me before I went inside. He was visibly rocked by what went down. "I swear, man, I didn't—"

"I know." I moved around him and headed for my room. I needed a hot shower.

Cray and a few of his men stayed for dinner. Seven tables were pushed together, and Rail filled the guys in on what happened to the San Diego crew.

"I'll pay for the family to stay at the Hilton," Cray chimed in. He glanced at Moe, who shrugged. Moe barely felt much inside. I understood that and made sure he was directly under Cray in ranks. Unemotional people tended to screw up less.

"Yeah," Moe said. "I'll send someone to get them."

"Did you find anything?" I knew the answer was no. I would have heard if Moe had gotten his hands on the Harmos family.

"Nah, skipped town."

I nodded and nursed my beer. Morgan finally joined us but remained quiet. The whole situation played on him, and he needed to get over it.

This was all my father—what he did best. Fuck with people's heads.

"Trigger?" Big Joe stood in the doorway with a box. "This just came for you."

I flicked my head at Jace, and he jumped to get it. He set it in front of me and cut the tape along the top before he stepped back. Rising from my chair, I slowly opened it and pulled out Gator's leather cut. I slammed it on the table and lifted out the rest of the cuts piece by piece.

Anger surged. The guys were waiting for me to explode, and I was about to let fly when I saw there was an envelope taped to the bottom of the box.

What the fuck was this?

I glanced at Gus before I ripped the paper and freed the note.

Eight down. Who is next?

You want this to stop?

Step into the ring.

"It's a trap," Brick hissed from behind me. "He knows you can't resist the ring."

Gus made a strange noise, and I looked over.

"What?"

He shook his head, but he still cleared his throat, which meant he was going to give me his two cents anyway. "It's just what he wants."

"Did I say I was going to?"

"No, but addicts slip, and he's playin' you."

Fuck. I needed to be alone to work off some of the tension that was building. My fists were clenched tight, and I couldn't relax my fingers.

"Get these cuts cleaned up, and we'll give them

to the families," I barked at Jace, and he quickly gathered them up without a word.

The door swung open, and my newest prospect, Rich, looked around the room, his excitement obvious.

"Excuse me." He blinked to find the right words for interrupting my fucking meeting. "Trigger, I saw some of them."

"Who?" My entire body immediately came to high alert.

"Five men from your father's army."

With a quick glance at Brick, we all stood and grabbed our weapons and followed Rich out back to where we had parked our bikes.

We didn't need a plan. We'd make one once we arrived and checked the place out.

"There." Rich pointed at a group of men who looked like they were part of a kid's birthday party being held at a park just outside the border of my territory on the Stripe Backs' land.

"How many kids?" Brick checked his phone.

"Ah," Rich craned his neck and looked around, "seven, no, ten. Ten kids in total. Including the baby on that chick's tit."

"You and Rail go around and draw them out. Brick and I will meet up behind."

I motioned for Cooper to go and headed around the cars to the other side.

"Ready?" Brick and I stood on either side of the line of Stripe Back bikes and tipped them in toward each other, so it was harder to stand them up in a rush. It would buy us an extra ten seconds or so.

We rushed in the opposite direction to create a

distraction that would pull the Stripe Backs away from us.

Just as we rounded the area near the restrooms, we saw Cooper nail one of my father's men in the head with a rock. They jumped to their feet and started to chase them through the garden area and up to the road.

"What the fuck, Samuel!" One of the Stripe Back members had a kid by the collar. "I told you not to touch the bikes."

"Poppy, I didn't!"

I signaled for Brick to follow me. We stayed low and made our way through the path and up the hill where Cooper was getting his ass kicked, and Rail had one in a neck hold.

My knuckles were curled tight as stone, and my heart jump-started into high as I ran in and swung with all my might. One man flew into another, and they both went down, which gave me a few seconds to take out the fucker on Cooper's back. I felt a blow to my shoulder and whirled to cave in the face of the first guy I could reach.

Pound.

Pound.

Pound.

My muscles screamed me on, and I reveled in each bone I broke. One by one, we took out each man, and every hit I took amped up my desire to kill.

"Where is Allen?" I heard Cooper shout at one of the men. "Where is he?"

The bastard laughed as blood drained from his mouth. "The Father is too protected, his army too big." His heavy accent made his words hard to follow. "You don't find him, he finds you."

"You're dead, anyway."

"*Sí*, but I die knowing where Father is. You," he poked Cooper's chest, "do not."

I stepped over and snapped his neck.

"He won't talk."

Cooper grabbed his legs and dragged the body to a nearby car. We had found it unlocked earlier and decided to fill the trunk with our gift.

I jumped back into the fight. Fuck, I needed this.

Rail's guy was huge, so I took over. I got lost in the fight. He was almost my size, but his swing was shit. He lasted at least a few minutes on his feet before he went down like a fucking tree.

My chest heaved with a cocktail of thirst and fuel. I needed more, but they were dead. I glanced back at the party and saw the Stripe Backs were aware of our visit, so it was time to go.

"Snap a photo, cut their fingers, and send them to the church. No note, just leave a bag of coke with our symbol. Whether he's still there or not, it'll get back to him."

"Wish I could see your old man's face when he opens it." Brick huffed and pulled out his phone. "Tess?" His tone was off. "Tess, hon, is that you?"

My legs were moving before my mind kicked in. He turned and caught my expression, and his face twisted with worry.

"You need to tell me what's going on."

CHAPTER SIX

Tess

The DVD was on a seven-second loop. I watched my beautiful friend Mags as she came into the viewing room at the house to meet her baby's father, and what happened next made me go cold with shock and throw up my dinner.

My legs went out from under me as I slid down the wall in the far corner of my room. My cell phone was still on airplane mode as it shook in my hands. I watched the little plane disappear and change to the cell reception icon. My knuckles were white, and I didn't know what else to do, so I gave in.

I swiped my thumb over his number and pressed call. Heavy, hot tears raced down my face, each one reminding me of my new truth.

"Hello?" His voice made my stomach hurt.

"Brick?" I whispered. I needed him so much right now.

"Tess." There was a pause. "Tess, hon, is that

you?" I pictured his face and how much he must hate me for leaving. "Are you okay? Where are you?" He stopped his chatter and waited a beat before he spoke again. "You need to tell me what's going on."

I tried to get my head to work, but the words came out jumbled. "He strangled her." I sobbed and rolled to my side. Everything hurt.

"Who strangled who, Tess?"

"Clark," I choked out. "He killed Mags! George was there and helped get rid of her. Mom ordered them around. I can't breathe. I always thought it was George, not…" My heart fought for room in my chest. Air was trapped half way up, and everything was tangled up inside.

"Shit." He covered the phone and said something. "Tess, are you there now?"

"Matt," I sobbed out his real name, and it felt good to say it, "I'm so sorry—"

"No," he shouted. "I don't know what black shit is going through your head right now, Tess. But you have nothing to be sorry for. I'm going to fly out to you tonight. I'm going to take you home, okay?"

"I can't." I felt so tired. My body needed sleep. It always shut down when things became too much. "I don't know everything yet."

"I think you got your answers."

Before I could explain that wasn't what I meant, he hung up. I needed to lie down for a while. I didn't bother changing, I just slipped on a robe and climbed on top of the covers.

I raced up the slippery steps of the old wheat

mill. You had to be so careful where you stepped. It had been abandoned about fifteen years ago. Rusty nails, broken windows, or trash could take you down in a flash.

I reached for the metal rail for support as my heart beat out of my chest and vibrated up my throat. The three guys were only two floors below and were gaining on me fast. It had been a stupid move, me trying to get the blanket back. They had grabbed it the night before last, and I'd nearly frozen to death without it. I thought they were out of it drunk when I pulled it free, but I had underestimated their street smarts, and they were on me pretty fast.

I hit the top floor and frantically glanced for a place to hide or for a weapon to use.

Nothing.

I raced for the stairs on the other side of the room. Just as I flew through the open the door, I heard them yell.

I dodged all the weak-looking patches on the steps and leapt down three, nearly falling on my ass.

My mind raced to figure out a game plan once outside. This exit led to an alleyway, and if they beat me down there, I would have no way of getting out.

I knew I could kick and knee hard, so I focused all my energy on that as I burst through the door and fell at a hit to the back of my legs.

Shit.

"Wow." One guy grinned down at me, and it took a moment for my brain to clear.

"*I get first dip.*" *Another groaned as he held his dick with his dirty fingers.* "*Let's see what we're dealing with.*"

Two hands clamped down on my ankles. I kicked and twisted, but another grabbed my wrists.

"*No!*" *I screamed and bucked with all my might, but they were too strong. I wasn't sure how many there were, but I could tell who the ringleader was. He bent over me and tried to wiggle off my pants while the others held me tight. My head jerked, and I tried to bite at the closest arm.*

"*Stop! Get off me!*" *My lungs nearly burst when I sucked in and screamed again, hoping to scare them off.*

The man above me started to cut my jeans off with a blade while yelling at the others to hold me still. In hindsight, I should have been more scared of the pocketknife skimming past my flesh, but better to get a wild infection than be poked by this sick son of a bitch with his whore of a dick.

"*Damn, no panties!*" *He licked his lips.*

"*You touch me, and I promise I'll bend your dick like a goddamned balloon animal.*" *I hissed and thrashed again and was able to knee his friend in the face.*

"*Fuckin' bitch!*" *The guy held his bloody nose.* "*Do it, already, Glen!*"

"*Mm, I love how soft a girl's thighs are.*"

I wanted to puke, but instead I focused my energy on where I was going to head butt next.

His hands moved higher up, and I prepared for when he bent down. Tears gushed, but I hardly felt them. My muscles were locked in place when his

81

fingers reached my upper thigh.

"No! Help!" I screamed and bucked, but he was ready for it, and a heavy roar from an exhaust drowned out my cries.

"Relax, darling. You're going to love this."

Oh, my God, this was going to happen, right here, in this alley below a bright green neon sign that advertised the show girls next door. It would be the day I died inside. I thought the house was rough, but this...this was something else.

I felt him move into position, and I squeezed my eyes shut and waited for him to make any kind of move.

Someone will make a mistake.

Just when I thought his dick would tear into me, I felt him jerk off me. My eyes flew open, and there was a guy I'd never seen before beating the shit out of him. One by one, he fought them all off, plowing one guy's head into a wall. His hand rose and fell with a sickening sound. I wasted no time getting out of there and ran back into the mill where my stuff was hidden in one of the corners. Somehow, I managed to put a pair of shorts on and got my stuff swung over my back.

I raced to the window and looked down. My attackers were all on the ground, knocked out cold or dead. I didn't care which. Then I heard a noise and whirled around as the guy found me. He had short, messy hair, wore a hoodie, and had a backpack of his own.

I was trying to decide on an escape route when he held up his hands. "I'm just making sure you're okay."

I held my stuff closer to my body. "I'm fine." I stepped back and wondered why he helped me. In my experience on the streets, no one ever helped, fearing they'd become a target too.

"Okay, good." He looked around then back at me again. "Are you here by yourself?"

"You care, because…?"

"Because you'll only get jumped again if you are."

I shrugged, and my defenses went up. "Been doing pretty well on my own so far."

He smirked. "Bet you have to keep moving."

"Yeah." He was right about that, and I didn't need to lie. Truth was, I didn't have a spot that was my own. "So?"

"You always this friendly after someone helps you out?"

I couldn't help myself and responded to his warm smile. I sighed and dropped my pack to the floor, exhausted. I followed suit and sat back against the cool wall. "Sorry." I tried to relax, but the memory of what almost happened began to surface. "That was fucking scary."

He slowly approached and sat warily but at a respectable distance, which I appreciated. "It was."

We sat in silence for a few moments before he moved in a bit and held out a hand. "Matt."

"Tess."

Sirens filled the room, and we jumped to our feet.

"Shit." He rushed to the window. "I dropped the brick I was using on them down there. We need to go. Can you run?"

"Yeah."

"Good. Hold my hand." We disappeared down the stairs.

***

Trigger

We stopped for gas and something to drink at the M Resort Casino just off the Fifteen Freeway. It had been pouring all night, so our drive took much longer than normal. Even on a bike, splitting traffic was a bitch. Every driver in any vehicle would be so intent on keeping themselves from hydroplaning they sure as hell wouldn't see us on the road.

"That semi drenched me." Brick wrung out his pant leg. "I wanted to blow out his tires."

I grunted out an agreement and poured a shitty cup of coffee from the corner store tucked into the side of the entryway. I eyed the creamer and saw a layer of curdled dairy on the top. I tossed it in the trash and grabbed a fresh one from the fridge.

"Sir, you can't—" The young clerk's sentence trailed off when she took in my annoyed face. "Never mind."

I grabbed a protein bar and held out a twenty to the girl then wiped my hair out of my eyes. Her cheeks were pink as she slid it away from me and proceeded to make change.

"You guys staying at the resort?" She glanced at me again.

"No." I left a five and headed out with Brick behind me. I stopped under a dry spot and lit a joint.

The rain was still heavy and showed no sign of letting up.

"How far?"

Brick lit his and blew out before he answered me. "Fifteen. I've never been past the gates, but if Jace got in, you know you will. It all comes down to the money."

I eyed the pack on the side of my bike and hoped Eli had come through with what I asked.

"Jesus." Brick shuddered like he had just had a nasty thought. "That house has some crazy shit darkness inside."

I tilted my head back to stare up at the clouds and hoped she was alone right now. I knew I would kill someone if she wasn't.

"What happened that made her go back to that house the last time you guys split up?"

Brick closed his eyes. "Well, I want to know why she stayed away for six years more."

I didn't point out he avoided my question. He'd told me a lot, and I respected that. For now.

"Come on." I tossed my joint into the dirt and started my bike. As I eased out, I caught sight of a man in a truck staring at us.

Do I know you? His face tugged a recent memory, but I couldn't place him.

Once we hit the road, I clicked the button on my helmet.

"You see the tan truck as we left?"

"No."

"Tan, Chevy, two-door. Keep an eye out."

"Copy that." He gave me a thumbs up.

Lightning shot across the sky as we turned into

the Wynn parking lot around three-thirty in the morning. We pulled up to the valet and handed the kid our keys. One glance at my cut, and he handed me my ticket. I hated the idea of someone else riding my bike, but I knew the kid would probably roll it into place by how scared he looked.

"You good?" He nodded at me. "Look after it."

"Of course."

Inside, Eli was in the lobby waiting for us, dressed like he owned the place. Well, maybe that was because he was the owner's stepson.

"Nice to see you again," he greeted us but took note that I wasn't in the mood to gamble or drink. "Please follow me."

We headed to the elevators where we joined an older couple. The guy had a tiny poodle thing stuck in his arms that whined when we came closer.

Don't blame it. The couple shifted closer to the far wall and turned the dog to face away from us.

Once on the thirty-ninth floor, Eli took us to our room. He opened the door and pointed to the table. The place had glass floor to ceiling windows.

"Everything you will need is here." He pointed to my ID, bank account number, and car keys. "And, of course," he motioned for me to look, "your pick of clothing." There was a garment rack thick with outfits for me to try.

I glared at Brick, who had already broken into the fully stocked bar. "Suck it up, Trigger. If you want to get in, you need to play the part."

"Fuck." The last time I wore a suit was when I won my last fight. My asshole father scammed a gambler, and I had to play a part in that shit too.

86

Hated every minute of it.

Eli waved around. "The kitchen is stocked, bar is too. You have the room for however long you need." He stepped closer and rubbed above his lip. "You need help, you know my number. All I ask is keep it out of my hotel."

"Like you did my club?"

Eli had enemies too and brought them right to the steps of my club. He owed me, and he knew it.

He pressed his hands down his suit uneasily, but before he left, he plastered on a smile and said, "Enjoy."

Brick set a bottle of whiskey on the counter. "You'll need this before you go."

I downed about a quarter before I moved to look out over the Strip. An unexpected memory of Tess drew my head elsewhere.

"Does the name Lily mean anything to you?"

I watched Brick's reflection in the window, and he went still and hesitated before he answered.

"Tess didn't have many friends in the house until a girl named Mags arrived. She was from North Carolina and had dreams of being a showgirl. Of course, she got tangled up in some shit and ended up at the house looking for fast cash. Mags and Tess hit it off right away. A few years later, Mags got involved with a client who got her pregnant and then proceeded to beat Mags whenever she didn't do as she was told. Lily was four when her mother was killed. They said it was a pill overdose in the living room, but now we know it wasn't." He sank into a chair. "I hate that Tess had to see that video."

"Where's Lily now?" I downed some more

whiskey.

"Parents. They're here now."

"The boyfriend?"

"He's around, draining her parents dry. I'm assuming that's why Tess cuts her paychecks in half, to help them out."

"Not her problem." I shrugged.

"It kinda is. Mags left Lily to Tess."

I turned around as I absorbed that.

"Yeah, but Tess doesn't want kids. She's got too much going on inside to raise a child. Besides, Mags's parents are good people. They wanted to raise her, so Tess agreed. Trouble is they don't have much money, especially after hiring shitty investigators to look into Mags's death. Their lawyer was bought off and ran off with their money."

"Shit luck."

"Hmm." He opened a beer and made a nasty face at the taste. "You should see Tess with Lily. They have a bond."

"I'll take your word on it." I didn't want kids. Never had.

Brick nodded. "You better get ready."

CHAPTER SEVEN

Tess

I started to wake, hating that feeling of being emotionally exhausted, but my body begged me to move. I stretched then felt like someone was watching me. I jolted upright and glanced around through dry, scratchy eyes.

Empty. The room was empty. Just like me.

With all my willpower, I peeled off the bed, showered, and changed into another house uniform.

I glanced at my phone to see if the doctor had emailed or called, but there was nothing. I pushed that dark cloud aside. Couldn't worry about something that hadn't happened yet.

I squeezed my eyes shut and held onto the counter for support.

Don't cry, Tess. You're stronger than this. That terrible video played over and over in my mind. How could I face them? I wanted to scream and tear them all apart with my bare hands. How could they do that to Mags? This place had taken so much from me. How I fucking hated it.

I had to pull myself together, as I had to in the past. I forced all grief from my mind and allowed the anger to flow through me and used it to steady myself. I moved purposefully to my bedside table and slipped a cuff over my wrist, dried the tears, and eyed my knife and envisioned it slicing through his skin and into his black heart.

Fuck. I shook off the craving and headed downstairs. It wasn't time. Soon, but not yet.

The main floor was busy, as usual. The bar was in full swing. That was Vegas for you. No sleep, just sex, booze, and endless amounts of money. I spotted Clark at a table with a young girl. I assumed it was the cocaine junkie's new replacement. He spotted me and nodded for me to come over.

I want to carve your heart out and jam it on a stick, so everyone can see your lies.

I loathe you.

I turned away and headed in the opposite direction. I wasn't ready to face him yet, and the odds of me losing it were high. Again, I pictured myself snapping off his balls and jamming them down his throat, and it made me feel a little better.

I noticed my mother flirting with a client in the living room, right about where she helped kill Mags, and my stomach rolled, but I reminded myself I was here for a reason. I hadn't felt this emotional in a long time, and frankly, I despised it. Nowhere was safe. Everywhere I looked, there were liars and murderers. How was I going to do this? How could I be here?

I could slice them both up and bury them under

the house. Lord knew how many bodies were already there.

I can't do this. I can't be here.

"Tessa?" Rachel called out, slapping me back to the present. "Can you come here, please?"

Shit. No!

"Wow, rough night?" She narrowed in on my face. I wondered if she knew the truth, and if she saw the video too. "Jesus, Tessa, what happened?"

"That's a loaded question." *I wish I had my loaded gun.*

She waved off my sarcasm, and her whole face lit up. "Well, snap out of it 'cause you have a client who requested you. Damn, you must be a freak in bed, girl."

Jace is here? The vise around my chest loosened a notch.

"Same guy as last time, right?"

"Nope." She pointed behind me, and I felt the vise tighten again.

Then, who?

My heart jumped into my throat when I saw him. Trigger sat in a chair, relaxed like he belonged there. His intense green eyes locked onto mine, and I felt the unforgettable hold he had on me. He slowly rose and buttoned his jacket with ease.

Jacket?

Wow. He was dressed in a dark gray three-piece suit. A navy-blue dress shirt peeked out from under his gray and black tie.

Wait…his hair was different. Shit, he looked more intense than ever.

My clit strummed to my wild heartbeat.

91

He strolled toward me, his broad shoulders a reminder of how large he was. He extended his hand and waited.

Breathe, Tess.

I hesitated, unsure if my body would work. Cautiously, I slipped my hand into his.

If it was possible to orgasm from a simple touch, it would be from his.

"Tess." He nodded and squeezed my hand, but didn't let go. "I've been waiting patiently for you."

Oh, my God, what was he doing here? I started to freak the fuck out inside. I hoped to God Clark hadn't spotted him, but he was deep in conversation with another man.

I battled with wanting to kill everyone and the fact that Trigger stood in front of me.

So many things fired off inside my head at once, I couldn't seem to find my voice.

He leaned toward my ear, still holding my hand, and I couldn't help but turn into him. Heat poured off his neck, and my head went light.

"Take me somewhere, Tess."

The fog lifted.

It was like his words brought me back to a sudden clarity. I dropped his hand, stepped out of his space, and glanced at the time on the desk.

"Well, I know I'm booked today, sir, but if you can wait, I'm sure we can work something out."

He clicked his tongue as he absorbed what I said, and then he glanced around. "I have all the time in the world to wait for you, darling. I could use a drink."

"Tessa, dear, who is this?"

Fuck. My mother shot a fresh dose of panic through my veins. *This cannot be happening.*

Trigger studied her and made the connection quickly, as we are basically twins. He muttered something, but I couldn't make it out.

My mother extended her hand limply and gave him a slutty smile. "Felicia. I'm the owner of this house."

Trigger didn't acknowledge her hand, just stared at her.

Oh, shit. I hope he doesn't lose it. Well, actually...

My mother looked at me, confused, but kept her smile plastered on her Botoxed face.

Yes, mother, it's hard to believe, but you can't use sex as a weapon on all men.

"So," she came behind the desk, "who are you scheduled to see today?"

"He's here to see Tessa," Rachel answered for him. "He won't see anyone else."

"Tessa seems to be fully booked today, sir."

Rachel pointed to the screen, and my mother's face changed.

"My, my. Well, let me see what I can do."

Yeah, she saw his bank account.

"I'll just move Bret to your lunch break. Lord knows you could skip a meal here and there," she muttered, and I felt my face flush. She cleared her throat when she realized what she had said in front of a potential customer and tried to backpedal.

"Tessa knows I joke."

Bitch.

"Actually, we were just going to have a drink.

Come this way, sir." I pushed by her, and Trigger reached out to take my elbow. He kept a good pace as he steered us into the bar area but away from the other girls who were busy entertaining their own clients.

Clark glanced in our direction, but he didn't seem to recognize Trigger, or at least he didn't let on that he did. Many men like Trigger had come through our doors. As long as they had the money, they were allowed in.

Jesus. My nerves were shot. Once we were out of earshot, I forced a big smile at Trigger to keep up the facade.

"What the hell are you doing here, Trigger?" I was moments from losing my shit. My two worlds were colliding in the worst possible way. I should have known he might come after Jace filled him in. I was angry with myself as well as him.

"I needed to talk—"

"So, you thought coming here was the best idea?"

He brushed his tongue over his teeth and tugged on his tie. "What was I supposed to do? Call? Email? You're unreachable."

"You *told* me to leave, if I remember correctly." I didn't want to toss it in his face, but come on.

"I had to say that to you, Tess. I had my reasons. It's part of what I need to talk to you about."

"Hey, Tessa." Bret popped out of fucking nowhere holding a glass of scotch. Damn, he stank.

"Get lost, man." Trigger stood straighter.

"You can't claim the women here." Bret laughed. "Gotta pay for a spot." He reached out and fingered the corset between my breasts, like always.

Die, Bret. Just die.

Trigger reached out slowly and took Bret's hand and squeezed it so hard he had to let go, all the while holding Bret's gaze with his cold, green eyes. "Let's not make a scene here, but if you touch her again, I will kill you."

"Jesus, man. I pay a lot of money for this chick to ride me, and I've booked her right now."

I was about to blow. "I'm so sorry, Bret, but there was a conflict. Felicia wants to see you."

"Mm, I just might work out a mother-daughter combo." He sneered at Trigger.

I closed my eyes and moved the hair out of my face. I guessed my secret was out anyway. Trigger had made it quite clear he wasn't okay with who I was back at the church, so why should I care?

"Did you sleep with him?" Trigger didn't hide his disgust.

Oh, hell no!

"If I did?"

"Did you?"

"Un-fucking-believable." I covered my face to take a moment to think. I needed him out of here. "What do you want, Trigger? I really don't have a whole lot left inside me right now."

"I told you I want to talk."

"Now isn't a good time."

"When?" He crossed his arms. I tried hard to figure out something.

I looked around to see who was watching. "Look, there's a café down the street called Brew. Meet me there at four p.m."

"Fine."

I waited for him to leave, but he didn't. "Why aren't you leaving?"

He waved the bartender over. "I think I might stay, check the place out."

"No."

"Whiskey, top shelf."

"Of course." The bartender acted quickly.

"No, Trigger, you can't stay here."

"Watch me."

Fuck! Stubborn ass.

My hand landed on his arm, and he stared at it then closed his eyes. I almost forgot what it was like to be close to him. To touch him. To be the only one who could.

"There were reasons why I left, and one of those reasons is over there." I tilted my head. "You want to talk, and so do I. Please," I whispered. "Please don't start anything. I don't know how much more I can take right now."

He followed my line of sight then turned back to me. His gaze fell to my neck, and warmth spread between my legs. My skin heated, and I knew I wanted him to do something about it, but that would have to wait.

"I have to go." I was about to step back when his arm locked around my waist.

He leaned in and brushed his lips over my earlobe. "I'll make you a deal."

I could barely handle how close he was again.

"If you're not wet, I'll behave. If you are, it's fair game. After all, look where we are."

"Trigger." I nearly panted as his free hand slid

down my side, over my hip, and curled around the edge of my panties. Before I could stop him, he stroked my folds with the pads of his fingers. He chuckled and slipped his fingers inside me with ease.

"You lose." His voice vibrated through me.

I reached out and held his shoulder for support. The fact we were in public failed to matter. Trigger knew exactly how to stroke to build me up.

"D to the N," Shantee chimed in behind me. I pulled quickly out of his hold and pushed his hand away. Trigger looked like he might murder her. "I heard there was some new meat in the house, but no one prepared me for this." Shantee reached out to touch Trigger, and I grabbed her hand and pulled her closer.

"Shantee, meet…" I stumbled to come up with a name.

"Don't need a name, sweetheart." She bit her finger in an attempt to be sexy. "I just want to know what side of the road he drives on."

Trigger downed his drink as I asked for another. "Straight, but flattered."

I was pleasantly shocked by Trigger's manners.

"Well, give me time." She turned to me. "Venna is looking for you. Said you took her shift, and you need to be there now."

"Shit, that's right. Okay, thanks."

Trigger eyed me sideways. "Shift?"

***

Trigger

I sat in my car outside the gate and sent off a few emails and touched base with the guys. Cooper told me my father got the package. We were waiting for what would come next. Eye for an eye, bitch. I never started this war.

Truth be told, I couldn't watch Tess dance. I'd kill someone, and she didn't need that right now. She had agreed to talk later, and that was enough for me.

Brick: You kill anyone yet?

Trigger: Night's still early.

Brick: How is she?

Trigger: Guarded.

Brick: Clark's got his claws in her, then?

Trigger: Yeah.

A flash of purple raced by the window, and it took me a moment to squint through the rain to see it was Tess. She looked to be in a hurry in her high heels and house outfit.

What the hell?

I slammed the car into drive and eased up beside her. She stopped, closed her eyes, and muttered something before she opened the door and slipped in.

I blasted the warm air and moved my bag to the back seat before I headed out into the flow of the traffic.

"What happened to your shift?" I eyed her outfit, and she covered herself with the soaking wet robe.

"Couldn't do it."

"Why?"

"Trigger—" She stopped herself and looked out the window. "Just forget it."

She stayed quiet but wiped her cheeks a few times. Her damp hair made it hard to read her face, but she needed time to get over her pissed off feelings.

I pulled up to the Wynn and tossed the keys at the kid who jumped when I parked.

"Good evening, sir. Do you need any help this evening?"

"No." I pulled the bag from the back seat and wrapped my jacket around her shoulders. I placed my hand on her back to steer her to the elevators. Once inside, she put distance between us, so I closed the gap, and again my hand was on her hip.

I pulled the key free and opened the door and waited for her to come in. She hesitated until she heard the TV. She peered inside and saw Brick as he poured a beer into his Cheerios. He looked her over as if to see if she was okay before he went back to his show.

"You look like shit, Tess."

She rolled her eyes and came further into the room.

"Yeah, hell will wear you out."

"How was the bitch?"

99

Her shaky fingers tucked a piece of hair behind her ear. "She booked me solid."

"To dance?"

"No."

Brick flicked off the TV and turned to face her. All fun was gone. He started to approach her but thought better of it and stood back. "Tess, you didn't." He rubbed his head. "Please tell me you—"

"Venna is back. We made a deal that she'd take my clients, and I'd dance. She needed the money more." She glanced at me then quickly looked away. "It wasn't easy and took me to a dark place, but it was only temporary."

"Temporary? Why did you even go back?"

I slammed a glass on the bar and filled it to the top with whiskey.

"He's just pissy he had to wear a suit." Brick waved me off. "Tess, did Clark…I mean, did he do anything?"

Her silence pulled my attention in their direction. Tess shook her head and moved over to the bar. "Pour me one of those. I've things to tell you, but I need a shower first."

Brick pointed to my room. "Towels are under the sink."

"Thanks." She pulled my jacket off her shoulders and hung it on the back of the chair.

Brick waited for the water to start running before he joined me at the bar.

"Well?" I grew impatient.

"I'm glad we got to her when we did. It's obvious she knows something she's not ready to talk about."

"Any idea?"

"My guess would be the million-dollar question why Tess stayed at the house for six years."

I tugged the tie off and tossed it on the table and unbuttoned the shirt. I wanted to change into my cut and jeans, but Eli had advised me to dress the part of a businessman so as not to draw too much attention to the fact that we were here.

I ordered room service, and when the bellman arrived, he glanced over my shoulder and smiled. I followed his line of sight and found Tess in one of my t-shirts. A part of me was glad she didn't choose one of the dress shirts. I liked her in my clothes.

"You like your dick?" I snapped at the bellman, who couldn't seem to keep his eyes off her.

"Sorry." He straightened and handed me the slip. "If you could sign here."

I signed and shoved it back at him.

He pointed to one of the covered plates. "Here is your steak with sweet potatoes and—"

"I ordered it," I reminded him.

"Right." He peeked at Tess again, and my temper rose. "Is there anything I can get you, miss?"

Tess came to my side and shook her head. "Thank you."

"Of course." He didn't leave.

I pulled out my gun and checked the clip. It was full. The man cleared his throat then turned and left quickly.

She sighed. "That was rude."

"He was staring at you."

"So do you," she challenged.

"That's different."

"How?" She propped her hands on her hips and lifted her chin.

"You're mine."

For a split second, I saw her flinch, but she kept it together.

"Was," she corrected before she turned back to the bedroom.

"Where the hell are you going?"

"Bed."

"You need to eat, and we need to talk."

She glanced back at me from the doorway. "I do appreciate you ordering it, but I'm not hungry. I'm also super tired, Trigger. I need to sleep."

Fine.

Later that night, the rain turned into a storm and lit up the entire place. Tess took Brick's room, and he slept on the couch in the other room.

My head was chaos. The demons wouldn't sleep, so I drank to keep them quiet. I lit a joint and kicked my feet up on the rail of the balcony. Whenever the rain blew, I got sprayed, but the cold felt good on my throbbing head.

It was a habit to sit in the far corner of a space, so no one could sneak up behind me. Plus, fewer people would interact with the lurker in the shadows.

I wasn't a fan of Vegas. Too many fights held here, too many desperate women looking to trap a man into marriage.

My dick twitched when I saw Tess step out onto the balcony with her phone to her ear. I strained to listen over the storm.

"I'm sorry, Ven. I just needed to step back for the night." She sounded exhausted. She paused to listen then dropped her head. "Yeah, he's just someone from my past."

Just? I didn't like that word.

"Clark will be fine. No, I don't want to talk to him. Tell him I'll be back tomorrow." She rubbed her head. "Thanks, girl. I'll make it up to you somehow." She hung up and ran her hand through her hair before she caught me out of the corner of her eye. I drew back the smoke and let it coat my lungs, taking in her body under my shirt.

"Jesus, Trigger." She held her chest. "Miss your pickup much?"

I smiled at her comment; she had a point. I did. I liked how I could blend in the shadows in the back of my truck.

The wind blew her shirt back, outlining her body. Her nipples grew hard, and so did my erection.

"What are you doing out here?"

I flicked the joint then handed it to her. She thought for a moment before she stepped up and was careful not to make skin to skin contact.

She sat on the footstool and crossed her legs, hiking the shirt up further.

"Couldn't sleep."

She blew out the smoke and nodded. "Understand that one." She jumped when a clap of thunder burst above us. "I like your hair."

I was pleased she liked it and took that moment to lean over and pull her stool between my legs. Her hands landed on my shoulders to stabilize herself.

"You need to be closer."

"Why?"

I pointed to my head. "The only time they're quiet is when you're near me."

"It's all mental, Trigger. You can override that shit."

I leaned closer, using my size to prove my point. "No, Tess, only you can." My lips were close to hers, and I smelled her arousal lingering in the heavy mist around us. I wanted to attack her, dominate her, but I didn't yet. The Clark thing hung between us. He was too close and had sunk his claws in too deep.

She dipped her head to block my access. "We should talk first."

"Then, talk." I moved her legs apart and slid my hands up her smooth, cool thighs. It was as if someone draped a cloak over my demons' cages, granting me a moment of sanity. I suddenly became thirsty for her taste, my tongue begging to lap at her skin.

Her hands landed on mine, but it didn't stop me. She moved out of my hold and stood at the balcony. I covered her back with my front and slipped my hand into her wet panties. I parted her smooth folds and slipped two fingers inside.

Her head flopped back onto my shoulder, but I felt her desire to fight me. My mouth latched onto her neck and drew in her intoxicating taste. My erection was painful, so with a free hand, I let it out and lined up with her. Before she could protest, I dove in until I hit my base.

She screamed and arched her back. I held her

tightly and sucked harder.

I could barely think as her walls adjusted to my size. I hiked her leg up on the chair and leaned back to get a different angle. I drew out to my tip and slammed back in. She screamed my name and clawed at my arm around her stomach.

"Harder." She reached back inside my pants and cupped my balls. My switch was dangerously close to flipping. She drove me wild as her nails dug my flesh.

"Tess," I warned through a locked jaw, "careful."

"Careful?" she bit out and pulled away so I'd slip out. The loss of contact made me instantly angry. "Careful of what? Because you've lost your shit on me before? Or are you saying careful, like you might throw it in my face that I'm a whore?"

What the fuck?

"I never called you a whore, Tess."

"You may not have said the word." She stepped back when I came near her.

"Don't walk away from me." I saw red, and my dick grew hot.

"You screw anyone while I was gone, Trigger?"

I hated the head games, but I hated to be questioned more.

"I can fuck whoever I want." I marched up and backed her into the corner. "When I want."

Her hand rested on my chest, and her head dropped, but not before I saw the sadness in her eyes. "Then you don't need me."

That stopped me in my tracks and held me in place, and she slipped around me and disappeared inside.

I hated my fucking ego.

CHAPTER EIGHT

Tess

The next morning, I woke to a pounding headache. I showered and put my house clothes back on. Careful not to wake Brick, I searched for my shoes, but they weren't in the room.

Damn. I must have kicked them off in the living room.

Thankfully, the place was quiet, and I found my shoes by the coffee table. Just as I slipped the second one on, I heard the couch squeak.

"Tess?" Brick rubbed his eyes. "Where are you going?"

I stood and headed for the door. "I need to go to work."

"What?"

"I'll call you later."

"Hang on—"

I opened the door to Trigger holding a tray of coffee cups.

He used his bulk as he moved forward and

forced me to back up. He shot me the most pissed off look and handed me a Starbucks coffee.

"Brick." He held my gaze, and Brick headed for the bedroom, leaving us alone.

"I'm late. I need to go." I held up the coffee. "Thank you."

He beat me to the door and slammed it shut. His arms folded over his chest, and I got hit with the scent of his body soap. I flinched, and I knew he caught it.

"I didn't drive four and half hours, dress in a fuckin' monkey suit, and be in the same room with your goddamned ex just for you to sneak out on me."

"I never asked you to do that." I felt like a child with my response, but if he was going to use that excuse, I was going to remind him of mine.

He took a step closer, and I held my ground. "Do you want to be there?"

"No."

He threw his hands in the air with an exasperated sigh. "Then why the fuck are you going back?"

"Because of you!" I shouted, and his face twisted in confusion. "You may think I'm a whore, and that I'm beyond fixable, and you know what? I am. I don't wanna be fixed." I pointed to my head. "I deal with my fucking demons too. My past is way more fucked than even Brick knows." Tears streamed down my cheeks.

"Then share! You said you wanted to talk, that you had something to tell me." His voice made my ribcage rattle.

"Why? So you can throw that in my face too?"

108

"No, so I can understand!"

Oh. Well, he asked for it.

"I fell in love with a man at ten years old. He made me feel like I had a place in this world." My throat burned with the words. "That I wasn't just a fuck-up in the back of a dingy strip joint. He loved me. He talked to me and bought me shiny things. We had secrets. It was wrong, I see that now, but it felt so good. I was happy and felt loved." I angrily brushed my tears away. "My mother was and is a jealous bitch and saw he wanted her money. She hated what I had, so she used him and got him to marry her. I'm not stupid, and I know he saw an equal opportunity and went along with it." I yanked up my bracelets to show my scar. "Just another reminder of my failure as a woman. You wanna know what happened after my mother brought me back from the psych ward? She made sure I would see them having sex, or kissing. She wanted me to try this again," I held up my wrist, "and she still does."

I stopped to catch my breath, and he stared.

"Clark tried everything to get me to understand why he married my mom. Said he had to for us to be together. Didn't take that long for me to fall for him again. Love is like that, especially when you're young. My eighteenth birthday, he took me to on a weekend trip where we had sex for the first time."

I hoped that stung him as much as it did me telling this story.

"He stole my heart and my virginity. I thought things would be different then, but every time my mother won, and every time my world would crash around me. There's so many broken pieces of me floating around inside, I don't know what fits where, and what doesn't."

I couldn't go on. I couldn't go that one step further and utter the horror that might tip the scale too far. I was permanently scarred.

"The last six years after I left Brick at the warehouse…" My shame got hold of me, and I stopped. "Look…"

I took a deep breath, but it was no use. I was too vulnerable to be rational.

"I made a promise that I wouldn't step foot inside that house after I left, after he stole the very last piece of me." I started to cry harder.

"Why did you? What did you mean, you did it for me?" he asked softly as he kept a safe distance away. I didn't blame him. I was a mess.

I eased into the chair, too tired to stand. "It's what I wanted to tell you, why I came to you in the church. That day, I heard Detective Aaron on the phone, talking to Clark about how he had something that could destroy your club. Clark was pissed because Aaron didn't keep his end of the bargain."

"Which was?"

"Me for the information."

Trigger popped his neck.

"I hid in the van. Jace and Morgan had no idea. I just wanted to tell you, and I didn't know when you'd be back. But you…" I closed my eyes for a moment before I stood on shaky legs. "I need to go back before Clark sends someone else to find me or leaks whatever information he has on you."

"Tess…" He rubbed his face.

"Please don't. I don't want to hear an apology."

"I'm not sorry."

I huffed out a laugh. "Of course, you're not." I headed for the door, but he hooked my arm and swung me around to face him.

"I'm not sorry for lying. Brick never told me. I just knew you were hiding something, so I played dirty. You never listen to me, so I had to hurt you so you would. I know you're still lying about it. Maybe not lying, but you're holding something back. But," he moved closer, "that man dressed as a Father of the Church...is actually my own father."

What?

"But..."

"I would have said anything to get you as far away from that man as possible. You think I scare you, times that by ten."

"But I heard you killed him."

He broke eye contact and shook his head. "I'm still trying to figure that out."

Wow, I wasn't expecting that.

He cursed and looked back at me; his eyes held so much emotion. "You've seen many sides of me, Tess, and accepted me in spite of it all. But the hole that opened in me when I saw my father standing there, still with a heartbeat, did something to me I can't explain. When you showed up, I had to get you away from him. He may have looked like a man of the Church, but believe me, he is wicked fuckin' Satan underneath. We might share demons, darlin', but mine would seriously hurt you."

I stepped into him, unable to stop myself. Trigger, raw with words, was indescribable. I reached up to show my intent and ran my hand over his cheek. His eyes bore through me. I knew we were both shitty at the intimacy part, but I wanted to show I heard him. I wanted to show him I was trying.

"You…" He stumbled and tried again with a harsher tone. "You are the last person I would want to hurt."

"Okay."

He nodded once but kept his hand locked around my arm as if I grounded him.

"Do you still love him?" he blurted, and my hand dropped away.

I fought with the wall that wanted to shoot up.

"We have a history, Trigger."

"That's not what I asked."

"I know." I took a sip of my coffee and backed up. Surprisingly, he let me go.

"He killed your best friend. How are you going to tell me you still love him?"

He was right. I was sure I didn't, but for whatever reason, I couldn't say the words.

"I need to go."

He blocked my path just as Brick, who no doubt was eavesdropping, came into the room.

"Tess," he said, "I really don't think you should go back. Let us figure out what Clark has on the club, and we'll deal with it."

"How?" I felt wrung out.

"We know people."

"I need my stuff." It was true; I did. I wanted my camera more than anything else.

Trigger's annoyance was evident. "Stuff can be

replaced."

"*Stuff* has memories for me, Trigger. I don't have many things, and the few I have, I want to keep." I rubbed my head, not sure where to go from here. "Give me the weekend, at least, to get my stuff."

Trigger glanced at Brick, and they exchanged some kind of thought.

"Guys, I can't leave Venna there, not without an explanation. She was, after all, the one who saved me from working the house. She kept me from having to sleep with countless men." That wasn't entirely true. I was sure I would have left before that happened, but I knew it would hit Trigger hardest.

"No," Trigger ordered, and when I began to protest, he cut me off. "I'll drive you there, so you can get your stuff and talk to your friend, then we'll meet Brick here and leave for Santa Monica tonight."

"Tess," Brick took my hand in his, "do this for me."

Fuck.

"You play dirty."

He beamed when he knew he had me.

"First, I need to buy some new clothes."

Brick went behind the bar and handed me a bag. "Something from home."

I peeked inside and smiled.

*   *   *

Although I slept well at the hotel, it did nothing for my head space. In fact, it tossed me right back to

113

street survival mode. I peeled my tired body off the leather seat of the Lexus and stood on heavy feet. Trigger eyed me cautiously as he rounded the car and steered me inside.

"You okay?"

I nodded, but I was nowhere close.

He came up next to me, and I whirled around, confused.

"You can't come inside. Clark knows your face."

"Don't worry about it."

"No." I cringed. "They'll kill you, or they might release the information."

He shrugged and nodded toward the house, urging me forward.

"Hey," I grabbed his arm and felt the warmth that came with my touch, "you may not care, but I do."

He licked his lips. I knew it was hard for him to put himself in another's shoes. That was the problem with giving a fuck, but I was serious.

"I may not care about myself, but I…" He rubbed the back of his head as if he were annoyed.

"Fine," I huffed and headed up the stairs. "Stubborn ass."

He chuckled behind me, which only made me more pissed off. Just to add fuel to the fire, he reached forward and opened the door and waved me on.

Oh, sure, now you're a gentleman.

Gilbert stepped in front of Trigger and asked him to spread his arms.

"Gilbert, let him pass."

"You know the rules, Tessa."

114

I glanced at him, worried, as he felt Trigger's jacket, waistband, legs, and ankles. The entire time, I witnessed the battle in his head. I wanted to help, but I didn't want to draw attention to us either.

"All clear. Have a good day, sir."

I pointed to the bar. "Give me twenty, and I'll meet you here."

He shook his head, but when he realized I wasn't going to budge, he backed down.

"You have ten before I come find you myself."

Each step up the stairs ignited my anger further. Flashes of Mags made their way into my head, and as I glanced over my shoulder at the living room, something snapped inside. I unlocked my bedroom door and grabbed my stuff then landed on my bed in a heap of confusion.

Nothing was making sense. All I could focus on was Mags. Her body—her limp body—being tossed around by people I once thought I knew and cared about.

I cringed away from the mirror and hated what looked back at me.

Emptiness.

I fingered the handle on the night table and pushed the papers aside. I felt the smooth blade and drew it free, looked at it, then held it tightly by my side.

Hatred consumed me from my very core, and I rose in a weightless stance.

I made my way cautiously out of my bedroom. My steps never wavered as my subconscious pointed me in the right direction. I felt like I had been drugged; my body operated on its own.

I had lost control.

I turned a corner and heard footsteps but didn't care. I pushed on. Someone raced across the hall but didn't notice me. It was, after all, a house that never slept. Just sex, booze, and endless amounts of money.

My feet barely lifted off the carpet as one moved in front of the other. I was numb all over.

The dark cherry-wood door was locked, but I knew just how to wiggle the handle to get it to open. Once I heard the release of the pin, I took a deep breath, and with an internal kick to the gut, I gave it a turn and stepped out of the light and into the dark.

Little lights that shone no brighter than the moon lit the crisp, white sheets of their bed and *his* outline. The smell of sex was still in the air, and I searched for her clothes but couldn't spot them.

Hmm.

I knew my mother well enough to know that whenever she got some, she'd have her smoke in her office and finish up her paperwork for the day. She wouldn't be interrupting us.

The blade tapped my bare leg, a reminder of why I was there.

At the foot of the bed, I came to a stop, pulled up my sleeves, and like a cat, crawled over his body. Using my knees to support my weight, I lifted the knife, but he must have felt me, and his erection bumped my thigh. The cool sheet brushed over my legs and made my skin heat with lust and rage.

Stab.

Stab.

Stab.

Mags's lifeless face appeared in front of me and turned to look at me right before they rolled her up in the carpet. Disposable, just like he was.

I stabbed again and twisted the blade roughly through his flesh to tear it at the roots. There was barely any struggle as I sliced at his soul the way he did mine.

Stab.

Stab.

Stab.

I couldn't see where he began, there was so much blood. My legs slipped around as I attacked more of him. Years of pent-up rage poured out of me in my blind state of mind.

It felt so good. So right.

I swore I felt Mags by my side, fueling me on.

Stab.

Stab.

With the knife in the air, I froze and jolted back and stumbled to my feet. It was as if someone suddenly pressed pause on a movie. I slapped my free hand over my mouth as I focused on the bed.

It was Bret.

Then it hit me. My mother suspected Clark was sleeping with someone else. I just never thought it was Bret!

Oh, fuck.

His naked body drained of blood quickly, and I was stuck in a fucking loop. What the fuck just happened?

I heard a sound and headed for the other door. I slipped and slammed into the dresser but managed to pull myself up and out of sight.

My ankle throbbed as I jolted out the door and down the hallway, holding the bloody knife with flesh still stuck to the blade.

My heart and lungs fought for room, and my stomach crept into my throat.

Slam!

I heard a stifled scream as someone pulled me upright and practically pushed me into my room and shut the door behind us.

"What the hell, Tess?" Venna jumped away from my bloody form. "Oh, my God. What did you do?"

"I-I…" I couldn't think quickly enough. "I killed."

"Killed who?" She grabbed the sheet off my bed and covered my shaking body while I stood like a zombie.

I couldn't seem to make myself answer, so she pushed me aside and frantically looked around. She spotted my phone on the side table and scrolled through it.

A flicker of light pulled my attention, and I caught the mirror again, only this time I stood straighter and stared directly into my own eyes. The knife still dangled from my fingertips, and I saw someone else looking back at me. A stronger me, not the me who always seemed to go dormant when I was here.

"Shit, Tess, where is Matt's number?"

Boom! The door burst open, and there was Trigger, lookin' fit to kill. He ran his eyes down my bloody body and quickly locked the door behind him.

He looked at Venna. "Tell me what you know."

"Nothing. She just slammed into me in the hallway, and I pulled her in here."

"Tess," he shook my shoulders, and I slowly met his eyes, "whose blood is this?"

"B-Bret's," I stammered.

Venna gasped behind me, and Trigger nodded, cool as could be.

"Is there a back way out of here?"

"Yeah, south side by the pool."

"In five minutes, make your way there, and I'll be in a blacked-out Lexus. Find me." Trigger dipped low to eye me one last time before he left.

Venna shoved the knife into my bag along with a few of my belongings and covered my bloody clothes with a clean, plush robe.

"No time to clean." Her hands shook as she turned me around and pushed me out the door and into the hallway.

Instead of going downstairs, she took us through the back way.

"It's okay, we're okay," Venna kept repeating.

Is it? I couldn't help but smirk at the power surge that raced through my core.

"Tess!" Clark's voice boomed through my head, and my veins froze solid.

No. Venna looked like she might pass out.

"Tess, where are you going, and what the shit happened to you?" He reached for me, and I pulled out Big Joe's gun and pointed it at him.

"Tess!" Venna screamed but remained by my side. "What are you doing?"

"Give it to me!" I pictured the smooth steel of the knife slicing through his blue shirt and into his

119

murderous heart. A heart I once loved.

"Give you what?" His hands were in the air.

I pointed the gun to his pocket, and he glared.

Come on, Clark. I know you're in there somewhere.

"No."

There he was. Clark had two personalities. Sweet and pricky.

"Does Mom know?" I tilted my head as I tapped into my new, wonderful state of mind. "Does she know you sleep with the man-whores of the house too?"

He did a double take then it clicked for him—the blood, my mood, us escaping.

"Tess," he started to move, but I raised the gun to his head, "I will give you one chance here to do the right thing." He sounded as though he was talking to a child, and that pissed me off further.

"It was *you* I came for."

"You wouldn't have been able to do it, Tess." He seemed so sure of himself.

"He's dead, isn't he?"

I relished the moment. My moment.

Clark's face changed, and his knees wobbled as though he was about to fall to the floor. He looked over his shoulder for a split second, and I took that moment to crack him over the head with the butt of the gun.

Down he went.

"Jesus Christ!" Venna nearly shouted. She watched as I dug in his pocket and grabbed his keys. "We have to go!" She grabbed my arm and pulled me out the side door to where Trigger was waiting.

As soon as we left the gates, the severity of what happened hit me like a brick.

"Don't check out on me, Tess." She touched my arm carefully in the one place the robe wasn't stained with blood. "I don't know him, and he terrifies me a little."

Her words didn't register. I couldn't stop shaking, my vison faded in and out, and my lungs couldn't get enough air.

I couldn't say how long we drove. Maybe fifteen minutes, just enough time for my head to freak out in loops of excitement, power, and full-blown panic.

When we arrived at the Wynn, Trigger pulled me to my feet. Venna followed with all my stuff. I was rushed into an elevator and felt my stomach roll as the smell of dried blood hit my senses hard.

Before I could say anything to Brick, who looked horrified, Trigger pushed me inside the bedroom and straight to the bathroom.

He ran the water and peeled my blood-soaked clothes off piece by piece.

I couldn't look at him, and he didn't look at me. He just kept himself busy until I was naked.

He ran his huge hands up my legs and around my body, checking to see if any of the blood was mine.

I couldn't help but feel the sick spark that we shared whenever anything like this happened between us, and by the way his hands flexed over my stomach, he felt it too.

"Get in," he grunted and pulled back the curtain.

I did as he told me, but mostly because I wanted Bret off me.

***

Trigger

Her blank expression told me she wasn't all there. The water beat off her face, and she opened and closed her mouth as if she was washing away the taste.

I stripped off my shirt, boots, and socks, and pulled the door open to step in. The water pounded my jeans and plastered them to my legs as I took her by the shoulders and turned her to face me.

"Lean back," I ordered and helped move her sticky hair under the spray. As gently as I could, I lathered the soap, coated her scalp, and massaged her head. "That feeling," I lowered my voice, "you'll get used to it."

She closed her eyes to shut out the hurt. The corners of her mouth lowered, and her chin exposed her true feelings. But she didn't break, which I admired. Tess was strong at times I wouldn't think she'd be.

"Arms." I tapped them once to get her to raise them. I moved the soapy puffy-fucking-thing all over her body to remove any sign of that man-whore that was left on her skin.

"I may have to patch you in," I joked.

Her eyes eased open, and I saw a hint of pride flicker across her lips.

"I'll get you something to wear." I stepped out and let her have a few moments alone.

"What the fuck happened to her?" Brick nearly tripped over his own feet when I came into the common area of the penthouse. His bowl of Cheerios stank like beer. I really wished he'd stick to one or the other.

I spotted Venna standing by the window. Her arms were wrapped around her, and she appeared deep in thought.

No doubt wondering how much shit she was in.

"Drink?" I held up a bottle of whiskey.

"No." She shook her head. "Got any vodka?"

I nodded at Brick to take over while I checked my phone.

"Tell me about Bret?" I asked over my shoulder.

Brick handed Venna a drink, and she took a sip and coughed. "He's…" She coughed again. Brick mixed a strong drink. "He's an asshole, although they all are. He's had it out for Tess forever. He keeps begging her mother for a threesome. If it was anyone but Tess, they'd have done it. Felicia is the freakin' devil stuck on a pair of legs. Well, a pair of freakin' good legs." She giggled darkly. "That's where Tess gets her looks. I think her father was some piece of shit who owned the strip joint her mom worked at…"

I tuned her out. Fuck me, I asked one simple question. I glanced at the bedroom door and waited for Tess to show herself.

"Why do you think Tess killed Bret?" Brick tried to force her back on track.

"She didn't mean to kill him. No," she corrected. "Tess and I ran into Clark on the way downstairs."

That caught my attention.

I whirled around and waited for her to go on. Her eyes widened as she stumbled over her own words.

123

"Tess made it very clear to Clark that she meant to go for *him*. Now she knows Clark was banging Bret, and she threatened to out him. He got pissed, but when he started to freak out, Tess hit him over the head with the gun." She shook her head. "All gangster style." She stopped herself. "No offense."

"Go on." I waved off her stupid comment.

"That was it. Oh, wait!" She tilted her head like she remembered something "She took the USB that hangs off his keychain. It's some stupid power trip thing he keeps over the employees of the house. I heard a rumor once that it holds a lot of secrets. I don't know, but Clark likes to play the flashy businessman. The dude is from Oklahoma, for God's sake. Just keep it real, ya know?"

The urge to kick her out was strong, but I wouldn't do that to Tess, so I'd keep her here…for now.

"Hey." Brick rose to his feet and greeted Tess with a hug. "You feeling a little better?"

She tugged at my t-shirt she was wearing and sank into the couch. "I'm…yeah, I'm okay."

"Hungry?"

"Very." She held her stomach.

"I got just the thing." Brick grabbed the hotel phone and prattled off an order.

Venna moved to Tess, and they started to chat quietly. Well, Venna did most of the talking.

Fifteen minutes later, there was a feast for six in the dining area. Wings, burgers, ribs, fries, rice, and potatoes sat in front of us. Finally, food I could get on board with. Vegas had a lot of pretentious food. I liked my meat.

I noticed Tess went for a burger and some fries. It was interesting that such a little woman could eat so much and stay that skinny.

"Nice to see you eat." Brick beamed behind a wing.

"Nice to want to eat." She sipped her water then glanced over at me. "What?"

"Venna mentioned you had a gun."

"Yup," was all she offered before she took another bite.

"Where did you get it?"

She swallowed then shrugged. "Big Joe."

What? Brick looked confused too.

"When was this?" He beat me to the punch.

She wiped her fingers then leaned back with a satisfied sigh. "Joe doesn't like Loose, and when Loose took me out for a walk, Joe got pissed and told me to take it just in case."

Joe needed a raise.

"Too bad you didn't use it on him." Brick snickered.

"Perhaps if I had a knife," she said darkly.

"Tess!" Venna gasped as she fought a smile. Her hand clamped down on Tess's, and she turned red from laughing. "Oh, it's too soon for that."

I raised an eyebrow at Brick, who looked shocked as hell. Who was this chick?

Later that afternoon, I settled everything with Eli. He seemed pleased we were leaving. I headed back to the room where I found Venna passed out on the couch, Brick at the TV, and Tess was…somewhere.

"Bedroom." Brick answered my unasked

125

question.

I found her curled up in the center of the bed. I could tell she was awake even though she had pulled the drapes closed.

"You good?"

"Yup."

"We're going to leave soon."

"Yup."

As much as I wanted to sink myself deep inside her, it wasn't the time. She wasn't in the right head space, and now Bret was most likely consuming her. I wouldn't compete with the dead.

***

Allen

"You think you can control yourself?" I pointed my gun at him to show I wasn't fucking around.

"Yeah."

"You sure?" I leaned forward and ran my tongue along my teeth.

He pulled at his jacket then flexed his fingers over his helmet. Little green eyes stared at me, begging me to use him again.

"Like I said, I got this. I really do. Last time, my head got away from me."

"Mmm." I flopped back on my seat. "If you can't get a good enough hold, don't risk it. Death is not an option tonight."

"Understood."

I glanced over at my hungry least weasels and pushed to my feet. They paced about their cages so aggressively that they'd shredded the bottoms of their feet.

"You six are just going to have to wait for your dinner." I turned to look over my shoulder at him to let him know I wasn't fucking around.

"Got it." He slammed his helmet over his head and rushed to join the others.

I smacked the cage and listened to the bloodthirsty screams from inside. I'd seen what these shits could do. You just drizzled a little rabbit blood over a human in a hole and let them feast.

They were the newest members in my army.

"Where do you want him?" Zay asked with his arm draped over a whore from the house.

"Out back."

"You have me confused!" the man screamed. "My name is James. I'm married with kids. Please! Please, Father, have mercy."

I straightened my collar and rubbed the dust from my arm.

"I'm very aware of who you are, Mr. Johnson. I just want to talk."

He knew better.

"Anything you want, but please don't hurt me."

"What do you know about Trigger?"

His gaze snapped up to mine. "Who?"

"Kill him."

CHAPTER NINE

Tess

"You can come with us." I hugged Ven again, but she shook her head.

"Maybe later, but right now I want to go see my brother. Thanks to you, I can."

"You need more?" I was willing to give her every last cent to thank her for all her help.

"No. I'm just happy to be out of there."

"Me too."

"Be careful, okay?" I nodded. "You go enjoy that fine specimen of a man."

I forced a smiled as she stepped up onto the Greyhound and waved when she found her seat in the back. I was going to miss her.

Trigger sat on the hood of the car, happy to give us some space. He didn't do emotion well, and I was sure with what I did, he looked at me differently.

I made my way over to him and ran my hands over my arms. The temperature had dropped, and the insane day was quickly coming to an end.

"Ready?" he asked as he put his phone away.

"Yeah." We really should get out of town.

He glanced at my pocket, and I knew what was coming. He saw the box in my bag, and when I tucked it away when he came into to the hotel earlier.

"What was in the box?"

I licked my lips, and my mouth went dry as I pulled out the engagement ring.

His eyes flickered up to mine then back to the ring.

"My eighteenth birthday, he asked me to marry him. It was one of our many secrets."

It wouldn't have been legal, but Clark wanted me to know he loved me as much as my mother.

Trigger nodded.

"It was a lie, like everything else. It was used as a control tactic that, sadly, I kept falling for."

"Did you go through with it?"

I hung my head, feeling so damn stupid and so hurt all at once.

"Almost."

"What stopped you?"

"Found him in bed with another girl. I threw the ring at him and left for a few days."

"Just a few days?"

"Look, Trigger, there's more to this…" I paused when I heard his phone alert him of a text, and Brick's name popped up.

"We need to leave." His voice almost scared me. I wished I knew what was going through his mind.

He headed for the driver's door, and I was left

feeling raw and slightly judged. I knew my past was fucked up, and it was why I didn't get close to people.

Instead of opening the door, I walked over to the edge of the cliff that dropped off into a canyon. I whispered a goodbye to the ring and threw it as far as I could. It glistened as it spun in the air, then it was out of sight.

"Hey," Mags's warm hand landed on mine and she gave it a friendly squeeze, "everything okay here?"

I glanced at my mother. She had her hands on a new client, who was asking for me to be his date for the evening.

No fucking way.

"George, is it?" my mother purred like the whore she was. "I'm sure there are several other ladies who would suit your needs better than Tessa."

My mother couldn't care less if I banged every man in the house, but because I wasn't cooperating, she had to divert the attention away from me and onto her. I'd get my ass handed to me later.

"It's her eyes." He ignored my mother and fixed his gaze on me. "They are a passionate mix of wild and worldly."

"If that's what you must see," she glared at me beneath her fake lashes, and I noticed they had peeled away at the corners, "I will see what Tessa's schedule looks like."

Mags read my terrified expression like an open book. There was no way that was going to happen.

"Hi, there." She stepped around me and offered her slender hand to him. He squinted before he tore his gaze off me and focused on my best friend. "I heard you said something about liking it rough?"

"I did." He held her hand so tight her skin turned white from lack of blood.

Something felt off about this ass even before he opened his mouth and showed his vampire- like teeth.

"Well, you're in luck. So do I." She winked, but I heard the hesitation in her voice. She felt it too. "Shall we discuss this over a drink?"

"What are you drinking?"

"Martini, dirty, hold the olives." She nodded to the bar and held her hand up to let him know she'd just be a moment.

"You don't have to do this, Mags." I pulled her closer to me so we could talk.

"Yes," she eyed my mother, "I do. You helped me keep this job after my little encounter with speed, and now it's time for me to take one for the team. Besides," her voice lowered, and she lovingly tucked a piece of hair behind my ear, "we both know this is not who you are. You're not like the rest of us, Tess. You're one of the good ones."

"So are you."

"I love you for saying that, but we both know who has more experience in this department. Besides, once he," she nodded at Clark, who greeted George at the bar, "gets wind that our new client is interested in you, there will be another dramatic episode between the three of you."

She was right on that one.

"There's something off about him, Mags."

"I know." She let out a shaky breath. "And I do plan on staying very far away from whatever the hell it is."

My mother strolled by with a look that could kill and hurried over to Clark to make sure she got her digs in on me. He may be her husband, but it was me he visited at night.

"Only three hundred and sixty-two more days, and then we'll be free of this place." Mags tried to pull my thoughts away from the matter at hand.

I grinned at her. It had been our plan since the day we met and realized how much we needed each other's friendship. "We'll live in a villa, a beautiful villa wedged in the side of a mountain. In Italy."

"With all the wine in the world."

"Wine and men," I corrected before she hugged me and left to sit next to the dark villain who would later shatter both our lives.

I shook the painful memory clear, and as far as I was concerned, Clark died along with Bret. He was nothing to me, history or not.

Trigger started the engine. I slipped inside the car and fell quiet with my thoughts.

It wasn't long before my eyes grew heavy, and I let myself drift off to an emotional sleep.

I woke to Trigger shaking my shoulder. It took me a moment to register him. He was back in jeans, black hoodie, and his cut. He smelled like weed and leather.

I had missed that smell.

"I let you sleep for as long as possible, but we

need get moving again."

Huh?

"Where are we?"

"State line."

With a groggy head, I stood on shaky legs and saw Brick's smile from his bike.

"Hey, beautiful."

I returned the warmth with a big hug. We were now going to be riding on the bikes. Well, shit. I looked longingly back at the nice, warm, comfy car, but knew I had to get my head back in the game.

"Here." He handed me my jeans.

I shimmied into them as Trigger watched. The man had no shame. Then he held out my leather jacket and threaded my arms through the sleeves like a child. He helped me with my helmet before he fired up the bike.

He waited for me to get on then nodded to Brick.

Guess we're leaving the car here.

The bike jolted forward, and I squeezed my eyes shut as he weaved down the on ramp and picked up speed on I-15. The air was freezing, and the further we drove, the colder it grew. It felt wonderful to press up against his back, my arms around his body and my thighs pressed around his ass. I felt at home on his bike. I rubbed my cold hands together whenever we had to slow down for merging traffic. Trigger unzipped his jacket pockets and urged my hands inside. They instantly thawed in his body warmth.

He might be an ass some of the time, but he could be incredibly thoughtful.

About two hours into the drive, my eyes started

133

to grow heavy. Between the hum of the bike and the setting sun, I wasn't sure I could stay awake. I leaned my forehead on his back and for a moment gave in to the urge.

"Tess." Trigger jolted me awake. "You asleep?"

"No," I lied, fiddling with the button on the helmet.

He reached back and squeezed my thigh. "Don't lie to me. If we need to stop, tell me."

"I'm fine."

He shook his head as he suddenly slipped in between two trucks. I ducked my head but kept my eyes on his patchwork. Anything to keep my eyes open.

We jumped off the I-15 and headed into the San Gabriel Mountains. His chest vibrated as he spoke to someone. I glanced back to Brick, who had pulled out a cell phone.

I began to feel like something was off by the way Trigger's head started to move around. The tenseness in his body gave me a bad feeling in the pit of my stomach. I pushed the button.

"Something wrong?"

"No."

I rolled my eyes. "Now who's lying?"

He didn't answer, so I started mimicking his movements. I wasn't sure what I was looking for, but I wanted to help if I could.

We got to a point where we were surrounded by mountains. Rain had started to fall in a cold drizzle, and it became hard to see very far through the mist.

I grew cold deep in my bones with his uneasiness.

I leaned back to stretch my arms, feeling them snap at the elbows. God, that felt great.

Then I spotted a single light off in the tree line, then another and another.

"Trigger…" My voice trailed off.

"I see them."

Fear licked through me at the word *them*. He placed a gun into my hands. "Point and shoot. Watch out for Brick."

Shit. It was one thing to shoot at a slow-moving target, but to shoot sitting behind someone on a bike that was moving around like crazy was something else.

Zip. Zip.

I yelped as two bullets whipped by my helmet.

So, point and fucking shoot. Got it!

I tried to aim at something and pulled the trigger, hoping like hell I would hit someone. Trigger fired back and swerved the bike around to make us harder targets. I heard Brick's gun as he fired, but all I could see were flashes of light. How could they tell if they were hitting them or not?

Trigger made a hand signal, and Brick disappeared. I wanted to ask where he was going, but now wasn't the time.

A different sounding motor caused a prickle up my spine and into my scalp. Two shots flew by, and one broke our mirror.

Shit! Shit! Shit!

My stomach dropped, and my hand flexed over the cold steel grip of the gun.

Fuck it!

I grabbed Trigger's waist, twisted around hard,

and concentrated on my fire. Each shot made my heart speed up. My muscles tightened and filled me with adrenaline.

I could tell by the light and the squeal of brakes that the bike spun out over the slick road. It turned completely around before he went out of sight in the ditch.

Trigger grabbed my hand and shoved it over his erection. His hand covered mine as he stroked it twice.

Jesus, I was wet.

We are seriously two fucked up individuals.

Just when I thought we were in the clear, two more bikes came up behind us. How did we not hear them?

Trigger popped one of them in the shoulder, but he didn't go down. The other tried to reach for me, pulling up alongside.

What the fuck?

I held up my gun and took the shot, but nothing happened. Shit! No bullets. He came up close again and grabbed my arm and tugged hard.

I slipped, but Trigger reached back and slammed me to him. He shot the guy to our right and got him in the thigh. He lost control, and his bike went flying into the trees.

Trigger waited until the guy went for me again. He suddenly turned and shot him under the arm.

Jesus Christ!

Trigger yelled something into his radio and revved the engine. We surged forward, picking up speed.

It was so fast, I had to duck to block the wind

because it hurt my neck so badly. I closed my eyes and counted my wild heartbeats until we finally slowed.

Holy shit.

Holy hell.

Holy Mother of Christ.

The words looped around and around in my head. I was trying to absorb what the hell had happened.

The bike hit gravel, and I was finally able to look around. Thick trees lined the road as we started up a big hill. We stopped at a rusty trailer set up on concrete blocks.

Once Trigger stopped, I hopped off, tossed my helmet, and headed into the woods. I had no idea where I was going, but shit, I needed a moment.

***

Trigger

As I tucked the bike away, I watched Tess fade into the darkness. These woods were safe, and I knew them well, so I wasn't worried.

"Heard you ran into some trouble." Gus appeared by my side. "I was about ready to send Rail and Cooper."

"Nothing we couldn't handle." I glanced at the woods again. "Brick make it back?"

"He did." He nodded at the woods. "That Tiger?"

"Yeah."

"You piss her off again?"

I smirked. "Turns out the girl can shoot, along with a few other hidden talents."

"Really?"

"Mmm." I threaded her helmet through the handlebar. "She needs a moment to come down, and so do we." I headed over to his fire pit, grabbed a beer, and set it on the stone. I opened another and eased into the metal contraption he called a chair.

Gus hobbled over and pulled back the tab. He always drank shit beer, even if I brought the good stuff.

"Stripe Backs. They had the advantage, and they could have taken Tess out, but they didn't. They tried to take her."

Gus set his beer down and rubbed his bottom lip as he thought. "She did overhear them in the desert, and they did try to attack her after Tiago. Maybe they just want to shut her up?"

"Maybe they have orders to take her." I played the Devil's advocate.

"You think Allen is behind this?"

"I think a lot of things."

He spat and took another swig. The sound of crickets filled the air, and I strained to hear Tess.

"How was the house?"

I shrugged. "Eye-opening."

"Meaning?"

"A lot of shit there." Gus knew about Tess and Bret, but I would deal with that later.

"Any part of it you can't get past?"

I tossed the beer in the rusty trashcan and grabbed another. "Getting past it would mean I cared."

"Cut the shit, Trigger. I saw your face that night in the trailer when we got her back."

I felt uncomfortable showing emotions, even with Gus.

His chuckle broke down into a nasty cough as he reached for another beer. "If Brick's sister was in trouble, you wouldn't have gone to the extent you did to get her back like you did Tess." He laughed again and nodded at the woods. "You're pissing me off. Just go get her."

"Whatever." I pushed to my feet and headed into the woods. It didn't take me long to find her at Gus's hideout near the brook. She was bent over the railing with her hands to her mouth in an attempt to warm them. She seemed to be restless and struggling over the day.

"Come on up. You're freezing."

"I'm fine."

"I wasn't asking."

"I know."

She just about drove me to the edge with all I had already going on inside me.

"Tess."

"Trigger."

"Why do you have to fight me on everything?" I bit out.

"Why do you have to be so demanding on everything?"

I rubbed my head and cursed.

"Trigger," she sighed, "I just had my ex play mind games with me, found out he killed my best friend, killed *his* lover, said goodbye again to an old friend, shot someone, was nearly yanked off a bike by what I assume was rival gang member, and am here with nothing but a backpack and a few belongings." She stopped to catch her breath. "I think I deserve a moment to stop my head from spinning."

"I get that—"

"No, you don't," she tossed back at me angrily. "You have a home, a family, and a sense of belonging. People would genuinely care if something happened to you. I don't know where the hell I belong. I'm just some girl who walks in and out of people's lives."

I stepped closer, and she held up her hand.

I grabbed it and pulled her to me. She looked pissed and shoved me, but I didn't move. She tried to do it again, and I wrapped my arms around her to pin her and backed her up against the railing.

"You are not just some girl, Tess. You belong with me at my club, and not with that mind fuck of an ex." I freed my hand and held her chin to look at me. Her eyes were wild, but there was a sadness behind it. I hated how it made me feel. I hated that it made me feel at all. "Let that shit go, or I'll make you."

"Try." Her face was flushed, and I saw what she wanted—no, what she needed. I also knew what it felt like to have all that adrenaline inside. We were both still riding the high from what we had experienced.

I unzipped her pants and split her folds to find her hot wetness. When she started to speak, I flipped her around and planted her hands on the rail.

"You might think you're in control, Tess." I

140

shoved up her shirt and undid my pants. My heavy erection twitched with need at her opening. "You might even think you want it." I leaned down and licked the entire length of her spine. "But I can assure you, when you're with me," I lined up and broke her opening with my tip, "you will give in to me." I eased in steadily, determined that this time we would finish.

Her insides squeezed me, and my fingers dug into her hips.

"Do you understand me?" I wanted to drive my point home. "Answer me." I slapped her ass, and she moaned loudly. I pulled out and waited for her to wiggle. When she backed up, I stepped back. I grabbed her neck, knowing she liked it rough, and tilted her head back. "Do-you-understand-me?"

"Fuck me, flip your switch," she snarled. "Make me scream."

I bent her over, plowed back in, and beat myself into her. She bucked, screamed, and begged for more. I didn't care who heard us. I was inside this woman, and I needed it as much as she did. The silence that took over me was bliss in itself. My balls smacked her clit, and she fought to chase the climax that ripped through her. Her skin broke out in a sexy pink, and my handprints on her hips marked my ownership.

Over and over again, I reminded her who was in charge, and with each thrust, I increased the speed. She could do nothing but hang on. Her hair was wild, and she jolted as she screamed my name. I loved that I could be me inside of her. No holding back, just pure, animal sex. We were meant to fuck this way.

I picked up the pace, changed the angle, and let myself coat her insides after weeks of frustration. She started to fall forward, totally done, but I held her to my chest, still inside her. Her breathing slowed, and I bit down on her neck.

"I will ground you next time. Now get dressed. Someone wants to see you."

I slipped out.

We climbed the hill, and I gave her my seat and took an even shittier one. Gus handed her a plate of shredded meat, tortilla, and salsa.

"So good to see you again, Tiger," Gus grunted and urged a beer in her hand.

She looked around for a moment and made the connection. "You live here?"

"My rusty slice of paradise." He grinned, and I huffed out a laugh.

Tess studied my face before she set her beer down and started in on the food.

"You here for good now?"

She paused before she took her next bite. "I'm not really sure of that yet."

My glare should have burned her. She tried everything not to look at me, but she felt it.

"Well," he sighed, "I sure hope you do."

My phone vibrated, and I saw it was Big Joe. I moved to the tree line before I answered it.

"Yeah?"

"There's a letter here for you."

"Open it." I glanced at Gus, who looked to be telling Tess a story. She tossed her head back and laughed. My dick twitched again. Fuck, she turned me on.

"Shit." Big Joe's tone brought me back to our conversation.

"What?"

"It's a flyer for a fight in Las Vegas."

"Toss it."

"Trigger." There was a pause, and before I could remind him how I hated long stories, he spat it out. "Your dad's making his first public appearance and calling you out to fight."

So, I didn't take the bait the first time, and now he's insuring it.

I felt my addiction for the cage surface for the first time in years. It was something I had buried for many reasons, the main one being that it changed me, turned me into an animal. I knew I would lose myself once the scent of blood in the ring freed the demons inside.

"Toss it," I repeated, feeling my body come alive.

When Big Joe didn't respond, I sensed something was off.

"No, brother, I don't think I can."

"Why?"

"If you don't fight, he said he'll come for her."

I glanced at Tess. She watched me, and I lowered my voice before I spoke.

"This stays between you and me."

"Got it."

CHAPTER TEN

Tess

Something was wrong. I could tell by the way Trigger's hands were clenched into fists, and when I added in his murderous expression, I had no doubt something big was up. Gus did everything to keep my attention on him, so I decided to use it to my advantage.

"Gus," I lowered my tone and traced the top of the beer can with my fingertip, "when I first arrived at the club, Brick told me the guys got their nicknames by the way they killed."

He nodded. "Yeah."

"I know Morgan isn't as high up as Brick and Rail, but why hasn't he gotten his nickname yet?"

He laughed. "He has."

"But I thought…" I looked at him, confused. What was I not getting?

"Trigger recruited Morgan from a biker bar in Palm Springs. Morgan smashed a bottle over a guy's head, jammed the jagged glass into his throat.

144

He used the same bottle on a few more. It was a real bloodbath." He waited for me to make the connection.

"A bottle of Captain Morgan." I smiled. "That's kind of funny."

"Yeah, he likes his nickname. Morgan doesn't like too much attention on himself."

"Reminds me of someone else we know."

Gus took a drink from his beer. "Sure does." He winked at me.

"So, if everyone has a nickname, that means they had different names first." I glanced at Trigger and back to Gus. "What's Trigger's real name?"

"You're going to get me in trouble, here, Tiger."

"Not my intent, Gus. Promise."

"I know." He glanced over his shoulder to make sure Trigger was out of earshot. "Nolan was the name his mother gave him at birth."

Nolan. Seemed different enough to suit him. I really couldn't picture a Scott or Eric.

"Why do you say 'at birth?'"

Gus rubbed his weathered eyes. "His father preferred *little shit* until his ability to fight without a conscience kicked in. Then it was Trigger. It was supposed to be a stage name, but as you can see, it fits."

"And now his father is posing as a *Father* of the Church?"

"Sick fucker will stop at nothing to become more powerful than his son. You need to be careful, Tess. Allen being back brings a whole new level of trouble to the club."

"You think he sent the Stripe Backs after us

145

tonight?"

"If you connect the dots, yeah, I think so."

"Dots?" I knew what he meant, but if he could offer some more detail, I'd be happy.

"You overheard a familiar voice in the desert, that night you also got attacked by Tiago."

"But they said he was a Serpent, talking to the mole."

"Yeah, but it was all part of Allen's twisted fuckery. He knew it was a matter of time before Carlos would make a deal with Trigger. He was getting worn down by the Devil's Reach at every turn. I think they sent in a Stripe Back to talk to whoever is the fuckin' mole, and he found out Devil's Reach had a weak link."

He held my gaze a little longer to make his point. I shifted uneasily.

"Before he could make his move, Tiago got to you first. Thus ending the Serpents' contract, and now Trigger has all of Santa Monica. The one town Allen has always wanted."

"Why?"

"It's like this. Every city has a value. Santa Monica is one of the highest, next to Oakland."

"Okay." I tried to follow.

"So, by running the Serpents out of town, more clubs will be chopping at the city limits. Trigger has more ground to cover and will need more men. Meanwhile, Allen will have the Stripe Backs do his dirty work of fucking with the club. One day when Trigger's not looking," he made a Hannibal Lecter chop noise, and my stomach lunged into my throat, "he'll take the one thing that will hurt the club the most."

"Which is…?" My nails bit into my skin.

He leaned forward, and the crow's feet around his eyes deepened as he become serious. "You."

My skin shivered as a gust of wind sent my hair all around me. "I wouldn't hurt the whole club."

"If Trigger's hurting, the club is hurting."

"Why?" I cleared my throat. "Why did he bring me back here if I'm the target? Why not leave me at the house?"

"Because he can't protect you if he can't be near you."

Gus let out an ear-piercing cough, and a moment later, I saw why. Trigger was approaching, and he didn't want him to hear us talking.

"Good?" Gus asked. Trigger looked a million miles away.

"Yeah."

I was so lost in my thoughts, I didn't hear Trigger speak to me. His hand landed on my thigh and gave it a little squeeze.

"We need to leave."

"Stay here if you like," Gus chimed in, and I nodded. I liked that idea better. "The hideout has heat."

"I'd like that." I smiled weakly at Gus and hoped he'd see I wasn't ready to go back to the clubhouse yet.

"Fine." Trigger sent off a quick text and pulled me to my feet.

We said goodnight and walked back down the hill to the little log cabin. He opened the door and started to make a fire while I stood in the doorway, unsure what to think.

"What?" he muttered over his shoulder.

"Just thinking."

"About?" He took out his lighter and lit the paper.

"Just some things."

He stood and scowled at me. "Why did you want to stay here?"

I looked around and covered one arm with the other. "I like it here. Feels safe, I guess."

"You don't feel safe at the club?"

"I do. I guess I just…" I fumbled for my words.

"Just what?"

"I think I'm just tired." I wished I hadn't said anything.

"Well, there's the bed." He pointed to a queen size bed up against a wall under a window. "Bathroom is over there."

I washed my face and brushed my teeth, my reflection showing the past twelve hours. Stress and a murder would do that to you.

I stripped down to my tank top and panties and crawled under the old quilt. It was beautiful, with light and dark blue threading that created pretty little flowers and swirls. Not at all something I would think Gus would own.

Trigger pulled up a seat next to the fire and nursed a glass of something brown. My guess would be more whiskey. There seemed to be an endless supply of it with this guy.

I rolled to my side and watched him study the flames. His profile was that of a man who had seen and done too much, but at the same time, there was this incredibly sexy sense of strength surrounding him.

"Trigger," I whispered, and he looked over at me. One side of his face glowed from the flickering flames, and the other was cloaked in shadow. Funny how true that seemed right now.

"Why did you come back for me?"

I could see he was mulling the answer. His jaw ticked, and his head bowed. I swallowed hard and wished I hadn't asked. I was fishing for some kind of warmth from him. I should've known better.

"You were in a bad place, and we thought it would be better to get you out of there."

I gave a little nod and looked away. I hated that my emotions were so close to the surface. Darkness started to eat away at my thoughts, and I fought back my insecurities, trying to pull on the inner strength I always managed to find.

My eyes grew hot with tears, so I gave up and flipped over and let them tumble down and hide in my pillow.

This was what happened whenever I stepped foot in that goddamned house. My entire body folded inward, and I lost my backbone. My mother had always undermined my confidence, and I still felt the control Clark had over me for so long. I really needed to pull my shit together.

The bed dipped, and Trigger lifted the covers and let in a rush of cold air.

"Tess," he grunted. "Roll over."

Afraid he would see my tears, I pretended I was asleep. He sighed heavily before he shifted and spooned me from behind. His arm slipped under my neck to cradle my head.

"Why are you crying?"

I dried my cheeks and shook my head. He shifted to reach above me, and I caught a whiff of a strong scent.

He reached down and took my hand and fiddled with the cuff, then undid the three snaps to reveal my scar.

My hand slapped down to stop him, but he moved it out of the way.

"Never hide yourself from me," he warned, but there was a softness to it.

I bit back my normal urge to pull away, but it was difficult.

Something wet touched my skin. I jumped, and he grunted, "Stay still."

He skimmed over my scar with a black Sharpie. I watched in fascination as his huge hand drew such delicate lines. He threaded some ivy through the scar and embedded a tiny lily toward the bottom. My eyes blurred when I realized he remembered my story. I wondered if Brick told him who she was. Lily was Mags's daughter, the only piece I had left of my best friend.

When I thought he was done, he started to draw something else. I sniffed, and he leaned over me. His weight felt good, and I relaxed and emptied my head of all but what he was doing. Soon, a skeleton key appeared and became entangled in the ivy, but it was at a strange angle. He continued to draw vines and left the key alone like a hidden secret among it all.

"It's beautiful," I barely whispered. "I didn't

know you could draw."

"I have a guy who can do this. I'll make you an appointment."

"The key?" I questioned, curious.

But he didn't say anything else. He went still, and I guessed he drifted off. The more I studied his work, the more I realized it was Trigger's way of comforting me. I pulled his hand to my lips and kissed his fingers softly then wiggled closer to him and closed my eyes.

***

Trigger

I woke with a jolt and noticed something was wrong. Tess wasn't in the hideout. I scrambled to get dressed and did a double take at the time. Ten a.m.

Shit. I'd slept like a rock.

I headed to where Gus was pouring a cup of coffee.

"Where's Tess?"

Gus splashed the coffee as he hobbled over to his chair. "She and I had breakfast, and then she went off for a walk."

"Where?"

He pointed in the opposite direction of the hideout.

"She's fine."

"We need to get back." I headed into the trees and scanned for her. My boots crunched over the sticks and rocks. I wasn't someone who could be

151

quiet. Hunting animals was never my strong suit. Hunting humans was a different game.

Something snapped loudly, and I turned around, but didn't see anything. Then something hit my back, and I whirled in the other direction.

Whack!

A pinecone nailed my thigh, but this time I didn't react.

"Come out." I listened for her footsteps, but all I got was another cone to the stomach. "I'm warning you, Tess."

"Your last warning," she said from above me in an old hunting blind, "landed me some great sex. I wonder what this will land me?"

I wanted to get mad, but all I could think of was my dick straining against my zipper.

"Ah, there's that look."

"Come down," I ordered.

She slowly unzipped her jeans, and I backed up to get a better look.

"I think I'll stay up here." She held up her purple lipstick vibrator. "I'm in good company."

I can play dirty too.

"Okay. You have fifteen minutes before we leave." With that, I left her up there and headed back to the trailer. My dick nearly turned blue, but I would get my way with her soon.

Ten minutes later, she came up the hill, looking flushed and sexually frustrated.

Perfect.

"Gus, you have a double A battery kickin' around?"

He looked at her oddly and pointed to a tool box

on the step. She held it up and excused herself.

I blocked her path and snatched the battery from her hand and replaced it with the helmet.

"Time to go."

"Just need five minutes."

I stepped closer, leaned down, and inhaled her smell. "I. Don't. Share."

Her breath caught in her lungs as I grabbed her ass and gave it a hard squeeze.

We said goodbye to Gus, and I rushed her onto the bike before she decided to find another way to get off.

On the drive back into town, I could feel her frustration through the vibrating bike. I couldn't help but smirk when we parked behind the club.

She was in a pissy, wound-up mood, and it was fucking hot. Her cheeks were flushed, and her glare was enough for me to bend her over my bike and remind her who she belonged to.

"Go get changed. Your shift started ten minutes ago."

She rolled her eyes but disappeared into the club as Brick came out with a newspaper held high in the air.

"Shit's gettin' real."

I tossed the keys at Jace to take my bike into the garage then removed the paper from Brick's hand.

Three men found dead this morning in an alley on the lower east side, apparently from an overdose of a tainted strain of cocaine. The local PD is attempting to match the symbol on the baggie to known drug runners. Detective Doyle of

SMPD reports they have a few leads but have made no arrests yet. We encourage anyone who knows anything to please call the nearest detachment of the SMPD.

"So glad we stopped distributing those drugs." Brick snickered sarcastically. "I want to kill the mole myself by feeding him some."

"We need to flush him out."

"How?"

"If I knew, he'd be in the slaughter room right now."

The sight of Tess behind the bar in tight black shorts and a red tank top made my pounding headache ease. Morgan looked less stressed and back to his old self. Loose wasted no time and was already on a stool nursing a drink.

Big Joe waited for me to be alone in the back of the bar before he came over with the letter.

"I checked on this, and it's legit. Sounds like Allen was in touch with Charlie himself and is working the angle of a father and son showdown. If you don't show, not sure what that will say about your reputation."

Fuck me.

"Don't give a shit about my reputation."

"But you do about hers." He flicked his head over at the bar. When I didn't respond, he went on. "Not like the old man will have much steam left, anyway."

I nodded. It would be an unfair fight, but a fight, nonetheless.

"There's something else you should know." He

checked over his shoulder at the guys. "Cooper and Rail have been in and out the last few days. I followed them, and they've been hanging out at the Flying Arrow."

"Okay." I needed a moment to digest that information. The Flying Arrow was where a lot of the Stripe Backs hung out. "Anything else?"

"You want me to find Loose something to do?"

I shook my head, and he walked back to his post at the door.

"Trigger?" Her voice made my head hurt. "When did you get back?"

Tess had spotted her too, and she made her way toward us with a bottle of whiskey in her hand.

Tammy fiddled with the ties on her dress and gave me the same look she used whenever she wanted me to fuck her.

"I thought your ass was kicked out of here, Tammy." Tess filled my glass like it was an everyday conversation.

"I left."

"But you're back."

"I need to talk to Trigger."

Tess glanced at me and lifted an eyebrow. "I'm sure it's something *really* important."

Tammy rolled her eyes and turned to me. "Can we talk in your office?"

"Regarding?" I didn't have time for her.

"Your father."

I flicked my head toward my office, and she turned and started to walk. Tess closed her eyes as she shook her head.

"Give me a minute," I muttered.

"Whatever, Trigger."

"What does that mean?"

"You do remember what she did, right?"

"Yes."

Her eyebrows pinched together, and she drew her lips in as she thought about something. Then she turned and headed back to the bar.

Women.

Tammy sat on my desk with her dress hiked up to her ass.

"Get off." I pointed to the chair. "You have five minutes to explain why you're here."

"What the hell do you see in that bitch?"

"Careful," I warned. "Four minutes."

"I'm dating Jet now." She waited for a reaction to her dating the rat from the Stripe Backs. Somehow, it didn't shock me. "He drills me for a lot of your club's information."

"That so?"

"Um-hm."

"What do you tell them?"

"Well, that depends." She grabbed the bottom of her dress and peeled it off over her head. She stood naked, in nothing but heels. "You take me back, and I'll let you stick it anywhere you want. If not, I'll tell Jet all your dirty little secrets."

I bolted from where I stood and wrapped my hands around her neck, slamming her to the wall. Her head bounced off the plaster, and her eyes widened.

"You don't know shit about my club!" I felt my switch begin to tick.

"I know more than you think," she spat. "I know

your chick of the month is going to destroy everything. I know she took a USB drive from a guy named Clark, and it holds information they want back. Allen will hunt her down and carve out her insides if the Stripe Backs don't get to her first."

"How do the Stripe Backs know Clark?" The words shot off my tongue.

"Dumbasses had a run-in with him and made a shitty deal."

I looked at her, confused. She gave a dramatic sigh, and I let my grip loosen slightly.

"You're not the only club that visits Vegas." She gripped my hands, but I didn't move, and she dropped them again. "I like Jet, but the Stripe Backs are one dumbass bunch of people. They made a shit deal with Clark, and then screwed him over. Clark found out something on them and now has leverage." Tammy nodded toward the door. "Allen wants her. And the USB."

My head spun, and the demons rattled in their cages.

She laughed, and her split lip bled. She touched a finger to her mouth, tasting it, then traced a line of blood down to her erect nipple. "Not such a dumb bitch now, am I?"

The door swung open, and Big Joe looked stunned. "Shit, I'm sorry. Find me later." Just as he backed up, I saw Tess's face turn white before she darted back to the bar.

Fuck!

"Whatcha going to do, Trigger? Run after her? Don't you want to find out what else I know?"

My chest heaved because she was right. I was

157

cornered. A pawn once again.

"What do you know about my father? Why Tess?"

"Loosen your fucking grip."

I did, a little, and she sucked in a few breaths of air. "He has eyes on you. He's feeding the PD information, and," she laughed, savoring her power, "he's going to kill her right in front of you."

"Where is he?" I slammed her head into the wall again.

"You don't get it." She smirked. "He's everywhere. Right outside your door, listening to your every word."

Fucking mole!

"Who's the mole?"

"Step into the ring, and you'll find out."

I squeezed my eyes shut and pushed aside the urge to fight.

No.

Don't even think it.

She opened her mouth like she wanted to give me head. I opened the door and pushed her out, and she landed on her bare ass. The entire room fell silent as a naked Tammy scrambled to her feet.

"Big fucking mistake, Trigger! I will ruin your club and make sure that blonde bitch gets what she deserves."

Brick looked ready to charge her, and I shook my head. At the sound of squealing tires, my senses went on high alert.

Everything went still, and I felt the chill as everything fit into place. They were here for her.

"Get down!" I yelled as bullets flew through the

window.

Glass burst all around us in slow motion. I raced to cover my nephew Fin, who had run out of his mother's hold. My hands covered his head as we raced behind the bar. "Gun!" I shouted at Morgan, and he handed me his extra rifle.

"Stay here!" I ordered Fin as tears streamed down his face. "Don't move, okay, Finny?"

"Where's Tess?" He covered his ears. "I want Tess!"

I scanned the bar, and as far as I could see, where the hell…?

"Morgan?"

He shrugged as more bullets sprayed the room. "She went out back after she saw you guys."

Zip.

Zip.

Zip.

Wood, glass, booze, and screams filled the air all at once. It seemed to linger before it fell all around us. Fin clung to my arm, his little hands white at the knuckles.

The place fell quiet once again as the tires screamed away.

A lot are going to die for this.

"Call out!" I shouted to the guys.

"Yeah," Brick huffed.

"Second that," Rail answered. "I think." He patted down his body. "Yeah, I'm here."

Gus wasn't here, so…

"Good," Cray piped up.

Morgan was good; Fin was too.

"Denton?"

159

"He's here with me." Vib screamed in a panic, "Where's Fin?"

"He's here too."

More people started to call out. Tammy, on the other hand, had been hit several times. I assumed she was set up for this shit storm.

"Trigg—" She fought for breath as her lungs filled with blood. "Help."

"I'm not the one who can help you." I leaned down to get a closer look at the bullet holes.

"Morgan," I ordered and heard him whirl Fin around so he wouldn't see what I was about to do. I raised my foot and slammed down on the shred of glass sticking out of her jugular.

Crunch.

Her cold, lifeless eyes stared at me. I kicked her torso, and her head flopped to the other side. Fuck, I hated that bitch.

"Trigger?" Fin pulled at my shirt. His snotty nose made his voice sound muffled. "Where's Tess?"

"Brick, Rail," I said calmly, and they spread out. "Get Jace and Loose to clean this shit up."

"Let's not forget," Loose pulled a piece of glass from his arm and tossed it on the floor, "who started all this. You want this cleaned up, you do it."

My head became tight as a drum as I slowly turned to look at the ungrateful little prick who had lived under my roof for far too long.

"You didn't seem to have a problem spending my money, living in my home, drinking my booze up until now."

"Well, now I do."

I sucked in a deep breath and looked down at my frightened nephew. He didn't need to see anyone else die right now. It suddenly hit me that two of my men didn't check in.

"Morgan," I pointed to Loose, and he ripped the cut off the cunt in front of me, "put him on ice."

"Fuck you, Trigger! You know what?" He stepped up to my face, and my men all pulled their weapons and waited for my command. "You don't deserve her." He held up his middle finger as Morgan pointed his gun at Loose's head and dragged him out of the room.

I wanted to kill him. I wanted to rip his throat out and beat him to a pulp, and I would, but right now I needed to find Tess. "Morgan, find the others then check in with me."

***

Allen

"How many?" I leaned back in my chair and lit my cigar while Fox, a member of the Stripe Backs, gave me a play by play on what happened at Trigger's club earlier. Fox was a loose cannon. He almost killed Tess in the desert and could have potentially fucked up all my hard work.

"Three."

"Including the snitch slut?"

"Yeah."

Three wasn't the number I hoped for, but maybe it would convince Trigger to fight.

"The girl?" I squinted and dared him to lie to me.

161

Fox rubbed the top of his bald head, which made my urge to rip out his throat stronger.

"We didn't think she'd go back to work the first day she came back. I can't confirm if she was hit or not."

I snapped my pen in half and considered what Fox would look like with a piece in each eyeball. Pulling out my phone, I sent a text.

Allen: Come in.

"Who were the other two?"

He sat a little straighter when he realized I wasn't going to kill him right now.

"Moe and Maze."

I dropped my head with annoyance and beat the desk. "Fucking amateurs! The club's runner and a beef-head? That doesn't mean shit. Fucking Christ!"

Fox looked around like we might get struck by lightning because I cursed in a church.

I leaned over and glared at the six-foot-two wannabe thug. "What the fuck? You got religion or something? Do some real damage, or I will." I turned toward the door and yelled out to the others. They were probably dick high in cocaine. "Where the fuck is Zay?"

"He's out trying to see if the girl is alive," one of my prospects answered with powder all over his face.

I dropped my head into my hands. "Waste of human beings. Go away." I waved dramatically at Fox. "Your face makes me want to kill you."

162

He left a lot quicker than he arrived. I rubbed my temple and wondered if I would need to deal with the girl myself.

"I can't keep meeting you like this." My shitty mood instantly evaporated at the sound of his voice. I couldn't help myself. I felt like a child getting his first look at the pretty puppy in the box.

"You're fast."

He came into the room and sank onto a chair. He hated being here, and I didn't blame him. He shifted in his cut like it was uncomfortable, or maybe he felt his disloyalty burning through the Devil's Reach patch.

"Do I have a choice?"

"No." I grinned. "You really don't." I kicked my feet up and leaned back in the chair. "Now, tell me everything."

CHAPTER ELEVEN

Tess

Wind whipped my hair and blocked my view of the choppy sea. My feet dangled over the edge of the pier as I held on to the rail and watched three surfers decide if they wanted to do battle with Mother Nature tonight.

One man, who looked to be in his forties, raced into the water, duck-dove under the whitecaps, and surfaced a few yards from shore. He looked back at the other two, and they waved him off and headed back up toward the parking lot.

He paddled out farther past the break. His movements were smooth and thought out. Once he got to a certain point, he hiked up to a seated position and watched the waves as if he were counting them. Or maybe he was waiting for just the right one. Either way, he seemed calm and fearless.

His sense of serenity seemed to pass over me as I relaxed into the cool wood.

I brushed my hair out of my face and held it down to the side with one hand. A raindrop hit the tip of my eyelash, then another and another. It didn't matter if it poured. I wanted to watch him.

To be so fearless, faced with such a great force, was hypnotizing. I could almost feel his rush as his body tensed. The wave he was watching began to rise, and it gained height and speed as it plowed toward him, its power building. I stepped up to get a better look, gripping the wooden post between my legs to steady myself.

He turned his board and started to paddle with all his might. Just as he was on the top, about to be toppled over, he stood and effortlessly glided along the inside of the tube. The curve of the wave chased wildly behind him.

Water sprayed with the chaos of the wind. The moon fought to shine brightly through the heavy clouds. Yet another moment I wished my camera was attached to my hip.

My breath was caught in my throat and my hands were white, unsure of how he was going to end his ride.

It was graceful beauty the way he showed respect to the sea, and the sea to him. His hand reached out and skimmed the water as if to say thanks before he jerked and tumbled beneath the surface.

Wow. I stood motionless as the dark water swallowed him up and he disappeared. Their moment was over.

I laughed at how wrapped up I was in it all. Growing up without the coast, you never really understood the draw, but now I did.

My phone rang, and I saw there was a missed call from a Vegas area code.

Hmm.

I tapped the play button and heard my doctor's tired voice telling me I need to come back in, but since she knew I wouldn't, as I'd avoided all her other calls, she would like me to call the office tomorrow for a phone consultation.

Well, shit, that can't be good.

"I hope you can swim."

I turned to find the surfer behind me with his board in hand. He was aged and weathered, but the smile in his eyes left no doubt how young his soul was.

"Well enough."

His eyes crinkled as he came a little closer. "You'd be dealing with a strong current and one hell of an undertow."

"Good thing I didn't fall in, then."

"Yeah, Trigger would open Pandora's box."

I carefully eased off the railing and tugged my shirt back down in place.

"You know Trigger?"

He motioned for me to follow him back down the pier.

"Everyone knows Trigger and his club. They're good people, despite their rep." He flung his wet hair out of his face. "Known him for about ten years now. He's my best client."

I couldn't help but laugh, and he eyed me strangely.

"Can't see Trigger on a surfboard."

"Ha! Like cats and water, they don't mix." He joined in my laughter. "No, I have a tattoo parlor in the back of my surf shop. I've probably done eighty-five percent of Trigger's tats."

"Really?" I raised an eyebrow, curious what he knew about Trigger.

"Yup." He lifted his huge board into the back of his topless Jeep. "You need a lift back?"

I shook my head. "Honestly, I'm not ready to go back yet."

"You can't stay here."

"Why?" I shrugged. "It's peaceful."

He opened the passenger side door and rested his arm over the top. "Storm is coming in, and this is neutral territory—which really means fair game."

"Serpents are gone," I reminded him.

"Yeah, but the Stripe Backs aren't. Besides, Trigger would have my head on a stick if he knew I saw you and didn't take you back."

"I appreciate it, but I'm good."

He rubbed the water from his face and smirked.

"He certainly didn't sugarcoat your stubbornness." I rolled my eyes. "I could use the company at my shop. You can hang out there until you feel like going back."

I hesitated. Just because he said he knew Trigger didn't mean he did. He must have noticed my mood change, as he pointed to his forearm.

"Under his right arm, he has the words *Forever Damned* written in script. I promise you, I'm the least of your worries."

He came around to his side and started the Jeep. I looked over my shoulder before I hopped inside and

167

closed the door. Trigger wasn't one for letting people get close, and he did have that tattoo, so I felt a little more relaxed.

He held out his freezing hand. "Name's Mud."

"Tess."

"I know." He smiled and backed up and headed down the street.

Mud's shop, housed in his garage, was the ultimate man cave. Pin-up models lined the ceiling and walls, a flat screen hung on a back wall with a chair strategically placed in front of it, and I saw a no doubt fully stocked Coca Cola fridge. Fans shot cool air from all angles. Pot hung in the air, and a heavy metal band could be heard throughout the room. It was oddly comforting.

"You have any clients coming tonight?" I asked as I admired his bonsai tree and the sand swirled around it.

"Nah, my buddy got caught up with his old lady. I was supposed to fix his train wreck of a tattoo he got in Reno." He lit a joint about as thick as a hotdog.

I took in the needles, ink, and blue gloves.

"Come here." He nodded and stared at me strangely. He turned my arm over and examined Trigger's Sharpie work. "You want that done professionally?"

"Maybe." I shrugged, but the more I thought about it, I knew I did. "Yeah, I do."

"First tat?"

I nodded.

"Good way to hide the scar."

My other hand slapped over it as I turned to stare

at the photos. I felt naked without something to conceal the evidence of my past.

"Sit here." He pointed to the chair. "Let me outline it before the marker wears off."

"I don't have much money right now."

"Don't recall asking for any."

I didn't like it, but he seemed determined to outline it, so I sank into the plush chair and gave him my arm.

"Here," he handed me his joint, "it will help."

"I think I'm okay."

"I like that you're tough, Tess, but this shit will hurt."

Fine.

I sucked back a few long puffs and soon felt as if I were flying out of my body and around the room. I jolted at the needle, but there was no pain. I felt free.

"Your hotdog of a joint is fantastic. My arm feels independent from me." I giggled.

He smirked. "Who drew this?"

"Trigger." I moved my arm to the left and felt like I was across the room looking at us.

"Why?"

I laughed and then cringed at the sound of the needle. "That's a good question, Mud. He drew it while we were in bed. I think it's his way to speak without having to."

"That key," he pointed, "you know what it's to?"

I rolled my head to look at him. "That would require him to use more than three words at a time."

He laughed and took the joint from me. His hand was incredibly steady, which made me calm.

169

"Do you know the DR well?"

He nodded and tapped the joint to drop the ash at his feet. "Been doing their tattoos for years."

"You do anyone else besides Trigger?"

"Morgan, Brick, and Rail."

"Impressive."

"Thanks." He nodded in agreement.

"I find it interesting that you've done Trigger's."

"Yeah?"

"You're the only person I know who can touch him."

"Besides you," he corrected.

"True." I shifted my weight to my other hip. "Wait." I tried to catch up with my thoughts. "Do you know what this key unlocks?"

"Yup."

"Well?"

"Well, I'll let you figure it out."

"Where's the fun in that?"

"Oh, trust me, Tess. There's a lot of it."

I closed my eyes and enjoyed the ride of the high. Clearly, Mud wasn't going to spill the truth. I asked a few questions here and there and loved that he would go off on a long story and let me picture it. He mostly shared stories of him and his waves and how a great board makes all the difference.

"You want me to stop?"

My eyes opened, and I saw he had outlined everything. It was dark and gray and fit me so well. Mud expressed what the scar meant to me without even knowing my story. I cleared my emotions from my throat and smiled at him.

"No, keep going, please."

"You want color?"

"Honestly, you do what you think would look the best."

"My favorite kind of client."

***

Trigger

It didn't take long for the smell of blood to fill the room. Tammy was pretty much drained before her naked ass was dragged out to the shed. We'd dispose of her later when there weren't as many eyes on the club. Rich was on his fourth bucket of cleaner before Jace slipped and fell in her juices with a disgusted moan.

Gus was with Vib and Denton in the back. Fin was still glued to my side.

My men's deaths weighed on me, but not Tammy's. She'd brought hers on herself, but Maze was loyal, and Moe had been around for a while. They were good men and shouldn't have gone out that way. They were family, and family didn't come easy.

"Rail," I called out, and he hurried over. "Where's Brick?"

"It's okay. Last I saw, he was with Tess." He rubbed his face. "You think this was—" He glanced down at Fin, who still appeared to be in shock. I stepped away, and he mirrored me like he was a third leg.

I shook my head, unsure what to do with Fin.

"You think it was the Stripe Backs?"

171

"No, this was an order from above." I looked around again. "Where the fuck are Brick and Tess?" I looked at Rail. "You know anything about this?"

"Why would I know any more than you?"

He looked genuinely shocked at my question. I didn't think Rail would be stupid enough to cross me.

"You want to ask me somethin'?"

I cracked my neck. What the hell was happening to my club?

"You and Cooper have been hanging out at the Flying Arrow."

"Yeah, we have."

"Making friends with the Stripe Backs?"

Rail crossed his arms and held my gaze. "Been by your side for a long-ass time now, worked my way up your ladder, and you stand here accusing me of something?"

"Just asking."

He licked his lips and dropped his arms heavily at his sides. "Not sure who is puttin' shit in your head, Trigger, or if you're just trippin' over Tess, but don't ever question my loyalty to the club. I say that to your face, knowing the consequences of my words right now."

"Careful," I warned but was pleased he had the balls to speak his mind.

His brows pinched together, and he let out a frustrated sigh. I needed to find Tess. My guess was this hit may have included her too.

"Fin, come!" Vib barked from the doorway. She looked like shit. No doubt she'd done a line out back. Such a fucking mess. "I said come here."

Fin didn't move. He just stood there, eyes locked on the floor. When his mother got closer, his hand latched on to mine. I flinched at the sudden contact, but forced myself not to shake him off.

"When I call, you come!" She reached for him, but I pulled him behind me and raised my free hand to stop her.

"Go lay down for a bit, Vib."

Her face twisted. "Give me my son."

"You think he wants to be with you when you're strung out? The boy's just seen some pretty bad shit go down. He doesn't need *your* shit right now."

"My shit?" she yelled when Gus appeared.

"Vib!" he hissed. "Get the hell out of here."

She turned to me and stuck a finger in my face. "He's not yours to make that decision for."

"Maybe he should be."

"Whatever!" She grabbed her jacket, kicked a chair, and marched out the door.

Gus glanced at me then dropped his head, tired of Vib and her crap. I felt for the old man. He helped raise me when I was at my worst, and now he had two little ones and a strung-out junkie wife who'd fuck any pair of legs around.

My phone vibrated in my pocket, and I reached for it, hoping it was Tess.

"Yeah?"

"Just heard. Everyone all right?"

"Lost Maze and Moe."

There was a small pause before he spoke again. "Sorry, man. What happened?" Mike sounded like he was in a helicopter, judging by the constant roar in the background.

"Stripe Backs came to shut up a snitch. My men got in the crossfire."

I reached for the drink Morgan handed me and tried not to trip over Fin. I covered the mic on the phone. "Find Tess."

Morgan nodded and rushed out back, and I grabbed my keys.

"Is Tess okay?"

"Yeah, she had left just before it happened."

"Good. Look, man, I need to meet with you next week. You got some time?"

I downed the glass and pointed for another when Morgan returned with a shake of the head.

"Yeah, when and where?"

"Friday, Courtside Pub. Bring Tess."

"I don't want her involved in anything."

"Should have thought of that before you fell in love, buddy." He laughed while I dismissed his comment. "Be there at nine p.m."

"Yeah." I hung up.

I looked around at the mess that still littered the floor and wanted to kill someone.

"Morgan," I muttered, "find her. Fin," I turned to my nephew, "go to my office where it's quiet." He didn't say anything as he slowly turned and did what I asked.

"Yeah, boss." Morgan whistled at Jace, who was cleaning the glass. "Let's go."

I hurried outside, needing to clear my head before I fucked with any of my own men. Just when I got on my bike, Minnie showed up.

"Where the fuck are Tess and Brick?" I called out as I pulled my helmet back off.

"Brick is with me. He's parking out back. I haven't seen Tess since the shooting."

"Brick told me she's okay. Said she's with Mud," Big Joe called out from his post. "Brick texted her, and she said she was okay."

"You think you can hold me here?" I heard Loose bark at Ryder. "I could break your face like that." He snapped his fingers.

I tossed my helmet and rushed through the back door and plowed Loose football style into the side of my pickup truck.

I didn't have the time for this.

"Ahh!" he shouted as he held his broken ribs. "What the fuck?"

I was so tired of his shit.

I swung and smoked his jaw so hard it tossed him around in a circle.

"You disrespected me." I elbowed him in the nose, and he stepped back a few feet, but I closed the gap. Blood dripped everywhere, and his expression changed to fight mode. "You disrespected my men and the club." I sent a knee to his balls. "You hit on my girl." I stopped walking when I had him where I wanted.

"She doesn't know the real you," he huffed in an attempt to look tough. "If she did, she'd see what I do. A monster."

"Too bad for you."

For a split second, he was confused, and when it finally hit him that I wasn't about to let him live, I punched him in the throat and he flew backward into the pool.

I bent down, grabbed his hair, and shoved him

175

back under. With a throat punch, your body naturally drew in deep breaths, so I held him down while he slowly killed himself. His struggle satisfied my years of hate for the man. Loose was a weasel, and with the way my club was these days, I needed every last piece of shit gone.

I waited an extra minute before I let go. His body drifted away, the reaper's face smiling back at me from his club shirt.

"Morgan," I barked into the phone. "Pool."

"Copy that."

I went back to my bike and turned over my engine and tore off down the street. The air had a nip to it and felt good over my churning head.

How the hell did she get tangled up with Mud?

Why am I not told anything?

Mud was outside when I arrived. He pulled down on the garage door and gave me a wave as I parked.

"Tess here?" I tried not to sound annoyed.

"Yeah, man, inside."

"Why?"

He smiled behind his joint as he locked the door with a padlock. "You think I'd touch something of yours?"

"Mud." The demons started to tempt me for a good fight.

"I called you twice."

I pulled out my phone and saw he did. How did I miss that?

"Why is she here?"

He waved over his head for me to follow. Once inside, I found her asleep on his long leather couch.

My body relaxed, and the noise settled inside. I moved closer and checked her over.

"She okay?"

"Yeah."

"How did she end up here?"

"I was out catching the storm, and I noticed a woman watching me from the pier. As I got closer, I saw it was your girl. She seemed off, so I told her I'd bring her back to you, but she wasn't ready. Couldn't leave her there, man. It would only be a matter of time before the Stripes found her."

"Appreciate that."

I bent down and rubbed her shoulder, but she didn't open her eyes.

"Tess," I whispered harshly.

"Might be a bit hard to wake her."

"What'd she take?"

"She had a few puffs off my Dragon Butter."

I couldn't help but smile; she must have felt pretty damn good.

Mud handed me the bottle of whiskey I kept under his work bench. "She'll wake in a few hours. Sounds like you could use a breather. I heard about your men, and I'm sorry."

"Me too."

I sat at her feet and listened to Mud tell me about his day. His stories were short and to the point. I liked that he skipped the mindless details.

By three a.m., the shop was cleaned, and we had finished off more than half the bottle.

"She's good people." Mud nodded at Tess.

"Yeah."

"Brave too."

I chuckled at the sleeping tiger next to me and thought about how much she pushed me and how much I'd let her get away with. I was still trying to understand that one.

"She is."

Tess stirred, and her eyes fluttered open. When she saw me sitting next to her, she moved to sit upright.

"Ohh," she moaned and held her arms out to steady herself. "When did you get here?"

"Few hours."

She licked her lips, no doubt suffering from cotton mouth.

"Here." I handed her a beer. She took a little and closed her eyes, trying to wake up. She tugged on the sleeves of her jacket.

"Where is my phone?" Mud leaned over the table and handed it to her. "Thanks." She glanced at a missed call and went to the voicemail but hesitated when she caught me watching.

"Thanks, Mud." She stood and kept her back to me. "I appreciate what you did for me, and I'll pay you back for the…" She trailed off.

"You won't. Consider it a gift. Just stop by once in a while, okay?"

She nodded and headed for the door. I looked at Mud, confused, but followed her out.

I caught up to her and grabbed her arm.

"Hey, what's with the quick exit, and who called you?"

She rubbed her head. "You jealous, Trigger? Oh, no, wait. That would require feelings."

"Who called?" I hated that she wouldn't tell me.

"You fuck Tammy?"

She hadn't heard yet?

"Hard to fuck the dead." It was a poor joke, but I was pissed she'd implied it.

"What?"

"Stripe Backs hit our club after you left. Killed Tammy, Moe, and Maze."

Her hands flew to her mouth in disbelief.

"Oh, my God! I'm so sorry, Trigger."

I crossed my arms and waited for her to tell me about the phone call.

"And everyone else is fine?"

"Physically, yeah. Mentally, Fin is suffering."

"Poor baby." Her hands moved to her hair, and she turned away from me as she processed it all.

"Tess—"

"It wasn't Clark." She cut me off and stepped closer to my bike. I could tell she was ready to go back to the club. "I wouldn't do that to you."

Good. One less person to kill...right now.

I nodded once before I handed her the helmet.

"Tammy did try to get me to screw her, in exchange for information. I didn't."

She let out an unsteady breath and slipped onto the back of my bike.

I wouldn't do that to you.

CHAPTER TWELVE

Tess

Big Joe held the door for me, and I saw the damage the Stripe Backs had done. Bullet holes dotted the walls, and the bar was only half stocked. Morgan gave me a stressed smile before I headed out back.

"Oh, thank God, you're back!" Minnie wrapped her arms around me and whispered, "He's such an asshole when you're gone. Can you believe what happened?"

I caught Trigger's annoyed expression as he muttered something mean next to us, and Morgan cleared his throat with a warning. Minnie missed the tension and pulled back and looked at me before I could get a word in. "You look thinner. Are you eating? Lord, tell me your secret!"

I shifted in embarrassment. I knew I was thinner. It was what happened when I was at the house. "No sleep."

"Oh." Her gaze fell, and she stroked my arm. "Date night tomorrow? I could use some girl time."

"Sure."

Trigger's hot hand landed on my back, and I knew he was growing restless. I waved goodnight and let him lead me in the direction of his room.

He disappeared into the bathroom, and when I heard the water running, I took that moment to head back to my room and get cleaned up. My tattoo was stuck to my shirt, so I cleaned it and rubbed in the sample lotion Mud gave me and quickly slipped into a silky, long-sleeve nightshirt. The USB was in my night table, and I hesitated as it gnawed at my curiosity. What was on it? Did I want to know? I pushed that aside and grabbed my book instead.

I tucked myself under his cool sheets, happy I chose a long-sleeve shirt, and pulled the comforter up under my chin to will my body to stop shaking. I was frozen. Trigger liked to sleep in a temperature reminiscent of the Arctic. Once I created a warm spot, I rolled over, clicked on the little light that hung over the spine of the book, and felt the rush that came with a second book in a trilogy.

Hello, old friends.

I was so lost in my fictional world that I hadn't heard Trigger come in. The bed dipped, and he lifted the blanket, destroying my hot air bubble.

He missed my glare, and I went back to the words in front of me. I couldn't help but sneak a peek as he lay facing the ceiling, one arm under his head, his muscles flexed as he thought about something.

God, between the story and this man, I'm doomed.

"What's on the USB?"

181

I hated that he interrupted me, but I was waiting for that conversation.

"All I know is he guards it with his life. I wanted to hurt him, so I took it."

"You haven't watched it yet?"

"No."

He stayed quiet after that, so I went back to reading.

The pages couldn't turn fast enough. I knew it was coming, but when? My eyes and my mind were in a battle as to which could absorb the story faster. My heart was in my throat. Mike was hinting at something, but what?

Suddenly, I gasped and felt my eyes prickle.

"Yes!" I blurted and heard the pillow slap as he turned to look at me. I ignored him and kept one hell of a grip on my book.

I could feel his eyes on me. They made my skin heat up, but so did the scene. He rolled to face me and stared harder.

"Read me what part you're at." His tone was raspy and hit me in the center of the stomach.

"I can't."

"Why?"

I tried to think of a good excuse, but I was fresh out. I licked my lips. Why the hell not? I dropped my tone to a low, raspy whisper.

"Mmm, you were ready for me." He groaned as he pushed his fingers in further, feeling her velvet insides squeeze around him.

"I'm always ready when it comes to you, Cole." She flopped her head against his chest. "Please, I

182

need you. "

I flicked my gaze up to his and was caught off guard by his expression. He looked hungry or pissed. I wasn't sure which.

"What?"

"Does that turn you on?"

I blushed, thankful the moon wasn't overly bright tonight, and the little book light was turned away from me.

"Maybe."

"What exactly about it does? Cole or the sex?"

I wanted to run and hide. Men would never understand the feelings behind a romance book. It wasn't that the men were sexy, so much as the *fantasy* was sexy. They were fictional characters, created to make women feel something amazing, make us feel wanted no matter our flaws, something that barely existed in this world. But, shit, there was always hope.

However, I knew this book was based on a true story, so I decided to tread carefully.

"It's not Cole that turns me on. It's the way he is with her."

"Meaning?"

My book flopped out of my hands when I rolled onto my back. I couldn't look at him. Trigger didn't do deep feelings, so it was hard for me to open up with him, but I was willing to try.

"Meaning he's primal, alpha, protective, but all the while she knows he loves her beyond anything else in this world. It's just so…"

"So…what?"

"Right, I guess. Cole shows romance here and there, but not all the time—"

"You like romance?" He pushed for more answers while I fought to find the right words.

"Not all the time, but yes, sometimes, just to know you matter enough, you know, that they are thinking of you, and you only." I rubbed my face. I wasn't good at this—*we* weren't good at this. "That no matter what, however angry the guy was, or if there was another girl in the room, you know they only have eyes for you."

"And Cole is that way?"

I shrugged and rolled my head to look at him straight on. "I don't know. I've never met him. The author sure paints him that way." I tucked my hands under my cheek so I could see him better. "Can I ask you something?"

"Maybe."

I rolled my eyes dramatically. "When I was gone, did you sleep with anyone?"

"No."

"Kiss anyone?"

He flinched, and I got the answer. I hated that it hurt so much.

"You?"

"Never slept with anyone."

His eyes flickered with anger but paused when I reached out and ran my hand along his tattooed chest.

"Doesn't feel good, does it?" I stopped to make my point. "To know the one you care for had a little kiss with someone else."

He took my hand and held it over his heart. I

wasn't sure what he was thinking, but I went with it. Slowly, he reached out and skimmed his finger along my jaw and stopped at my lips. His gaze landed there and narrowed in on them.

"How did your body react when Clark kissed you here?" His thumb brushed over my bottom lip like he was wiping away the memory.

I went with the truth, because the truth was all I had right now.

"It was confusion mixed with comfort." I swallowed hard. "But," his eyes turned up to mine, "it took me a moment to realize what I wanted."

"What do you want, Tess?" he whispered as his hand brushed over my brow.

You.

To myself.

I swallowed past the giant lump that formed in my throat. My mouth felt dry, and I was sure he could see my panic. I was always nervous to show anything remotely romantic with Trigger. He and I had both made it clear we didn't want more from each other. I didn't want to rock the boat. I just got back, and already so much had happened.

"I'm not sure."

His hand stilled, and I knew he felt my lie.

"Try again." The force of his glare dared me.

"Fine." I stared into his eyes and secretly begged his softer side to show itself. "I want what I've never had. I want someone to love me." I thought about Matt and how he'd always loved me, but in a brotherly way. He filled that void, and I, in return, had filled his, but that was different. "Someone who can see past my wall, past all my flaws and mistakes." I thought about my tattoo, hidden from his view under my shirt. I wasn't ready to show it to him yet. I didn't regret it. I was waiting for the right moment. I ducked my head down when I felt my face flush again. "Things like that don't happen to girls like me. We are unlovable, broken pieces of someone we could have been." I stopped when I realized my mouth ran away with me. "And you wonder why I read," I muttered to lighten the mood.

Just when I thought he was going to say something, he grabbed my waist and rolled me over. He pressed against my back and tucked his arm around my midsection.

I let a sad smile creep across my face. I was sure I had just made another wall go up. Trigger wasn't built to understand what I had said. Though he had his moments, I wasn't sure how to get through to him, or even if it was possible. For now, I'd hold on to the fact that I was the one in his arms tonight.

"What's wrong?" I sat next to Clark on the bed.

"I need to tell you something, something that is going to hurt you, but you need to hear me out before you freak out, okay?" I heard him, but his face scared the shit out of me.

"I don't know if I can take any more hurt."

His mouth opened, and the words came out, but I soon felt like I was falling down a black hole. My stomach dropped. How could this happen? He just kept going, and the last words that ripped me apart were...

"I'm still here, just in a different way now."

I shifted to smooth my shirt over my leggings, but

it was really so I could buy some time to let the words sink in.

"I don't understand."

Clark reached out and cupped my chin. "I love you, but I also love your mother."

My heart ripped from its anchor and floated around inside, bumping into other organs.

"I want to be with you, Gumdrop, but in order for that to happen, I need to marry your mother."

"Have you slept with her yet?" I didn't want to know the answer, but at the same time, I needed to know.

"Yes."

I stood on shaky legs and leaned against my dresser. "I'm confused. You say you love me, but you sleep with my mother. You say you love me, but you are marrying my mother."

"I know it's confusing."

"No." I laughed because if I didn't I would cry, and that was pointless here. "What's confusing are things like when I had a boy over to help me with a project and you sent him home. I got an F on that project. You act like we're together, but you're marrying my mother." Oh, God, I felt sick.

"I don't expect you to understand. This is a grown-up matter."

I glared at him. We both knew I had grown up entirely too fast.

"No, what I understand is that you want to have your cake and eat it too."

"Gumdrop." He lifted off my bed and tried to hug me, but I stepped out of his reach.

"Answer me one question."

"What?"

"Was this just a game to get to my mother?"

"No." His actions didn't match his words. "Of course not."

Punch to the gut.

I was done.

"Clark!" My mother's voice ripped through the thick tension. "Open the door."

Clark slowly went over and opened the door. "Felicia, I was just telling Tessa the good news."

"Well," she paused to grab our full attention, "we may need to speed the wedding up."

"Why?" Clark looked interested.

My mother's hand rested on her stomach, and she smiled up at him.

No.

"Really?" His face lit up. "How far along?"

I shoved him out of the way and slammed the bathroom door in their faces. I sank to the toilet and covered my eyes. My entire world was crashing down, and there was no way to stop it. Sick. This was all a sick, twisted game they were playing. How could he? He was mine. I saw him first. He was closer to my age than hers.

I pulled at the tissues that stuck out of the drawer, tugging it open. Something caught the light, and my fingers brushed over the sharp edges.

I glanced in the mirror and saw how pathetic I looked.

It had never been clearer. I was unlovable, used up, and disposable now.

I took a deep breath and...

My eyes jolted open, and I jumped in the darkness. My skin had a layer of sweat across it, and my heart raced to play catch up. I was not in the house. I was safe, away from them.

I carefully padded across the icy floor and over to the door where I slipped out, leaving Trigger to sleep.

***

Trigger

I slept like the dead. The demons reminded me that I was never free. My father hovered on the edge of my dreams, taunting me to agree to the fight.

I knew it would be a slippery slope if I stepped into the ring. I had a love-hate relationship with it, but, fuck, I felt alive between the ropes.

Sunlight burned through the gap between the curtains. I could use another few hours, but I knew my head wouldn't allow it.

I flipped the covers off and rubbed my head as I rolled to the side of the bed. I already sensed Tess wasn't there. I went for my gun when I detected movement.

It took me three seconds to register the little shit on my couch, rolled up like a burrito in his beloved green blanket.

He was dead to the world, and I saw a wet spot on the corner of the blanket where he had been crying. His snotty nose was a bit of a put-off, but I felt sorry for the kid.

Fuck. He is too young for this shit.

189

I scooped Fin up and tucked him in the middle of my bed. Maybe one of us would get some more sleep.

I wondered when Tess had slipped out and where she was. Last night was heavy, and I was still trying to figure out how to take what she said. Why the fuck were women so damn complicated? I figured I was safer to keep my mouth shut because I didn't want to say the wrong thing.

"Hungry?" Peggy asked when I slid into my booth in the back.

"Yeah," I huffed into my hands. "Normal."

"Coming right up." She swung her hips as she walked away. Peggy needed to stop trying. If I hadn't made her my old lady by now, it wasn't going to happen.

Morgan brought me a coffee, and I rubbed my face, fighting the fog in my head. So many things were on my mind, not the least of which was how to get Tess to hand over the USB she had taken from Clark. I had a feeling it wasn't going to be easy to convince her. I was still working on the problem when I heard her voice.

"Want some company?"

Tess was dressed in jeans, a tank top, and an oversized sweater that hung open in the front. Her hair smelled like that stuff I liked when she blew it dry.

"Sure." I signaled Morgan to bring her some coffee. He put the mugs down and left us alone. "You get much sleep?"

She wove her fingers through her hair and let out a long sigh. "Enough."

190

"What time did you get up?"

"Three something, don't know." She sprinkled some sugar into her mug. "I just went back to my room. I didn't want to wake you."

Peggy slid my bowl of oatmeal and toast in front of me and glared at Tess.

"What do you want?"

Tess shook her head but granted her a genuine smile. "I'm fine, Peggy, but thanks."

"Good. One less thing to do," she snarled and turned, but I caught her arm.

"Bring her what I'm having."

Tess waved her hand. "Really, I'm good."

"No, you're not." I sent Peggy off. "You need to eat more, Tess."

She looked me square in the eyes and then glanced over her shoulder. "I lost my appetite earlier this morning."

"Oh?"

"I decided to open the USB drive."

I dropped the toast from between my fingers. I knew I was on that thing and what it might show, but I also knew there was a lot more there I needed to see.

"Detective Aaron planted coke on some business guy, and then proceeded to smash his head in."

"Really?"

"Yeah." She stirred her coffee, lost in her thoughts. "It was weird, though. He kept looking at the camera on his dash, and when he was finished, he said, 'There, I did as you said.'"

"Hm." I bit into my toast and let my mind wander over that.

"Your coke has the reaper hood stamped on it, right?"

I squinted at her, wondering how the fuck she knew that.

"Why do you ask?" I'd never let her get that close to it. "You been poking around? Old ladies are not allowed in the back room."

Her elbows fell to the table, and she put her head in her hands.

"Having a conversation with you, Trigger, is maddening. Remind me to keep shit to myself."

She stood to leave, and I cursed. "Tess, I didn't mean to—"

"To what? Accuse me? I feel like I've been down this path before, only that time you believed me. What's changed now?"

Peggy, of course, showed up at that moment and tossed Tess's food on the table. The toast flipped off the plate and fell on the bench seat.

"Five second rule." Peggy picked up the bread with her bright orange nails and dropped it on the plate. "All good."

I grabbed her arm and twisted hard, and she yelped. "Get her some new shit, Peggy, now!" I ordered, and the entire room went silent.

"Fine." She left with her hand in the air.

"When?" Tess had her eyes closed, and her tone told me she was close to being finished. "When will you see I'm only looking out for the club?"

"You ask a lot of questions. I'm not used to a woman being this involved in my club. It takes a while for any member to be trusted enough to know as much as you do now."

"Have I ever made you doubt my loyalty?"

I leaned back and crossed my arms after I pushed my breakfast away from me. She hadn't, but that didn't mean I could lower my guard. It just wasn't in my nature.

"Tammy was here a lot longer than you, and she flipped."

The second I mentioned her name, I saw the fire ignite inside her.

"Don't you *ever* compare me to that skank."

I wanted to lash back at her tone, but I could see she was moments from making a scene.

"She wasn't always a skank."

She chuckled, and I could tell I wasn't going to like this next part.

"Now you're defending her." Her head fell backward as she took a moment. "Why did you bring me back here, Trigger?"

"You didn't belong there. It wasn't safe." I hated being asked that question.

"Let me get this straight. You brought me back, for what? An apology to Brick? For lying to me? And here I am trying to help you connect the dots to something so much bigger, and you question me? You want to see some fucking loyalty?" she hissed in a whisper then yanked up her sleeve and showed me the tattoo of the drawing I had traced on her arm.

Holy shit.

"Screw you, Trigger." She turned on her heel and headed for her room.

Holy shit. She actually got the tattoo, and it looked fucking amazing. By far one of the sexiest

193

things Tess had done yet. It was right up there with her ability to shoot a goddamn gun. My dick screamed at me to go after her, but the bar was filled with members waiting to see what my reaction would be. Sure, they only caught some of it, but I sure as hell didn't need to look pussy whipped.

"Fresh toast." Peggy snickered. "Where the fuck is she?"

"Take it back." I flicked my wrist at her and pulled out my phone.

"Un-fucking-believable!"

I waited for as long as I could before I went to her room, and just as I was about to knock on her door, I heard her talking. I pushed open the door a bit and listened.

"Why are you leavin', Tess?" Fin was on her bed, sitting inside her duffle bag. Every time she'd put something in he'd take it out. "Take me with you."

She sighed and sat next to him and folded the shirt that would be going back into her closet in a few minutes.

"I'm just going to visit a friend for a while. Besides, that wouldn't be fair to your mom."

"Like she'd notice."

Tess reached out and ruffled his hair. "What about Gus?"

"He's okay." He shrugged. "But if you leave, Uncle Trig won't be happy."

"Trigger doesn't have any room in this club for someone like me, Fin." She grabbed her stack of shirts and tucked them next to his legs.

194

"But…" He sniffed, and it took me a moment to see he was panicking. "But what about me?"

She turned and knelt in front of him and tucked a piece of his shaggy hair behind his ear. Her head tilted as a frown broke out across her face.

"You have so many people here who love you so much, Finny. No family is perfect. You have to see past the bad to see the good. Your mom is just a little lost, but she loves you with all her heart."

"But I love you more." He lunged into her arms and buried his head in her neck. She leaned back against the headboard and held him as he cried. "I hate that he's making you leave."

"Who?" She rubbed his back.

"Uncle Trig. He's supposed to be my hero, but he's being an asshole."

For once in my life, I felt like an asshole. Apparently, it was something I was good at.

"He's not an asshole." She started to laugh. "Okay, well, yes, some of the time he is, but under all that crap, he has a huge heart. You two are a lot alike, you know?"

"How?" He wiped his eyes dry.

"You're both strong, smart people. You're both looking for love, just in different ways."

Her words hit hard. Shit, I really was an asshole. It was hard to hear her words, but it was eye-opening.

"Do you love him?"

I held my breath, unsure if I wanted to hear her answer.

"You're a little young to ask such a big question." She stood him on his feet and looked up

195

at him.

"I'm five." He stood a little taller and tried to look strong. I smiled at his feistiness.

"I want to love him." I hardly breathed at her honestly. "But what's the point of loving someone who can never love you back? I've been there before, Fin, and you know where it got me?" He shook his head. "It got me knocking on the reaper's door."

"He loves you too, 'cause you're pretty, and mom says you make his balls hard."

She laughed out loud. "Well, thank you, I think."

"For what?" His brows pinched together.

"For caring about me this much. Feels pretty nice."

"Can I tell you a secret?"

She nodded, and he leaned in and whispered something in her ear. Her smile dropped, and her gaze fluttered to the floor.

"That's…" She fought back tears. "That's the nicest thing anyone has ever said to me, Fin."

"See why you can't leave?"

"Trigger?" Brick called out, and Tess looked over at me. Our eyes met, her back straightened, and she made a point to return to her packing. "Oh, shit, were you creepin'?" Brick waved at Tess, not at all caring that he had outed me. "Sorry, but you need to make a decision."

He handed me the iPad and showed me the email informing me I had to register if this fight was going to happen.

I nodded once before I handed it back to him. "I'll deal with it tonight."

"Deadline is seven p.m."

"Yeah."

I felt a tap on the back, and Fin stared up at me before he sucker punched me in the balls.

"Come here, you little shit." I grabbed the back of his hoodie and hung him in the air in front of me. His eyes were bloodshot, and is nose was still snotty. "What the hell?"

He wiggled before he gave up, knowing there was no use. "Stop her, like you always do, or I'll never talk to you again."

"Fin," Tess shook her head, "it's not up to him."

"The hell it isn't!" we both shot back in unison.

"Jesus Christ, he's your damn Mini You." Brick tossed his hands up. "I'm not sure I'm ready for this."

I dismissed Brick's comment and glared at my nephew. "You wanna toss a punch, at least learn how first. Meet me in the ring in twenty."

His eyes lit up, and I dropped him to his feet and watched him hurry down the hallway. Nice to see the little shit was feeling better.

I turned to deal with Tess. "Where the hell do think you're going?"

Tess packed even faster, shoving her clothes in the bag. "I'm going to go stay with Ven and her brother. Take a break."

I closed the door behind me, then whirled Tess around and grabbed her face so she'd look at me.

Say it.

Fuck me, just say it!

Nolan appeared out of nowhere.

"I do trust you, Tess, more than most here.

You've proven your loyalty more than once, but this…" My fingers found her arm and held it up to show her. "This is unbelievable." I leaned my forehead to hers and breathed in her scent. Her body made me feel alive for the first time in…ever. Oh, shit.

Say it.

My entire body vibrated. The truth made me feel weak and vulnerable, but fuck me, she couldn't leave.

"Don't leave."

I felt her shoulders rise and fall before she leaned forward on her toes and kissed my cheek tenderly.

"I'll stay under one condition."

I raised an eyebrow, curious what she was willing to bargain.

"What does the key go to?"

Oh, shit. She already knows, just doesn't remember.

"Pick another one."

She glared at me, but just as I thought she was going to start packing again, I saw a familiar dark expression flicker across her sexy eyes.

"Kiss me here." She pointed to her cheek.

I almost laughed but didn't hesitate. My lips skimmed her cheek.

"Now here." She slid her finger to the side of her jaw. I obeyed, thinking I had the better end of this deal. "Here." She pointed to the spot on her neck. "Here." Her collarbone.

My jeans felt crowded as I licked every spot she wanted.

"Right here." She pointed to her chest. "And

here." She tapped right between her breasts.

My body hummed as her flavor sank into my taste buds and drove me wild. I skimmed her spine as I sucked at her neck again. I drew in her skin and grazed it with the tips of my teeth. Lost. I was lost in the moment, wanting to suck on other parts of her, when she stepped out of my hold and pressed my arms to my side.

"I'll unpack."

"That can wait." I grabbed for her, but she stuck a finger in my face with a smirk.

"The deal was you kiss me where I said. I never said a thing about anything else."

I moved to stand in front of her, but her hands fell to my chest.

"I love your alpha-ness, Trigger. That's no secret." She bit her lip as she stared at her hands sprawled across my chest. I was sure she could feel my need for her. My blood was screaming her name.

"But, you need to stop lashing out and assuming things about me. So, from now on, when that happens, you can't touch me until I say otherwise."

Ha!

I reached for her again, but she grabbed my hands.

"And if you care about me at all," she studied me, searching for some trace of my feelings, "you'll respect me enough not to cross that line. If not, then take me." She stepped back and held her arms open.

Fuck me, she plays dirty.

I dropped my arms and held my switch down.

"I need to work." I ran a frustrated hand through

my hair. "And I need to be away from you right now."

I stopped at the door and turned.

"Only for you, Tess." Her eyes lit up, and my gaze roamed her body one last time. "Game on."

Her eyes widened as my words hit her.

CHAPTER THIRTEEN

Tess

"What in the ever-loving fuck are you wearing?" Brick scowled at me as I slid behind the bar. "I feel like I'm committing some incest crime just being in the same room as you."

I rolled my eyes and started to turn all the bottles so the labels were facing outward.

"Wowza," Rail yelled from across the room when he saw my tight leather pants and matching leather halter top that stopped a little below my breasts, and as an added bonus, gave me some massive cleavage. I had pulled my hair into a ponytail, which hung down to the middle of my back.

"Hey, Brick, from this angle I can see side boob!"

"Does it look like your mother's?"

"Oh, come on." I smacked Brick's arm.

I was happy about my encounter with Trigger earlier. It was always baby steps with him, but every little step seemed like a milestone to me and made me feel a little more like my old self.

"Hey, Tess!" Minnie came up to the bar and wrapped her arms around Brick. He held her tightly and kissed her hard. "Hey to you too." She beamed at my best friend. It made me unbelievably glad Brick had found someone who truly made him happy. He deserved it.

"So," she leaned over the bar top, "you ready for girls' night?"

Oh, my God, I almost forgot we had plans. Jesus, I almost left. What an asshole I would have looked like.

Morgan chuckled and shook his head. "What's one more night with Peggy?"

"You clear it with him yet?" Brick nodded toward Trigger's office.

"I have to clear it with him first?"

I don't fucking think so.

"Where do you want to go?' I asked over Brick's shocked expression.

"Well, you want to go dancing? Or dinner?"

I handed her a shot, picked up one myself, and raised it to her. "Both?"

She let out a whoop and slammed hers back. Yes! A girls' night that might actually be fun.

"At least tell him," Brick warned then pulled out his cell phone and sighed. "Fucking Jilly."

"Don't, Matt." I reached over and pushed the phone away from his view. "She only wants money."

"What if she's in trouble?"

"When you were in trouble, where was she?" I

knew my point hit home. "Take it from me. Don't let life's anchors drag you down from being happy."

"Tess!" Fin screamed from the hallway. "You're still here!" He raced under the bar and slammed into me for a hug.

"Hey, how was the ring?" His body was hot and sticky.

"Cool! Uncle Trig taught me how to throw a punch. Watch." He did a little karate kick.

I laughed at how seriously he took it. "You'll be able to take Den on soon."

"Yeah, he better watch out. Uncle Trig told me if I kept up bein' good, he'll teach me a choke hold and a roundhouse."

"That sounds like a good deal." I handed him a bottle of water. "You hungry?"

"Yes, I want a burger."

I eyed him. He knew better than to ask for that shit from me.

"Um, you pick."

Smart boy.

I headed to kitchen and ordered him a veggie plate, with chicken strips and milk.

When I returned, I grabbed my bag from under the bar, hugged Morgan—though he acted like he didn't love it—and headed for Trigger's office. I knocked and pushed the door open.

He was sitting at his desk, shirtless, sweaty, and staring at his computer screen.

He plays dirty too, I see.

"Hey," I whispered, just in case it was something serious. I didn't want to break his train of thought. "Got a sec?"

He looked up and lifted an eyebrow at my outfit. "I do."

"Morgan's covering my shift. I forgot I had plans tonight with Minnie."

He folded his arms, and I knew it wasn't going to be easy getting out of here, but my stubborn nature was standing right next to me.

"Where?"

"Not sure. Some place Min knows."

"What are you doing?"

"Dinner and dancing."

He tilted his head as he leaned back in his chair and thought about what I was saying.

"You need to change first."

I rolled my eyes. He was something else. "I'll see you later." I began to leave but made a sudden decision. "Um," I stepped closer to his desk, "Trigger, I knew about the logo on the coke because Big Joe explained that each bag was marked with a little symbol so the buyer knew what they were getting." I pulled out the USB stick. "I think you should watch it. I haven't watched a lot of it, but I know there must be stuff on there that's important, or Clark wouldn't have been so upset that I took it. Who knows, maybe you can find some dirt on Detective Aaron on there. A little blackmail never hurt anyone." I winked as I set it on his desk. "I have my own copy, if you want to keep the original. I might get time to look at the whole thing one day."

He leaned forward and examined the little piece of technology that held too many secrets.

"All right." He flicked it through his fingers like he did with his joints, and I waited for more, but

204

there was nothing. *Man of few words* was an understatement. "Take Jace with you."

"No." I held my ground. "Don't even think of it."

He leaned forward, pushed to his feet, and started a slow walk toward me. His chest rose high and fell hard, then his eyes turned dark, and it took all my effort not to run to him.

That's what he wants.

"Trigger, the last time I got a day off I went to the beach, and you had Jace watch me the entire time. Then you showed up and took me home. I'll be with Minnie, and that's it." I raised my chin to look a little taller. He towered over me, and my eyes blazed at him. I hated that his sweat turned me on, and I felt the rush of heat that pounded between my legs.

He leaned his head down and brushed his lips over my ear.

"If I want to protect what's mine, I have the goddamn right to," he growled but backed off. "Text me when you change locations. Do you understand me?"

"Fine. We're in agreement, then." I could handle that. He slid a hand into my hair and kissed me hard—to make a point, I was sure. But as fast as he swooped in and stole my breath, he was gone behind his desk, buried in whatever he was doing.

I didn't question it and left.

***

"Where the hell did you take me, Min?" I

laughed as she took the menu from me and prattled off something to the waiter.

We were in the basement of a clothing store in Venice. There was red velvet wallpaper glued to every inch of the walls, gold chandeliers dangled above us, and round leather tables with matching half cup seats were scattered as far as the stage. I felt like I was stuck on the set of *Moulin Rouge* where the sinful atmosphere was laced with dark and dirty promises.

"We, my friend," she removed a glass of champagne from the waiter's tray and handed it to me, "are having a true girls' night." She tapped the delicate rim of her glass to mine. "To *finally* having a girl around I don't want to smash in the teeth with a shovel."

I tossed my head back and laughed. That was possibility the best toast I'd heard in a long time.

"To us." I took a long sip of the crisp, bubbly drink then relaxed in my seat and pulled out my phone.

Tess: At the Rusty Diamond

Trigger: What the hell is that?

I laughed at his reaction. Minnie questioned my sudden outburst.

"Trigger wants to know where we are."

"Tell him to Google it."

We both waited a beat and burst out laughing together. Trigger didn't Google.

"Give me your phone."

I hesitated but thought why not. He'd be less apt to kill her than me.

One eyebrow slowly rose as her fingers tapped on the screen. I could only imagine the things she'd write, but before I could ask, the lights flickered out, and a spotlight illuminated a man standing at center stage. He was dressed in a black suit, his hair hung a little shaggy, and there was an intriguing grin on his face.

"Min—?" I began, but he beat me to the punch.

"Ladies and, well, dirty gentlemen," he flashed a wicked grin, "you all know the drill, and if you don't, here is a quick rundown." He swaggered across the stage. "Keep your arms and legs outside your seat at all times. If you need assistance, kindly slap the nearest ass you can find, and if you need to use the restroom, good luck, because I cannot help what may happen to you along the way. Now," he slapped his hands loudly by his head mic, "are you ready?"

The crowd screamed so loud my ears rang.

"I said, are you *ready*?"

I shook my head, and Minnie mouthed, "Girls' night, baby!"

Smoke rose from under our feet, and an under-glow of color engulfed us. Then a roar started from the corner of the room, and a man was slowly lowered from the roof and landed like a panther about five feet from me.

Drums beat to a familiar tune, and it took me a moment to recognize it. The man closest to me pointed in my direction just as a spotlight lit him up. He started to lip sync to "Comin' to Your City" by

Big & Rich.

I grinned at Minnie. She had the best expression on her face, like a kid in a candy shop. She had taken me to a country drag queen show! Holy shit, it was perfect.

My train of thought was interrupted when a man started to come toward me. I closed my eyes. Fuck me. If Trigger showed up, there would be a bloodbath in here. Although I had to say Trigger was surprisingly good with Shantee.

A finger lifted my chin, and by the thick scent of the cocoa butter, I knew it was the dancer.

"Smile, darling!" he yelled over the music with a dramatic wink. I laughed at his totally over the top gorgeous eyelashes.

Three songs went by, and I had never seen so much glitter, feathers, and sequins in my life, and that was saying something. The men were incredible, and I hadn't laughed so hard in a very long time. Who would have thought this was under Venice?

The song changed to "Fake ID" by Big & Rich, and the place went wild. I looked around, puzzled at what was I missing.

Minnie hopped up on her seat and waved her arms. The guys started pulling people up on stage and dressing them in costumes.

I grabbed my friend and pulled her down into her seat while I signaled for another round of drinks. Oh, my God. This place was beyond fun, but my ass was not about to go on stage. I didn't dare risk a photo that would set Trigger's switch off for damn sure.

"You have got to be fucking kidding me!" I yelled, and anger licked at my insides. "He's impossible!"

"What?"

I leaned over and carefully pointed at the man back by the door.

"No way." She started to get up, but I stopped her.

"Wait. I have a better idea."

I hurried toward the stage and grabbed one of the men and whispered my idea to him. I handed him a twenty. He refused it, saying it was "all his pleasure."

"What did you do?" Minnie shouted, her champagne breath in my face.

"Just get your phone ready."

I waited for the song to switch, but it took all my power not to look in his direction.

My entire body jumped when I heard the beat. I scrambled to grab my phone as the man dressed like a horse raced toward him.

"Save a Horse" burst through the speakers, and the moment Rail caught sight of the man coming toward him, his horrified expression shot over to me.

I gave a little wave and held up my phone.

Three men circled Rail and rushed him up to the stage. They stuck a brown cowboy hat on him and looped a pair of reins around his waist. He tried everything to fight them, but they were too fast. Clearly, they'd dealt with people like him before.

When the song got to the chorus, the entire place went wild with the words, and guys pretended to ride him.

The look on his face when he locked eyes with me was that of man who was going to spend the rest of his life making sure mine was miserable.

Oh, Matt, this one is for you.

As soon as the song ended, they stripped him of his get-up and made him bow with the rest of them.

Rail pointed at me, but all I could do was laugh so hard tears streamed down my face. Minnie buried her face in her hands, but I could see her shoulders shaking.

"I will never forgive you for that." He pulled out a chair and downed the rest of both our drinks then grabbed a waiter. "Whiskey on *her* tab." He pointed to me.

Five more songs, some bubbles, and a lot more mist, and the show ended. We were finally served dinner, and I was starved.

I was surprised to see a lobster tail smothered in garlic sauce, and scallops paired with baby potatoes.

"You wouldn't think one of the best seafood chefs around worked here, would you?" Minnie bit into the scallop.

Rail ordered a steak and cringed when the man brought him his food wearing ass-less chaps. The music was turned down, and we were able to talk a little easier.

"I have never wanted to kill so many half naked men in my life." Rail dumped a half a bottle of A-1 sauce on his meat.

"Serves you right." Minnie stuck her fork at him. "We don't need an escort."

"I wasn't really sent *here*." He madly cut into the

overdone cow. "I just got back to the club, and Trigger told me to check in on you. I wasn't going to stay. You weren't even supposed to see me."

"Well," I lifted my hands dramatically, "that makes it even better, doesn't it?"

***

Trigger

The cursor flashed over the *submit* button. I knew it was a bad idea, but what choice did I have? I either said no and this shit storm stayed, or I ended it once and for all.

My phone rang, and I quickly scooped it up.

"Yeah?"

"Boss, there's someone here who wants to speak to Tess." Morgan cleared his throat as I leaned forward in my chair. "You got a minute?"

Who the hell was here?

"Yeah." I hung up and clicked the button. The demons went wild and stirred up my hot blood to a dangerous level. My hands formed into fists. Who the hell would come here looking for Tess?

Blood could be shed, and the reaper might be rewarded tonight. I could almost taste it. I needed it.

I swung open the door, disappointed to find a medium-sized man dressed in black at my bar, a beer held between battered hands. Hands I recognized had seen a fight or two.

He felt me come up and slowly turned and took a moment to let my appearance sink in. I knew I was big, and I knew I fit the biker look. I'd let my beard grow, my hair was shaved on either side, and the rest hung in a messy, long mohawk that flopped to the right. Tattoos inked my skin, and my past was as evident as his was across my knuckles.

"He's clear," Joe chimed in and held up the gun he had taken from him. "Offered it at the door."

"Got no beef with you, man. Always carry it like my wallet." He stood and offered me a hand.

Morgan slid over a bottle of whiskey and two glasses. I ignored his hand and folded my arms, not wanting to touch him. The demons were so loud I could barely hear, and I knew he had better have a good explanation why he wanted to see Tess.

"Why do I know you?" I couldn't place him.

"I, ah…" He stumbled at my coldness. "I live in Vegas and know some friends of Tess's. I overheard some shit I thought she might want to know about."

"Like?"

He sank back onto the stool and looked around. "No offense, but I'd rather speak directly to Tess."

It wasn't lost on me that he called her Tess and not Tessa. He either did know her, or he'd heard about her recently.

"If you want to talk to Tess, you talk to me first." Just as the last word came out, Big Joe backed up and let someone in.

"Honey, I'm home!" Minnie called out as she and Tess stumbled into the bar, looking more than half in the bag. Rail was behind them and seemed relieved to be back.

Shit.

"Oh, look, Tess! We have company." Minnie

giggled, and Tess grinned, but it was obvious she tried with her all might not to join in.

"Shh, you'll make him mad," Tess whispered loudly. "Although I kinda like Trigger angry. It's real exciting." Her expression turned devilish.

"You had fun tonight, Tiger?" Morgan broke through her dirty thoughts to try to make her see our unknown visitor.

"You know what Min and I did?" She pointed. "Railey wouldn't let us dance, so we came here to get the party started."

"She's all yours, man." Rail raised his hands. "Please don't ever ask me to check on them again. This one," he pointed at Tess, "thought it was cute to slip out of the club to make a phone call alone, then went back and did endless shots."

Tess broke out in a loud laugh. "Three men made Rail their bitch!" Minnie had to hold onto the stool to stop from falling over, she was in such a fit of laugher. "I will never forget his face when they bent him over and rode him with reins."

Morgan glanced at me and waved over Brick as he came in from out back.

"Hey, ladies, how was—" He stopped when he saw how piss-eyed drunk they were. "Damn, I really missed a fun night, hey?"

"Oh, Matt, you have no idea." I glanced back to her. I hated that she had used his real name in front of the unknown guy. They had their names for protection and honor, and their old names had no place here in the club. "I have an early birthday gift for you. Or maybe it's mine. Whatever. We can share."

"Die. All of you, die." Rail grabbed a beer from behind the bar. "Who the fuck is this?" He nodded to the guy who was staring at Tess like he was way too friendly with her.

"Brick, take Minnie to bed," I ordered. He caught my tone and scooped Minnie up and whisked her out of the room. "Morgan, coffee for Tess."

"Sure thing, boss."

Tess stood straight and gave me a salute, giggled, and stumbled as she peeled off her coat. I caught her arm before she fell.

"I would love to snap my fingers and have everyone jump to my command." She finally seemed to notice the guy next to me and dramatically offered her hand. "You look kinda familiar. How are ya?"

His face relaxed, and he broke out in a smile, taking her hand in his a little longer than I would have liked.

"I'm a friend of your mother's."

Tess yanked her hand free, and she immediately lost all sense of fun. "My past just keeps comin' to knock me down, and all I wanted was one night to have a little fun."

My attention moved to her face, and I saw something flicker across it. What did she mean? And what the hell? The guy never said anything about her mother.

"I'm not here on her behalf. I'm really not. I'm here to warn you about something."

She glanced at me, her eyes heavy with sadness. Or was it fear? Slowly, she leaned into the side of

214

the bar in front of me and took the coffee Morgan handed her along with three Advil.

"No disrespect, but I really don't give a shit what happened to those people."

He nodded but then looked over at me and downed his beer. "Can we talk somewhere private?"

I considered his words and looked around the bar, which was littered with my men and a few random women, then back to Tess.

"This is my family, so my business is their business," she said.

I felt a sense of pride at her words. My hand slipped around her waist, and I pressed her against my side. She sagged into my hold.

"Okay." He cleared his throat. "You took a USB from Clark?"

"And if I did?"

"Have you watched it yet?"

"Only a little of it. Why?"

"So, you haven't gotten to file thirty-three?"

She shook her head.

He purposefully glanced down and then back to her eyes again. It only took her a moment before her entire body went stiff. She pulled herself free of me and stood off to one side, holding his gaze.

"Trigger, could you please get me the USB drive I gave you?"

"Rail, third drawer, left side."

Rail returned a moment later and handed it to Tess. She tossed it on the floor and jammed the heel of her shoe on it, crushing it into pieces.

"Shit!" Her hand covered her mouth. "How do you know—I mean, is that what you're here to warn me about, or is there…Jesus!" She grabbed the bar top and looked like she might pass out.

"Tess?" I reached out for her, and she gripped my arm. Her hands were ice. "What is in file thirty-three?"

"Not my place, man." He shook his head. "I'm here to let you know Clark won't give up. He's already headed this way."

"What? Tell him I destroyed it. I want nothing to do with all that crap. It's just a stupid stick full of lies. I only took it so he would know how serious I was about being done with him and the whole house."

"Do you have a copy?"

"No." She didn't miss a beat. I knew she had another copy, but I didn't know where.

"But it's not just about the USB, Tess. He wants you."

My blood thickened at the thought of Clark touching what was mine. He had his chance, and she choose the club—she chose me.

"I hate him! I've made that very clear. I loved him once. Well, actually, I'm not sure I ever really did. Not the way I love—the club." She whirled around. "Trigger? Can we borrow your office for a minute, please?"

No. No way in hell.

Her expression stopped me. I gave a nod, and she motioned for him to follow.

"Wait." She turned to him. "I never got your name."

He smiled. "Name's Zay."

I was pissed with this whole thing, and when the

door closed, I turned to face Morgan. He stared at the barrier that separated us from them.

"Something feels off, man." He turned back to me and started wiping off the counter. "You think Clark is really coming?"

"No fucking clue."

"And what the hell is file thirty-three?"

I looked down to the broken USB. "Something bad, I assume."

"I hate that she can't have one night of fun."

"Mmm," I agreed. I couldn't help myself. Her phone was face-down on the bar, and I flipped it over and swiped the screen open. I tapped the phone log and saw a couple of Vegas area numbers had repeatedly called her.

Who the hell was that? Just as I went to call the number, a text came through from another number.

Clark: I'm sorry, Gumdrop. I don't blame you for what happened, and I took care of it. You were upset, that's all. I can't go another day without touching you or hearing the sounds you make when you're turned on. I NEED to see you NOW. I know where you're staying now. If you won't come to me, I'll come to you.

Oh, hell no! So many ways of killing that bastard flashed through my head.

"Dude has texted her three times tonight." Rail broke through my murderous state. "Look." He held up his phone and showed me a picture he took of the text messages. "I deleted them so she wouldn't see them. Look what good that did." He snickered.

Clark: I need you.

Clark: I'm tired of your damn voicemail! PICK UP, DAMMIT!

Clark: I miss me inside you.

The door to my office opened, and Zay came out, followed by Tess. She looked totally done.

"Sorry for the nature of my visit, Trigger. I meant no disrespect to you or your club. I just needed to warn Tess of what was happening."

I nodded at him but kept my eyes on Tess as she moved to the bar and leaned against it.

"You seem good here, Tess. I'm glad to see that. I'll do my best to keep Clark away."

"Thank you, Zay," she whispered.

"Take care."

Big Joe handed him his gun at the door, and he disappeared into the night.

"You okay, Tiger?"

I glanced at her.

"Not even a little."

I needed to get a look at her copy of that damn USB.

CHAPTER FOURTEEN

Tess

My breathing was heavy by the time I got to Trigger's room. I knew better than to go to my room; he'd only insist. I had no fight left in me.

I never used his bath before, but it looked inviting, so I ran the water and stripped off my clothes. I almost giggled when I found bubble soap under the sink. I decided I wouldn't go there, then I helped myself to some.

I eased into the hot water and tuned in to the soothing sounds around me. Rain pelted off the window, and I stared at the glass as the wind drove the drops in random patterns on the panes. Even the weather matched my mood. Cold, dark, and chaotic.

My eyelids grew heavy from my pounding head, so I let them lower and rest. I must have passed out for a bit because when I opened them, I was surrounded by candles and a glass of red wine.

"Trigger?" I whispered, hoping to hell it was him and not Brick.

He appeared in the doorway in only his jeans.

"Did you do this for me?"

He nodded, and his hair flopped forward in a sweet, messy way.

"Thank you." I felt the pesky tears brew in my lower lids.

"I do listen." His voice was low. "I may not be good at it, but I hear you."

My lips turned up, but my burning eyes held the truth. I was hurting from a very old wound.

"It's a big tub." I tried to focus on something else.

He smirked. "Never sat in one before. You enjoy it."

"You just ruined this for me."

"Why?"

"You had this bubble bath under your sink. Am I to assume you had other women in here?"

He sat on the bench next to the shower. His muscles looked even sexier against the flickering flames that highlighted his lean, toned body and cast yummy shadows in all the right places.

"Fin likes to pretend he's a shark." He shrugged, but I noticed his eyes crinkled when he spoke about his nephew. He cared about both the boys, although he pretended he didn't. They were part of his family. I understood that, and they really were pretty sweet when you considered the life they were being brought up in. "I never let anyone in here but me, and, well, maybe the kid."

"What makes me different?"

His lips sucked inward as he thought. "I'll make you a deal. You answer a question for me, and I'll answer one for you."

"No vetoes," I added. For once, I wanted some answers, and I was ready to share some truths.

"All right." He waited for me to start. "You don't want to go first?"

"Truthfully, you need to hear about my past in order to answer the question I'm going to ask."

He flipped his hair out of his eyes before he pulled a joint free from his pocket. "What's on file thirty-three?"

"It's my biggest regret." I pushed the bubbles around, unable to look at him. "My mother faked a pregnancy to trap Clark into rushing the wedding date. Everyone thinks I cut myself because of their wedding, but it was really because they would be forever tied together. I knew that baby would be loved the way I never was. Selfish, I know, but I was eleven and mentally warped." I wiped a tear that rested on my cheek. "When I was twenty-six, I had been living on the streets with Brick for some time. One night, he met a girl and left me to go spend the night with her in a motel. I ran into a pack of guys who were always causing trouble, and they tried to attack me. Before I knew what I was doing, I raced back to the house, which I said I would never do, and that night, I ended up in bed with Clark."

I tried to speed past the dirty details. I didn't need to make this any worse than it was. "I took off again the very next morning and met up with Brick, but I couldn't bear to confess what I had done. I couldn't admit to him that I had gone to see Clark after I got away from those guys. Brick would never forgive himself." I let out a long sigh, trying to gather enough strength to go on. "Three weeks later, I knew something was off with me. It didn't take long to figure out what had happened. I was so ashamed." The tears fell harder. "Brick risked so much for me to stay away from that house, and the one time he left me alone, I got into trouble and ran back there. I couldn't face him. He would never have understood. I don't deserve his forgiveness. So," I sniffed, "I packed my shit and went back to the house. Left him a note saying where I went and that I needed to work some stuff out. I left him all the money I had on me and thought I could live without my best friend."

Trigger's phone rang, but he turned it off and tossed it on the counter. He waited for me to continue.

"My mother was livid and tried to figure out why I'd come home. One night, she overheard me crying to Venna about how awful I felt." My voice trailed off, nervous of his reaction. "I was about a month pregnant and terrified." I glanced up, only to find his face like stone. "I didn't want children. I knew I'd be a horrible mother. What kind of role model would I be, sleeping with my stepfather?" I stopped to let the hurt rip across my chest.

"My mother grabbed my hair, dragged me upstairs to Clark's office, and shoved me to my knees. She screamed at him, called me a whore, and all Clark did was stare at me. He never protected me. He just looked at me like I was someone else, not someone he had made love to a few weeks before." Heavy, hot tears raced down my face, running away from me like everyone else in my life.

I shook off my emotions and pushed on. "A few nights later, three men who worked at the house woke me up and forced me downstairs into one of the back rooms." I swallowed hard, as the next part was a haunting blur of pain. "Venna said they could hear me screaming for hours. She tried to help, but they had the room guarded. Clark paced the room but didn't even try to intervene." Trigger's throat contracted, but the rest of him was still.

"I couldn't believe what they were doing to me, my own mother and the man I thought loved me. They stood there and watched while I was held down and my baby ripped out of me by some cold-faced stranger. They killed my child. Whether I wanted it or not, they took a life. I checked out, and it took me a long time to find the will to even bother to leave that place. I fell into a bad crowd. Sex and alcohol were all I cared about for four years. Funny how quickly time passed when you've been stuck between two lives." I took a moment to remember. "It felt good, helped me cope. That was where I learned how to turn *it* off. Just stop caring. I guess we all have a switch somewhere." I shrugged. "I just didn't give a damn what happened to me. Until one day I reached out to the only person who had ever loved me."

"Tess," Trigger started, but I wasn't done.

"The number that keeps calling me is my doctor. I had some liquid courage tonight and finally called her back. I saw her when I was at the house for the pain in my side. The Serpents really did a number on my stomach. It really took a long time to heal.

Turns out my doctor had more *great* news. What happened to me at the house years ago…well, that rent-a-doctor didn't do the procedure right and did a lot of damage. Since I never dealt with the old injury, my new one flared up the scarring, and…I guess my loving mother took yet another thing from me."

I laughed darkly and dried my cheeks. I was a mess, but at least he now knew the whole truth.

"Tess—"

"I'm fine, Trigger, really. I just wanted you to know, so you can decide what to do."

He huffed loudly. "Do with what?"

"With me. I can leave tonight if Clark is really coming. You don't need this shit right—"

"You're not going anywhere."

"Trigger—"

"That's three times now, Tess. You interrupt me again, and I'll tie you up and gag you myself to make you listen."

The anger in his voice shook me to the core, but it also awakened a foreign feeling. He still cared. I wasn't expecting that.

"I don't want kids. Never have. I'm sorry you went through that, but fuck me, I'm damn happy you never had his kid. As for your mother, I will deal with her myself. If Clark shows…I hope he does because I can't wait to give him the full clubhouse tour."

Ah, yes, the slaughter room.

"As for you," he twisted to sit on the side of the tub, his eyes dark in the dim light, "you're not going anywhere. I can't protect you if you run off again."

His finger curled around a fallen strand of hair that was stuck to my chest. He peeled it free, running the back of his finger down my hot skin.

"I don't want to be a problem."

His hand disappeared into the water and gently urged my legs open. He found my opening and circled my clit. My stomach tightened as I bowed upward and tried to direct them inside.

My eyes closed when the delicious warmth tingled up my skin, preparing me for what was to come. I snapped my hand around his wrist and pushed him to where I needed it.

He suddenly stood, leaving my feverish body to fend for itself. He kicked off his pants and briefs and stepped into the tub in front of me. I grabbed his hips and swallowed his erection before he could stop me.

"Jesus, Tess!" My name vibrated from deep inside his throat, and he grabbed a handful of hair and held me in place as he set the pace. His tip rolled over my taste buds, so I curled my tongue to cup and caress the velvet slit.

I took him deeper, and he hissed loudly.

"Enough." He pulled out and eased me backward into the water. He hovered over me, legs on either side of mine, and pinched my nipples. His expression was one I hadn't seen before, like he was contemplating something. His brows drew together, and his eyes widened. Before I discovered what it was, he broke his hold on me.

"Turn over," he commanded. I wasted no time and flipped around. He took hold of my waist and pulled me onto his lap as he sat on his knees. "Lift."

His voice was tight. "Now down." He slammed up as I dropped down.

I screamed at the sudden fullness. He hit the end of me with a force that took my words away.

"Again." He nipped at my neck, and I obeyed.

And again, I rose, completely at his mercy. His hands started to roam as I repeated the action. The water splashed onto the floor with each thrust. I'd never had sex in a tub before, and as awkward as it seemed, Trigger made it easy. Maybe because the space was so large, or because it was exactly what I needed at that moment. I needed so much to feel something other than shame and disappointment.

"Stop." He turned my chin to look at him. "When you're with me, you're with me. Nowhere else. Ever."

I nodded and tried to let the ugly thoughts go. Easier said than done, and I knew he felt my struggle.

When I rose to slam back down, he pushed me to my knees and placed my hands on the side of the tub. He slid in fast and took me from behind. I could barely think at the pace. My vision blurred, and I struggled to catch my breath. He slapped my ass and pulled my attention back to him.

"Give it to me!" He was close to losing it. "Now!"

I leaped off the edge and burst into a hundred million pieces. Colors of every shade sparkled behind my eyelids and pricked at my sensitive skin. My heartbeat strummed a wicked melody as I floated back to reality. Sex with Trigger was like unwrapping a present. The outcome was always wanted, but it was seriously unpredictable.

He nibbled my neck to see if I was back with him.

"Mmm," I moaned because it was all I had in me.

"I will kill anyone who touches you."

***

Trigger

I couldn't stop touching her. Her skin was like silk, and each time I inhaled her scent, she calmed the raging storm inside my head. It wasn't lost on me that I was becoming addicted to Tess. So much of me wanted to push her away, send her back to Clark. Go back to my familiar hell. But the other part told me I deserved her. I'd put in my time to the reaper. I did his dirty work, and I had the savages in their cages to remind me that I wasn't free.

My father popped into my head, and I flinched at his image. I'd need to start training soon. I knew I had this, but I needed my head in the game.

I reached for my phone and sent a text.

Trigger: Call me.

It rang three seconds later.

"Been awhile," I whispered as I rose off the bed and moved out to the hallway.

"Am I to assume you contacted me because you're heading back into the ring?"

I waited for the door to click shut behind me before I answered him.

"Yeah."

Langley paused, and I knew what was rolling through his mind.

"Spare me the whole 'you go to the dark side in the ring,' Lang." I pushed my anger aside. "I need your help."

"I've taught you everything you need to know. Not sure why you'd call on me now."

I rubbed my head and thought about getting a drink, but my liver needed the break, and my body needed to be in the best shape it could be.

"What's really going on?"

I licked my lips. "My father is back."

"Impossible."

"I would say the same thing if I hadn't seen him myself."

Langley let out a puff of air, and I heard a chair scrape along the floor.

"But you—"

"I know. I'm out of ideas on that score. I know I have a mole. I'm just not sure how long he's been around or who the fuck he is. He's tied to my father, I know that much, and they screwed with my drug route and killed some of my men. Now he's got…" I glanced at the bedroom door and pictured Tess so small in my bed.

"Got what?"

"He's got leverage over me."

"What, a video or something?"

"Something," I repeated, unsure how to describe Tess.

"Oh," he chuckled, "well, now I really need to come."

I closed my eyes and wished to hell people would stop making comments about the situation. They all saw something that wasn't there. I cared for Tess, I needed her, but I wasn't in love with her. That was something I simply wasn't capable of. Neither was she.

"You got room for me there? I don't do motels."

"Yeah."

"I'll be there tonight."

"Morgan will be here. I have something to handle tonight."

"See you soon, son."

I lowered the phone and watched as the call disconnected. No turning back now.

Tess worked the bar with Peggy in the morning. Morgan had to help Cooper with a family problem. Peggy was a raging bitch, but Tess ignored her and did her own thing.

Rail and Brick worked out the details for the fight in my office away from anyone who might want to listen.

Jace hovered around the bar, trying not to trip over Maze's cousin, who came by to collect his shit. She was a cute little one but was barely twenty-two and clearly had hang-ups of her own.

Cray: Last shipment has been collected. You are no longer walking with the white witch.

Trigger: Now I walk with the monsters.

229

Cray: Not that long now, my friend.

My head pounded. I was about to signal Tess when she appeared at my table with a double whiskey. She set it in front of me then stepped up and ran her hands through my long hair. I hooked my arm around her waist and pulled her closer. She studied my face, and her hands slid down and ran along my brow to my temples.

"Do you always carry such heavy shadows with you?"

"I could ask you the same."

The corner of her mouth twitched before it faded away.

"I guess it makes it easier to spot them, then." She touched her lips to mine then sighed. "You can talk to me, you know. I know I'm not one of the guys, but—"

"No, you're not." I forced a smile, but I knew she saw through it.

"Okay." She tried to step back, but I locked my arms.

"We have plans tonight."

"We do?" She looked confused, then her face fell. "What kind of plans? I will not hide out, if that's what you're thinking."

"As tempting as that sounds, no, you have been requested at my meeting tonight."

"With who?"

I grinned at her sudden interest. She made the little things fun again.

There was a loud crash, and I jumped to my feet and shoved Tess behind my back.

"Slippery little fuckers!" Peggy cursed at the pile of glass in front of her.

"Karma's a bitch when you're a bitch," Gus muttered at his empty glass, which made Tess laugh, and Peggy glared at her.

"You gonna just watch me or actually be useful around here?" She raised an eyebrow at Tess.

"I just figured you spend so much time on your knees it would be like you were home down there."

"Screw you, bitch!"

"Not if you paid me."

Peggy picked up a bottle of vodka by the neck like she was going to throw it.

"Peggy!" I barked as Gus began to get up. "Get this shit cleaned up and get the fuck out."

Her hands went to her hips. "You're seriously pussy whipped, Trigger."

"Enough!" I felt my switch tremble. "I don't need this shit right now."

Tess ran her hand up my back, and I swung around to grab it. I held it tightly in mine, wanting to crush the bones, but my head stopped me.

I brought her hand to my mouth and kissed it. The urge to hurt someone was right below the surface. As much as Tess calmed me, I couldn't always control my temper. Yet another reason we shouldn't be together.

"When should I be ready?" Her voice was low. I wondered if I scared her.

Fuck.

"Eight." She looked about to leave as I hooked her waist and pulled her to my chest. I leaned down and whispered a warning in her ear. "Don't wear anything sexy."

Her devilish stare made me hard. I slapped her ass as she sauntered away.

I scanned the room and spotted Rail. "Rail, suit up."

His eyes widened, and he cursed. "Why me?"

Three hours in the ring with Rail, and he was done. He heaved over the ropes to catch his breath and held his side in pain.

I was jacked up on adrenaline. My body had at least five more hours left in it, and all I could get Rail to do was stand there while I did circles.

"Come on, Uncle Trig. Nail him in the sack!" Fin squealed from the corner of the room.

"Shut up!" Rail huffed. "Don't you need to be in school or something, shit?"

"Not my fault you hit like a girl."

Rail straightened. "Seriously, why the fuck is he here?"

"School's closed." I tossed a punch at his shoulder, which did dick for my mood. I had to wear gloves with the guys or I'd kill them.

"Nipple twist him!" Fin screamed again.

"No, don't," Brick laughed from the doorway. "He likes that."

My arms fell when Rail glared at Brick. "So does your momma."

"Yeah, and so does yours." Brick gave him the finger then licked the tip.

"Fuck me," I hissed and knew another pissing match was on the way.

"Can I play?" They fell silent as I whirled around and saw Maze's cousin in a little pair of tight shorts and a sports bra.

She ducked under the ropes and smiled up at me. "You think you can take me?"

"No chicks in the ring," I muttered, brushing past her. My head wasn't in the mood for another child right now.

"Is he always so friendly?" she whispered as I tossed off my gloves and slicked my hair back.

"No," Brick and Rail said in unison.

She appeared at my side, her oversized blue eyes blinked up at me. She was pretty, but in an annoying way. You could tell she'd be high maintenance once she roped you in.

Ignoring her, I grabbed my towel and headed to the front of the club. I didn't have much time before I needed to get ready.

"So, I, ah…" She rushed to match my strides. "I was wondering if I could stay here for a while."

"Why?" I didn't care for the answer, but I wanted her to know this wasn't a hangout for strays.

"Maze paid for my apartment, but now that he's gone, I'm being evicted. Got nowhere else to go."

I snatched a water bottle from the fridge behind the bar and caught Tess serving Cooper and a few of his friends.

She didn't spot me right away; the bar was in full swing.

"So?" I vaguely heard the girl as I moved around the bar. Just as I was about to approach Tess, a hot hand clamped around my forearm.

The entire place went quiet when I stopped and whirled around, feeling the demons flip the fuck out inside. Acidic rage coursed through my bloodstream, rushing to the surface and scarring the inside of me.

I dropped my gaze to her hand then backed up. She was confused but didn't let go.

Morgan whistled from behind the bar and glanced at her hand with a warning. Finally, she got the hint, and her arm fell with a thud.

"So, you don't like to be touched?" she asked in disbelief. "The great, almighty fighter can kill with his bare hands, but he can't be touched by a woman?" She nearly laughed, and I saw her death flash in front of me. A quick snap to her neck to shut her up would be ideal.

"How do you screw?"

"Bitches with mouths don't last long here," Morgan warned again.

My switch vibrated, and the maddening screams became ear-piercing.

"First rule in a club is respect, little girl." I stepped closer, and she cowered away from me. I almost smirked. Tess would have given me lip. "Maze's blood or not, you don't belong here."

"I'll vouch for her," Jace said, and I flicked my gaze over to him.

"Quit thinkin' with your dick."

"She's got nowhere to go." He shrugged.

"Yeah, man." Tat, one of Cooper's cocky friends, said and rose out of his chair. "She got no one since you got her cousin killed." He smirked at the girl, and I glared at Cooper. He knew better than to let a non-club member hear club information.

"Tat, shut the fuck up." Cooper punched his buddy in the arm. I knew that shithead used Cooper for free booze and tried to join the club a few years back, but I refused him. He never got over the fact I didn't let him in.

"That's the problem with this club. Everyone is expendable. Just takin' this one a little longer to see it." Tat draped his arm over Tess, and she sidestepped out of his reach with a hiss.

Red. I saw nothing but red.

I rubbed my mouth to take a moment to calm down, but it didn't work. I snatched the hunting knife Rail carried, held it by the tip, and whipped it with all my might into Tat's shoulder.

His eyes popped while he grabbed at the blade. Blood lined the wound and soaked into his shirt.

The girl screamed as Tat struggled to comprehend what had happened. I eased into the chair and took the drink Morgan set in front of me.

Tat shot up behind me, white as a sheet, and stuck a gun to the back of my head.

"No," Tess whispered. "Tat, don't." She started to move, but Brick stopped her. "Tat, look at me," she tried again as my patience fizzed away.

"How can you love such a monster, Tess?" Tat shouted, foaming at the mouth. I guessed I underestimated his interest in Tess. Tat's body was rejecting the sudden intrusion.

"Because," her voice shook, "I'm one too." She pushed Brick's hand away when he tried to stop her again. "So, point that at me, not him."

I sipped the amber liquid and watched as he tried to push the blinding pain away. If he so much as twitched in her direction, he was dead. Well, he was dead anyway.

Tess moved closer, and I tried not to reach for her. She was insane. What the fuck was she doing?

Tat blinked a few times before he focused back on me.

"I hope she watches you die by your father's hand," he whispered.

Flip.

CHAPTER FIFTEEN

Tess

Trigger flipped his hair out of his face and turned to the screaming chick in Jace's arms. The broken whiskey bottle was tossed to the ground a few feet away.

"Remove her, or I will."

"How can you kill someone like that?" she screamed. "Sick son of a bitch!"

"Now! Or she's next."

"Come on." Jace literally had to yank her along by the arm to get her to leave.

Trigger turned to me then closed his eyes. He was trying hard to get himself back under control, and it wasn't easy for him. "Everyone out!"

Within seconds, the room had emptied except Tat on the floor in a puddle of blood, myself, and Trigger. Trigger reached out and held onto the bar. I had never seen him like that. He seemed to be struggling with something.

"Trigger?" I whispered, unsure what the hell was

running through his head. "You okay?"

"No," he hissed and glared at me, and his pupils searched mine before he spoke. "Are you fucking insane?"

"You sure you want to pull at that thread?" I attempted to joke.

"I'm not fucking kidding!" His voice echoed throughout the room. I was thankful the music was still on, but I was sure some may have heard him.

"He had a gun to your head. What was I supposed to—"

"You let me deal with it, Tess! Not get him to point a gun at *your* fucking face!" He kicked Tat hard and covered his mouth and muttered something.

"I knew he wouldn't hurt me."

"How?" His bark made me jump. "How the fuck do you know what was going through that fucker's head?"

I felt my back go up.

"He asked me to leave you for him. He told me he wanted me, and that he could make me happier."

It was true. He had pulled me aside while Trigger was in the ring that afternoon. I laughed at first, thinking he was drunk, but when he leaned in to kiss me, I shoved him aside.

"And?"

Oh, please!

"We're planning our marriage right now." I dripped with sarcasm, and my fury burned through my eyes. Shit, when would he ever get that I wanted him?

"Be careful, Tess. I just killed a man. You push

me too far, and I'll kill again."

I stepped closer and pushed my chest into his. His heat smoldered around me, holding me tight.

"You saying you'd hurt me?"

"I'm saying I'd kill for you." He grabbed my face between his huge hands and pressed his forehead to mine. I clutched his shoulders and held him just as hard. He needed an anchor. "Don't ever do that to me again. Promise me. If anything happens to you, I…" He stopped himself.

"You'd what?"

"Promise me, Tess." His voice was strained, and I needed to stop pushing. It was enough for now.

"I'm sorry." I pressed my lips to his and let him devour my mouth. Right as I was about to grab his belt, he pulled away.

"We need to leave."

Just like that, the moment was gone, and just like that, Tat was forgotten. The MC world had no room for screw-ups or mourning, and if I was going to allow myself to fully fall for this man, I needed to learn that now.

***

"Who are we meeting up with?" I walked through the door he held open for me.

"Mike."

I grinned with delight. I liked Mike and was curious why I was brought along for the ride.

"Really?"

"Don't be too excited," he grunted, but I saw the humor in his smile.

239

Trigger's playful moods didn't happen often, so when they did, I relished them.

"Can't blame me. He has all the goods on the books…" I trailed off when I caught sight of a table full of beautiful people. "Oh, my sweet non-fictional heaven, what have you done?"

There sat the cast of the *Broken* trilogy. I knew because I Googled the shit out of them when I finished the first book.

Savannah was dressed in a pair of blue jeans and an oversized sweater. She wrapped me in her arms. "It is such a pleasure to meet you, Tess!" She smelled like heaven in a jar. "I'm Savannah, but please call me Savi."

All I could do was freak the fuck out inside while I played it cool on the outside.

"Please, the pleasure is all mine."

Her smile made me blush. She had a whimsical way of moving that reminded me of a ballet dancer. She had such grace and poise.

Then there was me.

Trigger and Mike stepped off to the side to speak while Savi introduced me to everyone else.

Mark was cute as hell. He was clearly a boy in men's clothes. Keith was the silent, broody type, and then there was Cole. Holy hell, there were no words to describe that kind of sexy. Not entirely *my* type, but I sure wouldn't kick him out of bed for any reason, ever.

Savannah handed me a glass of champagne when the waiter returned. I raised an eyebrow and wondered how she knew what I liked.

"Trigger filled us in."

"That so?" I laughed softly. "What else did he say?"

"Actually, a lot," Mark said with a wink. "Like how he wanted us to meet you for your birthday."

"What?"

Shit just got interesting.

"Yup, but something happened, and our last trip got canceled. So, when Mike said he was coming here for a meeting, we all tagged along."

"Wait." I flipped my hair out of my face, more to cool off my warm cheeks than anything. "Trigger planned for you all to meet me for my birthday?"

"That's right." Mike flashed me a killer smile. "First time I have ever heard him speak about a girl."

"Hmm." I tried to hide my smile, but Savi mirrored my mood.

"Feels pretty good, doesn't it?"

I tapped my glass to hers. "Kind of does."

I loved how Cole found some way to touch Savannah, or how he watched her tell a story. He was obviously captivated by her. Part of me was envious of how he didn't mind showing his affection for Savannah in public. His finger twisted a lock of her hair, which made her lean in and press her cheek to his chest. They were beautiful together.

They grilled me about Trigger. It was odd to think they were interested in us when I had a thousand and one questions to ask about them, but I went along with it. Truth be told, I rather liked it. I felt like I was in a normal relationship, or something like it, anyway.

Keith caught my attention though. He kept

glancing at his phone, and his mood seemed edgy. Finally, Cole picked up on it, or maybe he was just as curious as I was.

"Everything—" Cole started when Keith answered his phone.

We all went quiet when he spoke, obviously agitated. "No, you can't do that," he said then paused to listen. "I will not bail you out again!" He paused. "No, no way. I won't do it. I told you that the last time."

Mark tried to hold back his smirk. I guessed he knew who was on the other end of the line.

Keith leaned forward and tried to muffle his voice. "The boy is twenty-two. You cannot pinch his ass in the checkout line! I will not be a part of this—" He stopped mid-sentence. "No! I will not." He stopped again. "Dammit, Nan! Fine, but I'm callin' Mom." His eyes widened. "Watch me."

"He won't." Mark shook his head.

"Find your own way to bingo."

"Such a lie." Mark sighed, and I tried not to laugh while Savi pressed her lips together to hide her smile.

Just when I thought Keith was going to hang up, he lowered his voice. "See you Thursday."

"For bingo." Mark leaned out of the way of Keith's swat. "Nan puts a seventeen-year-old boy on prom night to shame."

"Not gonna lie, I kinda want to meet the woman." I made the table laugh, Keith included.

Trigger glanced over at me from the bar. He didn't smile, but he held my gaze. My lungs contracted and trapped the air, and I felt a rush of lust hit the center of my belly.

"I know that look," Mark stole my attention, "and I don't mean yours."

Savi beamed at me. "So, we have something for you."

"Me?" I shook off my moment with Trigger and sat a little straighter, intrigued by what was in the silver box in front of her.

She slid it over. I pulled on the ribbon and opened the top. There sat a paperback with the whole *Broken* trilogy.

"The author signed it, and we all did too." She laughed.

Holy...

"You did this for me?"

"Not entirely." Cole nodded at Trigger. "It was his idea too."

I gently pulled the cover back and flipped the pages in disbelief. "Can I ask some questions?"

"Of course." Savannah pulled her hair to one side and leaned in like she was ready to go.

Where to begin...?

"Keith." He broke out in a smile. I guessed he didn't think I would start with him. "I haven't gotten to your book yet, but I have to know. Why did you leave Shadows?"

"It wasn't easy." He glanced at Cole, who gave a slight nod. I assumed it was his way of asking how much he could talk about. "At first, it was so I could be closer to my family and to keep Lexi close."

"But now?"

"All I can say is Mike and I are getting things set up the way we want them, and it takes a while to get

243

a house to run smoothly. Will we stay there forever? Probably not."

Mark broke out in a boyish grin. "They're training some guys to run the house. Only a matter of time."

"Really?" I liked that idea. "I mean, I get it. You can't really have a safe house with kids running around."

"Well, that was the problem at first," Cole chimed in. "But after they left, the house hasn't been the same, so Savi came up with the idea of building some homes on the property. We are a family first, and special ops second."

"Life's too short to be without the ones you love," Savannah added with a laugh.

Keith reached over and squeezed her hand. Jesus, they were all such good friends. I had to admit I was a little jealous, but we had our *club love,* maybe just a little warped and sharp around the edges.

"Okay," Mike shook them off, "what else you wanna know?"

"Well, I have one for you." I leaned forward so he could hear me better. "Are you dating anyone?"

Everyone looked at him with smiles.

"Yeah, Mikey." Mark spat soda out of his mouth. "You datin' anyone?"

"Nah." He glance down at his colorful hands. "I'm not exactly the boy you bring home to meet the parents."

I thought I heard my heart break.

"I disagree."

"That's 'cause you're dating him." He nodded at Trigger. "You, Tess, are a rare breed, and I appreciate that a lot."

Warmth spread through me; I understood being an outcast.

"Savi," I grabbed her attention from Mike, "you play any more paintball?"

Cole's face dropped but lit up when Savannah smiled at him. "Not that I can openly admit to."

"Pardon me?"

"Bah!" Mark jammed at Cole's shoulder. "Great question, Tess!"

"So help me God, Lopez."

Mark held up his hands in defense, and it gave me an opener for my next topic.

"Okay, okay, one more, and I promise I'm done." I couldn't help but smirk. "Is Doc Roberts still dating Abigail?"

"*No!*" Mark yelled, but the entire table broke out in a loud laughter, and I was thrown a million and one *yesses*.

***

Trigger

"I don't know, man. Listening to all this sounds like you got a real shit pile going on." Mike rubbed his head while he nursed his beer. "Aaron and Doyle been joined at the hip lately. Those two are sure as hell on someone's payroll." He tapped the photos he brought of the two cops having coffee. "Clark has some USB drive with a bunch of secret shit on it, you have a mole, Tammy says there's more to this than you know, and now you've agreed to a fight."

"Yeah." I nodded slowly.

"You seem unfazed, my friend."

"Shit's coming. Just gotta be ready."

Mike nodded and asked for another drink. "Now that the coke contract is done, what will you do?"

"Between the garage, strip club, and debts owed to me, the club will be fine."

"If you ever need anything, you know we could use you at the house."

I smiled at his offer. "Appreciate that, but I think it's better for me to stay down here and you up there." I knew he got my reference. Too many skeletons kept me rooted in the dirt.

"The offer doesn't expire."

"Good to know. Oh," I pulled out my phone and brought up a still shot from the club's outside cameras, "know who this is?"

Mike took it from my hand an examined the image. "No, but if you send it to me, I can look into it."

"Yeah, okay. He said his name was Zay. Said he knew Tess's mother, and we both know him from somewhere." I sent it to his phone.

"I'll see what I can dig up."

I offered my hand—not something I did. He blinked before he took it. Mike had been a loyal friend to me for years and had helped me out even when he shouldn't have.

"Can I ask you something?"

I glanced over at Tess, her face lit up with excitement as she talked with her book friends, and nodded.

"Does your sixty-some-year-old father really want to fight you publicly?"

"Apparently."

"You don't think he's planning on bringing anyone else in?"

"Despite his huge ego, I'm sure there's someone or something else coming."

"Why not grab him right before?"

"My father is all about the attention, the performance, and the win. To bring him to his knees and prove I'm better is the victory I want. Whether it's with him or some jacked-up asshole he brings in."

"Then what?"

I allowed myself a moment to relish the darkness inside, my mood shifted, and I felt the old urge to hurt him fill me. "Then I kill him."

"What about everyone else?"

"My father has something on Doyle. He made that clear at the station. I just need to know what it is, so I can swing the power to my side. As for Detective Aaron, he was working for Clark to get Tess back. They have something on me, but I'm working on that."

"Any idea what it is?"

"Yeah, I might. You remember when that strip joint Billy owned went up in flames a few years back? There was a huge explosion, and they lost millions in their meth lab."

Mike thought for a moment. "Ah, yeah, bunch of guys were killed when it exploded, but quite a few more were trapped down below. Burned to death or something? Santa Barbara?"

"Yeah, well, I was in town that week for something else. A friend asked me to pay Billy a visit to discuss something. Things went south, but I left before anything went down. Billy was a piece of shit and not worth my time. I just did it for a favor."

"Any witnesses?"

"Just one, but she went MIA, and no one else would talk. It was ruled an accident, but my guess would be they have photos of me that day."

"Shit, seriously?"

"Look," I leaned in closer, "we both know I don't kill sloppy. When I do, I do it right. I walked into that one. Bad timing."

"You trust that friend who asked you for the favor?"

For a split second, I hesitated, but shook off the feeling. "I do. But it's no secret many people want to see me dead. If the info was brought to the cops and put the right way, it could look bad."

Mike dropped his head and squeezed his eyes shut and sighed.

"And Doyle? Any ideas what he has on him?"

"Doyle is a power trippin' little asshole who hides behind his badge. He's just lookin' to make my life shit. He's the least of my problems."

Mike grabbed some peanuts from the bowl on the bar and peered over at me.

"Say it."

He half smiled. "And for the elephant in the room? You think she's safe?"

"Nope."

"Your father knows how you feel about her. You don't keep women around, and you've never done something like this." He full-out smiled and waved at his friends.

I ran my hand down my beard and wished she'd never come to the church that day. Maybe the devil wouldn't have seen my fear.

"She can always come back with us, you know."

"I've thought about that."

"Where can I go?" Tess asked. Shit, the girl moved fast. She shouldn't be eavesdropping or butting in my conversations. She needed to know her place.

"You don't listen or interrupt me when I'm in a meeting." I grew angry fast. "You need to learn your role, dammit, Tess."

"And what is that, exactly?" Her hands flew to hips, and her eyes shot fire.

"You're the girl I'm fucking. Not an old lady or—" I stopped myself when I heard my own words echo back at me. Fuck my father. My own temper was going to kill me.

"Well, the girl you're just *fucking*," her eyes seemed to change, "wants to thank you for your thoughtful gift."

I took a moment to calm myself. I knew I needed to back off here, but the grin on Mike's face pissed me off.

"Mike," I controlled the urge to punch something, "offered his safe house for you until this shit with my father ends."

Tess's face softened, and her posture relaxed. She smiled sweetly over at Mike. He was enjoying this way too much.

"I deeply appreciate the offer, Mike, more than

you know, but for now, I'm fine at the club."

"Not your choice to make, sweetheart." I ground my teeth.

Her eyes flickered over to mine. "Funny how I just made it, *honey*."

"Tess," I warned.

"Trigger." She matched my tone.

Mike snorted a laugh as she walked back to the table. "You're fucked, Trig!"

We ordered another round and joined the others at the table. Tess was in the middle of a story Mark found hysterically funny. Cole had his arm around Savannah, and they both laughed, engulfed in her story as well. I felt Mike's eyes on me and squinted at him, wondering what the hell he was thinking.

Once Tess was finished, she looked back at me and smiled. Her eyes raked across my face.

"Tess," Mike called, "can I ask you something?"

"Of course."

"There's something to your story at the church that confused me."

Tess stood straight. I knew it wasn't a topic she liked to talk about.

She cleared her throat. "Okay."

"You got to the church by hiding in the ammo truck, right?"

"Yes."

Mike nodded. "You slipped out and raced into the church, where you found Trigger and Allen talking?"

"Yes, that's right."

"But then you went to the bus station."

She shook her head. "No, I went to the trailer to

grab my stuff, and then went to the bus station."

"But how did you get there?"

Her slim fingers skimmed down the long stem of the champagne glass as she considered her answer. "When I raced down the driveway, I ran into Tristan. He freaked out that I was there and took me back to the trailer."

"Really?" First I'd heard about this.

She nodded at me before she turned back to Mike. "I grabbed all my stuff, and when I went to find Gus, Big Joe said he'd give me a lift."

The table went quiet, and I could hear my heartbeat in my ears.

"Wonder why that was never shared?" Mike glanced at me.

"That's Joe for you. He's loyal where loyalty needs to be. He did nothing wrong," Tess said. "He wanted to stop me, but I told him I was leaving with either his help or with Loose." She peeked at me over her shoulder. "I'm sorry, Trigger, but I played dirty, and even he said you'd kill him if he took me. I promised I'd never tell, but to get me out of there."

My mouth went dry. Big Joe had always been loyal, but I knew he did bend the rules at times. I knew the club always came first with him, but the fact that he knew where she was when I was flipping out fucking bothered me. I wasn't done with him.

"If you're going to be mad at someone, it should be me. He saw the situation for what it was and did what he thought you'd want him to do."

"Well," Savannah broke the tension, "I don't

know about you guys, but I could use some food."

"Music to my ears." Mark snatched up the menu and started to prattle off the appetizers.

Tess leaned back in her chair and looked up at me. I knew she was worried, and in a way, it showed me how much she had protected my club by protecting one of the family.

"I'm sorry."

"He should've told me."

Her eyes closed, and I saw how much it bothered her. Without thinking, I rested my heavy hand on hers. She glanced down at the contact and slowly laced her fingers through mine. I tensed but didn't pull away.

I tuned back to Mark speaking with the waiter. "Mozza sticks—no, wait—sweet potato fries. No, you know what? Just bring one of everything."

"Watch your fingers when you place it in front of him," Keith joked. "He has sharp teeth."

"I have a healthy appetite." Mark shrugged. "Don't project your negativity on me just because I can eat whatever I want and look this fabulous."

Keith stuck a finger in his face. "What did I tell you about using the word 'fabulous' outside the house?"

Jesus Christ, you'd think they were married.

"Yeah," Cole laughed, "I really need to second that shit."

Mark rolled his eyes but rubbed his stomach when the plates arrived.

Tess appeared right at home with everyone, and she and Savannah seemed to like each other. They were all good guys, and I could understand why

Mike fit in. He was lot more outgoing than I would ever be. My bike and bar were my comfort zone. I liked space and didn't have much to say in a group. Never did.

The girls went to the bathroom, and Keith and Mike were talking. I finally relaxed and got out my phone.

CHAPTER SIXTEEN

Tess

Trigger was alone at the table when I returned. Savi took a call from Abigail, who was watching Olivia, and needed a few minutes.

"How are you doing?" I shifted into my seat next to him.

He tucked his phone away and leaned his arms on his knees to rub his face. "Fine."

I wondered if he was still angry that I hadn't told him about Joe. As always, he was hard to read. I decided to probe a bit. "You and Mike have a good chat?"

"Yup."

I took a sip of my drink, but decided to keep at it, even though I risked poking the beast.

"I know you don't like crowds."

"Nope."

"So, why did you do this?" I wanted him to say it was for me. Just once, I'd love him to say he was thinking about me out loud.

His attention was glued to the door. "Mike wanted a meeting, and he thought you should come along."

"So, it was all his idea to bring Savannah and Cole and the guys."

Throw me some kind of bone here, dude, just a little shred of emotion.

"You got something you wanna ask, Tess, just ask it." He stunned me for a moment. *Shit, let's dance!*

"I want to know why you did all this." I slapped my hand on the table to make him look at me. His eyes flickered with anger. I knew he hated when I took control. "Give me the truth."

"Why?"

"Why not?" I challenged.

"Jesus, Tess, not here." He glanced around.

I was never the girl who made a scene in public, or even remotely liked drama, but I really wanted him to say he had done something nice for me. It seemed important for him to say it out loud.

"Sorry, guys." Cole was suddenly at the far end of the table. "Don't meant to cut the evening short, but we need to go."

Savannah grabbed her purse and waited for me to stand. "Story of my life, but I wouldn't change a moment of it." She hugged me like she really meant it. "I'll call you. Happy late birthday, Tess. It was really nice getting to know you."

"You too, Savi." I really did mean it. "Thanks for everything."

The guys all wrapped me in bear hugs before they disappeared, and I was left with the memory of the nicest gift anyone had ever given me and the moody gift-giver.

I grabbed my stuff and pushed my chair in. "I think I'll walk back." Before he could speak, I headed for the door. I didn't get far before I heard him behind me. His arm swiped around my waist and pulled me hard against a wall. Trigger trapped my arms and pressed them back against the cold concrete.

"I don't do drama. I don't do public fights—"

"I'm not asking for a high school relationship, Trigger!" I snapped, knowing it pissed him off. "I just want *you* to know that *I* know I'm more to you than just a fuck buddy. You know my history, and you still care about me. I need to know I count for something in this fucked up world! I know you get that, Trigger, because you just proved it to me by what you did back there."

He grabbed my chin and held my head in place. His eyes burned into mine. He struggled for words then dropped his hands. Just as I thought he would walk away, he spoke with his back turned to me.

"You know I'm not good at all this feeling shit. I've never had to explain myself to anyone before. I feel this way, I feel that way. Fuck. You are my woman. That's enough." He shook his head.

Suddenly, it dawned on me. "I get a question that you can't veto, and you have to answer."

His mouth opened to say something, but he quickly shut it.

"I told you my deepest, darkest secret. That took me out of *my* comfort zone, and you promised me a question back."

256

He cursed then shook his head for me to go on.

I couldn't help but feel the power, but there was still a part of me that was frightened to hell.

"Tell me why you came back for me."

He didn't move. Said nothing.

"Never mind, Trigger. Just drop it. I guess I just wanted more." I knew I wouldn't get any farther, and now we were both pissed off. I wished I had let it go.

I started back toward the club. I struggled with the fact I let myself feel something, only to get rejected. We both agreed we wanted nothing from each other. So, what the hell was I doing?

I needed to stop pushing him or I would be seen as another Peggy, and that would be the end of us— no, the end of me.

I had to accept him for what he was. I had to get over my pity party and learn my place with him. I had the club and Brick. They were all family now.

When I got back, I noticed I was alone. I was so consumed with my thoughts I assumed he was behind me.

When I walked in, Big Joe's forehead creased as he pushed off from his post and looked around.

"You by yourself?"

"Just needed the quiet."

He turned back around to me, his head slightly tilted like he was listening to something. "Where's Trigger?"

"I think he went to visit Mud or something."

His puffy eyebrow rose to question my lie.

I pointed over my shoulder. "Brick inside?"

"Yeah." He nodded, but when I attempted to

move, he blocked my path. "Everything good? Trigger seem okay to you tonight?"

"Same as normal. Why?"

"He didn't mention anything to you?"

"Like?"

"Like…" He shook his head. "Never mind." He opened the door, and I moved inside. I was too mentally fried to ask what the hell he meant. "Watch your step."

My foot stepped down into something tacky, and then my eyes took in the mess.

"Oh, my God."

The place was trashed. Beer bottles were everywhere, not a table was clean, and all the guys were piss loaded drunk.

"Tess!" Rail called out from beneath a chick who looked half his age. "Girl, you missed out on one hell of a night."

"I can," I paused to kick a pink bra out of my way, "see that."

"Please tell me you got my text!" Brick said from the booth. Minnie was passed out next to him.

"No." I shook my head but froze when I saw Fin under the pool table with his blanket and book, looking at pictures.

It was past midnight. Why was he here? Where the hell was Vib?

"We had a party." Rail laughed from somewhere.

No shit.

I headed for my room, ignoring the others who wanted me to join them. I changed into yoga pants, a tank top, and a big, comfy sweater. I grabbed a blanket and pillow and set the box of books on my shelf for later.

My phone buzzed with an incoming message.

Savannah: Hey, I'll be in town next week. We should meet up.

Oh, that would be fun.

Tess: Sure, call me with the details.

Savannah: Will do!

I went back out and reached for Fin under the table. "Fin, come with me."

I wondered where his brother was and headed outside where it was quiet and clean.

"Where's Denton?"

"He's with Aunt Jaqueline. Mom is sick." I wiped the snot from his nasty little nose.

"Why didn't you go with them?"

"I don't like to go with her. I like to be with Uncle Trig."

I lifted him up on the back of Trigger's pickup then hopped in and covered us both with the fuzzy blanket. The pillow was tucked behind us, and I took the book from his hands.

"What are you reading?"

He shrugged. "Don't know, but I like the pictures. This one," he flipped a few pages, "is my favorite. I like the red rocket ship."

"It is pretty cool." I couldn't help but ask. "Fin, were you in there the whole night?"

He nodded with a small yawn. "I couldn't find

Dad or you, so I just waited."

"You were in the bar with all those people?"

He nodded, unfazed by my horror. It was bad enough he saw what he did in the run of a day, but it sounded like a whore-fest tonight.

"Tess?"

"Mmm." I tucked the blanket around my sides. The air was cold tonight, and the temperature was on its way down. I heard a small meow from underneath us and wondered who else was camping out here tonight.

"Can you read this to me?" His eyes were so hopeful I wondered if anyone ever read to him.

"Sure." I pulled the book from between his grubby fingers and opened the page.

We went on the journey of the choo-train that got each of its freight cars full by all the circus animals. Halfway through, Fin lifted my arm and curled to fit against my side. He rested his head on my chest and asked a few questions. At first, I wasn't sure how Vib would feel if she saw us cuddled, but the way he seemed at ease made me relax too. Clearly, he was starved for affection, and I guessed I was too.

***

Trigger

"Where have you been?" Brick handed me a coffee when I returned from a night of punching a hole in my Everlast bag. My hands were worn out, and my muscles finally stopped twitching from the workout.

"Out."

"I see that." He slipped into the booth across from me. "I'll take it last night didn't go as planned?"

We were out of sugar, so I whistled for Jace to bring me more. "Tess got pissed."

He chuckled with a knowing look. "What did you do this time?"

I needed to shed some anger before I blew up and killed another member of my own club.

"She wants too much."

Brick lowered his mug, and his humorous expression faded. He glanced over his shoulder then lowered his voice. "Too much in what way?"

"Too much from me, I guess." I rubbed my beard, unsure how to navigate the conversation.

"She said that?"

"More or less."

"What did she say, exactly?"

"She wants me to tell her she matters and how I feel about this and that. I don't do feelings. Why can't women leave well enough alone?"

Brick's eyes bulged, and I could tell he was thrown by this. He leaned back and let out a long breath of air. "You sure she said that?"

"Yeah."

"I find that odd."

"Why?"

"Just, wow."

"Wow, what?" I started to grow annoyed. He needed to spit it out.

"Look," he leaned a little closer to me in case anyone was listening, "Tess doesn't normally do feelings. Clark robbed her of that. He broke her in two then broke her some more. I've only heard her say she loved two people in her life, and Clark never counted because he brainwashed her. Seriously, that house fucks her up something bad, but if she's lookin' for more from you..." He shook his head. "I don't...I don't know what to say to that. I mean, fuck, you must have really gotten to her."

I leaned back and let out a heavy breath. My head swirled with all the words she had said last night, and then her face before I left her.

"Trigger, I think it's pretty obvious..." Brick started to say before my face made him stumble. "I mean, we've been friends for a long time, man, and I'm going to step over a line here." He paused to see if I'd argue. "You owe me this, okay?" I glared but gave a nod. He was right; I did toss him under the bus before. "When you came out of the church, I have never seen you like that before. Man, I think there's a pretty good chance you might love that girl."

My first reaction was no, but I couldn't say the words. I cared for her a lot. She calmed the voices and the chaos and blew me away sexually. Her touch was something else, but was that love? I wasn't sure.

"Trig," he stopped my internal dialog, "you can at least start with saying you do care for her. Tess isn't some chick who the moment you say it is going to be lookin' for a proposal. She just needs to know she matters."

He moved to slide off the bench, but I reached out to stop him.

"Who did she say she loved?"

Brick grinned big like I'd handed him a gun to kill a Stripe Back. "Lily, Mags's daughter, and me. One of the best days of my life."

"Should I be jealous?" I half joked.

"Only if you love her like a sister." He chuckled before he turned.

"Where is she now?"

He whirled around but kept walking. "Pickup truck."

I pushed open the back door and took note of the heavy clouds rolling in. They did say we were getting a storm, but I didn't think it was supposed to start until the afternoon. My coffee was hot and felt good on my sore hands. I was careful not to spill it as I made my way over to my pickup. As I got close, I saw her lying under a blanket, and I nearly spilled my coffee when I noticed she wasn't alone. Black hair stuck out from underneath the blanket. I reached over and pulled it back. There was Fin curled into a ball, his hand over top of Tess's. I felt a moment of jealousy looking at the kid lying there with my woman. Shit, he was just a little kid, snotty nose and all.

A small part of me felt a pinch of warmth. For someone who never wanted kids, she sure took to Fin.

As I pulled the blanket back up, movement caught my eye, and a little pink nose and dark eyes stared up at me. Carefully, I lifted the kitten, rubbed her back, and placed her inside the wheel well.

Tess's phone lit up, and I reached for it.

Unknown Number: I'm here in the city. I need to see you, Gumdrop. Please tell me where to meet you. Give me twenty minutes, that's all I ask.

I expected to see red. I expected to want to murder someone, but instead, I was calm. Maybe it was because of my conversation with Brick. I knew she was warped by Clark, but I also knew she didn't love him. It was me she wanted more from, and that felt pretty good.

Tess: 5627 Dustin Street, Helmond's Bar. Noon.

A moment later, I saw him typing.

Unknown Number: Will Trigger be there?

Tess: Yes.

Unknown Number: Can we meet somewhere he won't be?

Tess: No.

Unknown Number: How do I know you aren't setting me up?

Tess: I never asked you to come. Take it or leave it.

Unknown Number: Fine, I'll be there. Just

hear me out.

I tucked the phone back where it was and shook her shoulder.

"Tess," I whispered.

Her eyes opened, and it took her a moment to see where she was.

"Oh." She held her neck like it was sore. "Oh, my God, what time is it?"

"Nine."

"Shit." She looked down at Fin. "Is Vib freaking out?"

"No." I leaned my arms over the side of the truck, and the steam from my coffee swirled. "Doubt she's even noticed he's gone."

"I'm sorry." She tried to sit up straight.

"Why?"

"I didn't mean for this to happen. He spent the night in the bar waiting for you, and I felt horrible for what he saw. I started to read to him, and I guess we both fell asleep. I—"

"Why are you sorry?"

She looked at me strangely, her mouth pulled into a straight line. "He's not my kid, and I don't want to cross a line with Vib."

"Vib's done nothing more than give up an egg and a warm stomach to grow in. She has zero maternal instincts. That boy is looking for someone to cling to." I sipped my coffee and watched her absorb my words. "You're good for him, Tess. You're good for a lot of us."

She studied me for a moment before she looked over my shoulder with tired eyes. "About last night,

265

just forget what I said. I was wrapped up in Cole and Savannah's happiness—" She paused, and her gaze dropped. "I appreciate what you did for me. Nicest thing anyone's done in a long time."

"Tess—" I had no idea what I was going to say, but she interrupted me.

"Is there any coffee left inside?"

I handed her mine, and she hesitated but took it anyway.

"Thanks." She closed her eyes and sighed at the taste. "At least I know this isn't laced with anything. Fucking Peggy," she muttered.

She handed it back and woke Fin, who yawned and batted her hand away.

Her smile was one I hadn't seen before. I knew she was growing attached to him too.

Suddenly, she froze. "Shit." She scrambled to stand. I caught her waist and lowered her to the ground.

"Thanks." She stepped back and ran her fingers through her hair. "I need to get to work. Morgan needed the morning off."

With that, she was gone, and I was left with a grumpy Fin.

"Trigger?" Gus called from the door. "You're needed."

"So are you." I pointed down at Fin.

He squinted and limped over. "What's he doing there? Vib said her sister took them."

"The junkie lied. Fin and Tess had a sleepover."

"Would anyone notice if I buried that bitch under the pool house?" He snickered as he tried to wake Fin.

"Notice? No. Give a fuck? Hell, no. You need a shovel, I have plenty." I reached over and pulled the blanket by the sides and lifted the grump out like he was in a bag.

"Hey," he stopped me, "why is Langley here? You didn't agree, did you?"

"Submitted the forms the other day."

"Trigger, you think that's wise? You know how you get."

I glanced down at Fin. "You should get him to bed. Looks like the rain will start early."

I needed to train and get ready for our company.

"Trigger!" Rail popped his head out the door. "There's a fire, my garage."

I hurried to follow him next door.

CHAPTER SEVENTEEN

Tess

"You seem different." Peggy blocked my path when I went to wash down the tables.

"Go away, Peggy." I pushed her aside, but she followed me.

"You do." She stood beside me and stared. "But what is it?"

I closed my eyes and calmed my temper. The bar had a few stragglers, and I really didn't need her shit right now.

She sucked in a breath. "Oh, my God." She beamed with excitement. "Did Trigger dump you?"

"Fuck off, Peggy." I tried to ignore her, but my grip on the rag was tight.

"Oh, this is great! Don't feel bad, Tess. It was bound to happen. He gets bored. He's a fuck and chuck kinda guy."

"Good to know." I moved on to the next table.

She kept going. "You *love* him, don't you?"

It was too early for this shit.

I stopped and pinched the bridge of my nose. "Peggy, he's all yours."

She glared at me for a moment then one eyebrow rose with amusement. She pulled out some gloss and ran it over her fake lips. "Time to lube up the runway."

"What a bumpy runway that is," Rail chimed in as he whisked by.

"I've never blown you!"

"Yeah, 'cause I like my dick clean."

"I'm clean, you jackass."

Rail stuck his head around the corner. "Peggy, your vag is about as clean as a dirty hotdog in an alley."

"Please, some of us are trying to eat!" Cooper dropped his fork and pushed his food away. "Fuck me, I'm getting a visual. I'm gonna be sick."

"Are you fantasizing?" She licked her lips at Cooper, and he pretended to stab himself.

Jesus, what a crew.

I turned back to the table but froze. My stomach jolted, and vomit crept up the back of my throat.

"Wow, Gumdrop." Clark's gaze dragged down from my mouth to my thighs.

I was squeezed into a pair of tight jeans with a red corset-style top and heels. My hair was wavy because I didn't have time to dry it. How I wished I was in sweats and a sweater like this morning. My mind was in a tailspin. I looked around, desperate to find a way out, and at the same time was terrified Trigger would come in.

"Well, now." Peggy slithered into view like the slippery snake she was. "And who might you be?"

"Clark." He extended his hand, and she took it with a giggle.

"How do you know Tess?"

"Peggy, leave," I warned, but of course she didn't listen.

"I'm an…" Clark smirked at me with that smile he used to get me into bed. "An old friend."

I couldn't move. I was stuck in this fuck hole of a situation.

How? How did he know where I was?

"Everything okay?" Big Joe asked, and I shot him a dirty look. Why did he let him in?

"He was cleared, Tess."

What? Cleared by who?

Clark tossed a file on the table before he stepped forward and ran a hand down my arm. It burned like acid against my skin. "Damn, I've missed you." He leaned down to kiss my lips, and I shoved him away. He was ready for it and hooked an arm around my waist to hold me in place. He leaned down again, but instead he brushed his lips by my ear. "I forgive you."

"Get the fuck off me."

"Keep talkin' dirty to me, Tessa. I know how feisty you can get."

This was a dream, a horrible dream that had sunk its claw deep and rattled my bones. I desperately needed to wake up. Clark here in Trigger's club. It just couldn't be happening.

I wiggled to get free, but he was too strong. Cooper suddenly appeared at my side.

"She said get off her. Respect the lady."

"Respect." Clark laughed. "Right, when did the MC world ever respect their women?"

"We respect family, asshole, and if you want to keep that hand, you better get it the fuck off her." Cooper raised his voice. "Tess, you want me to get—"

"That won't be necessary." Clark cut him off and pulled his hand back. "I'm not staying long."

If that was true, I'd rather deal with Clark myself than involve Trigger. He didn't need to fight for me.

"Thanks, Cooper, but I'm okay."

He thought for a moment then headed out back, I was sure to find Trigger.

I needed to be quick.

"Ouch," I whimpered as he grabbed my wrist again and squeezed.

"You fuck him too?" Clark hissed at me. He was classic for mood swings, a sign that he was on steroids again.

"No." I glared at him. "Not yet, at least." I couldn't help myself. Clark was a jealous asshole when it came to me and men. He hated Brick but had never met him.

"Bet you're spreading for all these men." His tone was nasty.

"Most." I chuckled, and he lifted on his toes to use his body weight to squeeze me harder. I yelped, and he smirked. "How's your wife?" The words were like acid on my tongue, but it was my slap in his face that he fucked me over by fucking my mother.

He let go, and I stepped back and rubbed at the

sudden rush of pain when the blood returned to its normal path.

"I hate that you get me that crazy." He switched back to calm, loving Clark.

"I hate that you hurt me. I hate a lot of things about you."

"I don't want to hurt you, Gumdrop."

"But yet you have, many times. Let's start with you killing my best friend." Anger corroded my insides.

"You should never have seen that video."

"God!" I huffed in disbelief. "You're insane! You can't even see it. You killed her, and that very night, you came to my room. Have you no soul? No heart?"

He scratched his chin and turned away. "We've always had a unique relationship, haven't we?"

Wow.

"You call it unique. Others call it abusive." I glared at him and felt the surge of anger flow and take over the shock and fear his showing up had brought. The club was my home, and it gave me a sense of power. He was on my turf.

"Abusive? When have I ever truly hurt you?"

"Do you even hear me?"

His stare burned into mine, and I felt my power slowly being sucked away. I needed to move before Trigger got wind he was here. I was shocked he hadn't stormed in yet.

"Why are you here?"

His eyes flickered with a darkness I had only seen a few times in the past.

Shit.

"You told me I could come."

What? He was mad.

"When?"

"This morning. You sent me the address." He held up his phone and showed me his messages.

"I never texted you that."

"Someone did." He shrugged, and I felt sick when I realized Trigger had done it.

Oh, my God. So, where the hell was Trigger, since he set up this fucking meeting?

"Whatever. Look, I wanted to give you an eyeopener about the man you think you know."

I folded my arms and tried to control my temper. "Such as?"

"Here?" He glanced around.

Perfect. Just the moment I was waiting for.

I waited a beat, rolled my eyes dramatically, and waved for him to follow me.

"Don't touch me," I snapped when his hand fell on my back.

"I need to touch you," he grunted, but in a pathetic way. Funny how I was seeing things so clearly now. The tables had finally turned.

"You lost that privilege years ago."

"And yet you keep coming back."

I turned and faced him dead on. "*Children* who are mentally abused don't see their abuser as the monster. It takes time, but I see you now."

Before he could snap back at me, I changed our destination and skipped my bedroom. If we were going to do this, we were going to do it right.

I opened the door and waved him inside. His face dropped, and he choked on the smell.

273

"What is that?"

"Bleach." I fought back my own cough. I needed to be strong. I could not afford to look scared. "Sit." I pointed at a steel table with two metal chairs across from one another.

"Seriously? I feel like we're on the set of *Saw*."

"You wanted to talk alone, so talk." I eased into the chair.

He flipped the file open.

"I'm guessing I have about ten minutes before your boyfriend shows up." He pointed to the photo. "I thought you might like to know who you're sleeping with."

I slid the photo over and tried not to react at the image of Trigger doing a girl from behind at some party.

"Okay."

He tossed over another of a different girl and Trigger. One by one, he piled the photos on top of each other until there were about eight different girls. It stung, but I had no right to Trigger before now, and he had none to me. I only hoped these were all before me.

"Hope he wears a rubber." He snickered then pulled out another photo. "I'm guessing you're curious if these were all before you?"

"I don't really care." That was a lie.

"You should, Tess." He tossed another photo at me. "This was when you were with me. Check out his haircut."

Ouch. The girl was on her knees giving him a blow job, or at least it looked that way. Trigger said he cut his hair right before he came to get me. He said he needed a change.

"How did you even get this shit?

"Please," he sighed. "We both know Aaron is working for me. You give someone enough money, and they'll be your bitch. Plus, it doesn't hurt that I have something on him too."

"Which is?"

"Let's just say he's a dirty cop, but we're not here to talk about Aaron. We're here for you, Tessa."

"Shit, is that it? That's all you got? Him fucking a bunch of women?"

He picked up another picture. "Your twisted little biker family can go up in flames with one phone call from me, Tessa." He handed me the picture, and I blinked a few times to register what I was seeing.

Trigger had blood on his hands and seemed to be surrounded by dead bodies. Brick was next to him, standing over a man, a rope dangled from his fingertips. Morgan and Cray were off in the background, and Rail was on the phone.

Sweat broke out along the back of my neck, my ears rang, and my heart pounded.

"It's not proof they did it," I whispered, terrified that my voice was gone. I was right. It outed me for being beyond terrified that the club could go down for murder.

"Does it matter? Dead bodies, weapons, right place at the right time. They never called it in. They just checked the men for something and left. Stellar MC family you got here, Gumdrop."

His nickname made my stomach roll.

"So, now what? What now?" I could barely breathe as I eyed the door. Where the hell was Trigger?

He waited until I looked up at him. His face was serious, and his jaw was locked in place.

"I want you to come home for good. No more running. You will not date anyone else, and you will dance for the house, but nothing more. You will give yourself to me whenever I want. If not, I will hand-deliver these to the police tonight."

I laughed out of shock at what I was hearing.

"You're mad."

"I'm in love."

My anger burst through, and I knew my own fucking switch was about to be flipped.

"You had me! But you chose greed over love. You screwed my mother while you screwed me!" I dug deep for strength. "I have proof it was you." My words came out like a hiss. "Proof you killed Mags. You'd be lucky to become someone's bitch and not be sliced up under a bed sheet." My lungs nearly popped at how hard I was drawing in air. His face snapped up to meet mine. "Don't you get it? I came to kill *you*, not him."

"Tessa!"

"No! You listen!" I rose out of my seat. I couldn't feel my body as I pounded my fist on the table. "You knocked me up and let them butcher me! Forever scarring me, preventing me from ever having children. Now you're here threatening my chance at being happy with these pictures of sex and violence."

"Yes, I do!" he boomed as he jumped out of his

chair and around the table. He walked me back a few steps and let his temper go. "I've loved you since I met in you in the common room of the house."

"I was ten, you sick bastard! Ten and alone with no one to love me. You took advantage of a little girl and warped her so much that she will always second guess anything and anyone. How can you think that's okay?" I hated him so much it was painful. I turned off my rational side and let my mouth go.

"Took advantage?" He came closer, and I held my ground. "You baited me, Tessa," he gritted through his teeth.

"You're insane, Clark. How I ever thought you were my savior, I will never know."

He narrowed his eyes and hovered over me. "You know the best part of all this?" He pronounced the words perfectly, and my stomach dropped. "At least I know you can never have a child with Trigger. No chance at a family."

Done.

I reached for whatever was on the wall and swung. The steel pipe smoked him across the side of the knees, and he fell to the ground with a shout. He reached for me, and I swung again and pounded his wrist with all my might.

"You fucking bitch!" he screamed and rolled around holding his hands to his chest. "You want to know why I let them carve that baby out of you?"

I froze.

"I saved it. You would have been a shitty mother. A mother who tried to kill herself over a man? Pathetic, weak, unlovable Tessa."

I dropped the pipe and stepped back while he laughed like he thought he had gotten to me.

"I rest my case," he cried. "Worthless."

"I may be all those things, Clark, but you know what?" I waited for him to look at me. "You could have had one more blow to the head, but instead, I think I'll return what you've given me."

His eyes bulged as I slammed the pipe hard at his stomach.

Whack.

Whack.

Whack.

I pulled my phone free.

Karma really is a wonderful bitch.

***

Trigger

"Where is she?" I could barely see straight. The fire at the garage was small, but nonetheless a fire. We checked the cameras, and it wasn't arson. Seemed like a faulty line in the office. Once it was under control and the fire department left, I raced back.

I slammed the door to the bar, and Peggy jumped and almost dropped a tray full of beer.

"Peggy, where the hell is Tess?"

"Last I saw her, the guy's lips were on hers and they headed for her room." She swayed her hips, making sucky sounds as she handed the guys their drinks. "Seems to me she was excited to get her freak on."

"Was that before or after he grabbed her arms and made her scream?" Cooper barked. "She went out back."

"We all know Tess likes it rough," Peggy purred, and I wanted to slam her head into the beam next to her. "You can see where I got confused."

"Peggy, shut the fuck up or you're out of here," I warned, which made her blink. "Where is she?"

My phone rang,

"Where are you?" My heart pounded so loud I had to focus on her voice.

"Slaughter room."

"Brick." He dropped his beer and hurried over.

We headed to the slaughter room. My fists pumped with excitement, but I also needed to know she was okay.

"Watch the door."

Brick stood in place, and I tore open the door to hear Clark's cries. Tess was holding a pipe. She looked fuckin' sexy. She was breathing hard through her flared nose. Her eyes were shiny and wide.

"You okay?"

"Thought you should know your guest arrived." Her voice sounded husky.

I deserved that.

"Thought this whole little situation should end now. Revenge doesn't always end badly. It can be closure."

She walked around Clark, and the pipe made an eerie sound as it bounced over the grooves in the tile floor. The sound echoed off the walls, and

Clark's breathing picked up. He was sweating and bleeding and wasn't able to get up.

Tess suddenly swung and crushed his ribs with a hard blow.

"Ah!" He shook and tried to turn himself to see her. She dropped her arm and dragged the bar as she continued to circle him.

When she got to me, she reached in my pocket and removed my phone. I watched as she fumbled through my music and tapped on a song. It took a second, and then I heard Weezer's "Say It Ain't So." Interesting choice of music.

Clark's head flicked over to her, and something passed between them.

Tess started to circle again, and I popped my neck, wanting a piece of him. He hurt her, therefore, he hurt me.

Once the chorus came on, Tess screamed and slammed the pipe right next to his head.

"Fuck, Tess!" He shook and curled into a ball. "I didn't know you were watching us!"

"She did! She saw me watching you guys screw like rabbits while this fucking song looped over and over." She dropped the pipe, crawled onto his stomach, and punched his face. He grabbed her shoulders and shoved her off. She went flying to the floor, and I couldn't hold back anymore. I lunged and fisted his collar to haul him backward. He couldn't stand. His knees were broken, but he could still hurt her.

Once he was far enough away, I stepped on his leg and rolled my shoe to rotate the broken bone. He bellowed and clawed at the floor. His nails broke away, and he foamed at the mouth.

He started to laugh hysterically.

"She tell you I made it so she can't have kids? You can never have kids with her, Trigger!" He spat out blood.

I swallowed past my need to kill. I needed her to give me the green light. This was her kill, not mine.

She stood and walked over to the sink. I thought she was going to be sick, but to my surprise, she pulled the bleach down and poured it into a spray bottle.

As she drew closer, he started up again.

"I can still hear your screams for help as that doctor tore it from you. Sometimes it gets me off."

She grabbed a handful of hair and sprayed the bleach into his wild eyes. He bucked, twisted, and screamed.

"Bitch!"

I let her go until she exhausted herself, then I stepped in, hauled back my fist, and slammed it down on top of his head. He dropped like a stone.

Quickly, I checked his pulse. He was still alive. Good.

Tess dropped the spray bottle, looking fuckin' amazing. It took everything I had in me not to take her there. She looked at Clark, then at me, then turned and walked out.

A deep ache still burned in my chest. I dragged him to the center of the room, tied his hands and feet together to the hook above the drain, and flipped off the light.

"She's outside." Gus limped into the bar and saw my expression. "Although I say that loosely, as I'm not really sure Tess is home." He pointed to his head. "Tried talking to her, but she didn't answer me. She's just sitting there.

I walked past him and out the door to where she was sitting by the pool. I wasn't sure what to expect from her, so I approached her slowly.

When I got closer, I saw her cheeks were puffy and her eyes were bloodshot. Evidence she had come down off the high I knew only too well. This was one of those moments where I didn't know if she wanted me to say something.

I reached over and gently stroked her arm.

"What can I do?" I whispered as quietly as possible.

She didn't answer me.

Shit, I'm really tryin', here.

"Tess, are you okay?" I changed the pitch of my voice to take a new approach. She turned to me, and I knew that look. Her mind was racing.

Her head rose ever so slowly, and her eyes were a dark gray that showed the wicked battle that held her mind hostage.

"He deserves to die."

"He does. What did he say to you, Tess?"

"He told me something that will haunt me for the rest of my life, and I don't know if I'm okay." She fought the tears. I could see she was deeply wounded, and I knew the depth of that pain.

"Brick," I glanced over to where he hovered a few feet away, "the cameras are on in the slaughter room. Have Jace monitor them."

"Is she okay?"

I lifted my shoulders, unsure, and he walked

over, stopped in front of Tess, bent down on his heels, and slowly traced a square on the back of her hand. She gave a tiny nod, and he turned and raced off to the house.

Once we were alone, I leaned toward her. "What all did he say to you?"

She smiled. "Where to begin?"

"How 'bout the start?"

"After you took my phone and invited him to come visit," she glared at me for a second but broke eye contact before she went on, "he showed me a bunch of pornographic pictures of you and a bunch of women, then a photo of you and Brick, Rail, Morgan, and Cray standing around about eight dead guys."

"What?" My hands went cold, and my mind raced. "I wonder who else has copies of the pictures. They can't be the only ones."

Her head snapped up, and the feisty tiger was back. "I don't have any idea," she huffed, "but I think they're the originals."

"But you're not sure." I needed a clear answer.

"No, I'm not." She pointed to the house. "Why the hell do you think his knees were smashed and his hands were broken before you came in?"

I wanted to grin with pride, but now wasn't the time.

"I'll be back, okay?"

"I expect nothing less," she muttered, and I felt a ping to the chest.

What the shit was that? I rubbed my chest over my heart and hoped I wasn't about to have a heart attack. What fucking luck that would be. At least let

283

me know I had put my father *down there* first.

Three hours later, I cleaned Clark off me and felt pretty sure Detective Aaron had the original photos. I had Brick and Rail on their phones, so we would be ready when the shit hit the fan.

"Still alive?" Morgan slid a beer at me from the bar and handed me my lunch.

"Just." I bit into the burger and eyed Langley as he rounded the corner. "Don't want to rush his leavin'."

"Good morning, Mr. Morgan." Langley gave a polite nod.

"Morgan," he corrected. He hated being called Mister. It reminded him of his father. It was one of the many things Morgan and I had in common.

"Of course, Mr. Morgan." He stopped in front of me. "You've been fighting."

"Just dealing with something."

"That will mess with your head. Deal with it now, or regret it later."

"I'm not worried."

"I am." He pointed to a power drink in the mini fridge and thanked Morgan for it. "Oh," he smiled warmly, "you must be Tess."

I looked over my shoulder and saw Tess coming in from a run. When the hell did she start running, and when did she get those tight-ass leggings?

"Um…" She glanced at me, and I saw the weight still on her shoulders. "I am."

He took her hand. "It's lovely to meet you. I'm Trigger's ring trainer, Langley."

"Ring trainer?" Her eyebrows pinched.

"Yes, I'm here to get him back into shape for the

284

fight."

Her face dropped, and the little color she had faded from her cheeks. "I wasn't aware he was training for a fight."

"No?" Langley glanced at me disapprovingly.

She glared at me. "I should go. It was nice to meet you, Langley."

"You too." He smacked my arm once she was out of earshot. "You're an asshole."

"I get that a lot."

Guess I forgot to bring it up.

***

Three more nights to the fight, and I could barely sleep. Tess seemed to spend every free minute when she wasn't working the bar on her newfound love of running, which in turn left Jace exhausted. I'd given him strict instructions to follow her to keep her away from the ring. I was almost disappointed she didn't put up a fight when she found out about her escort. It was like she simply stopped caring in general.

I fucking hated it, and I needed to blow off the tension.

I felt around the wall and switched on the light that hung above him. His battered face tilted in the direction of my footsteps.

"Tessa?" Clark's eyebrows rose over the black blindfold. "That you?"

I snapped my knuckles, ready to end this fight once and for all.

His face fell when he heard it was me, and he

muttered something before he cleared his throat.

"I have money."

Pathetic.

"Don't want your money."

"I can get you any woman you want. I have connections."

"I have what I want." I peeled off my cut and shirt and hung them away from potential spray.

His chest heaved, and his neck contracted. He was scared, as he should be.

"Please." Saliva pooled at the corners of his mouth. "Please, there's got to be some—" He stopped himself and sat a little straighter. "I can share what I have on you."

My hand twitched as I pulled up a chair and settled in front of him. I was interested in what he thought he had on me, but at the same time, I did have a copy of the USB.

"It won't help." I grew annoyed with him, and my fingers ached for a good fight.

"I know you slept with Doyle's sister."

"Who doesn't?" I tossed my phone onto the table behind me.

"Y-you killed those men in that New York bar after your fight at fifteen."

I stood and kicked my chair away. "I've killed many."

"Wait!" he screamed with a jolt, and the chains slapped the wall, filling the air with an ear-piercing sound. "Does Brick know you've located his brother?"

With my fist drawn back and my body weight behind it, I froze.

How the fuck did he know that?

"Ahh." His demeanor relaxed. "So, he doesn't know…"

"Time's up!" I slammed my fist on the top of his head and caved it in. His neck snapped loudly, and he flopped to the ground.

Clark may have known more, but when you were faced with a life and death situation, most would spill their deepest secrets…or mine, and mine were hidden for a reason.

I nodded at the reaper who waited in the corner for me. His dark presence engulfed the room.

My part was finished.

***

"Coffee?" Morgan set the mug in front of me and eyed my swollen knuckles. "Are we down a guy?"

I started to speak when Tess came through the doors and over to the bar for a water. Jace tumbled in behind her and held onto a chair for support.

"Lookin' good." Brick laughed with me.

"Fuck off," he wheezed, unable to speak.

"Tess," I called as she went to leave, "come here."

She hesitated. "I need a shower."

"This will just take a minute."

"Yeah?" She stood a few feet away, holding my gaze.

"Clark is dead."

No emotion surfaced on her face. "Okay."

Not what I wanted or expected.

Even Brick was stunned and cleared his throat.

"You okay, Tess?"

She shrugged. "Why? I was part of it. I'm glad. Wish I'd finished him myself."

"Tess," Brick tried to get her to open up, "come on."

"What do you want me to say?" She checked her phone. "One down, one to go?"

Her phone vibrated, and her eyes scanned side to side as she read it.

"I gotta go."

Brick watched her leave before he turned around. "Christ, she's turning into you."

Lucky me.

CHAPTER EIGHTEEN

Tess

"Tess," Minnie stuck her head in the door and looked around my room, "are you ready for this trip?"

I sank onto the side of the bed. I used to love Vegas, but I couldn't get my head into this trip.

"Clothes-wise, yes. Nerves-wise? I have no clue."

She glanced over her shoulder before she shut the door. "Girl, you need to let whatever the hell is bothering you go."

I attempted a smile, and she narrowed her eyes.

"When was the last time you and Trigger bumped fuzzies?"

"Wow." I pulled up the handle of my suitcase. "Where my head just went was not okay."

"That long, hey?"

"I don't know. I have mixed feelings on the

289

e thought for a moment. "Whenever Brick and

are out of sync, I just need to get laid. I really

you need it, girl."

I glanced at the time. "You know he brought
Clark here by texting him from my phone."

"Yeah, but you got what you wanted, right?"

I shrugged. She was right, and I didn't know
why it bothered me.

Brick appeared at the door. "Ready?"

"Yeah." Minnie stopped me from following him.
"Do you trust me?"

She waved me off and dug out a silver tube.
"Stick out your tongue." She tapped a little white
pill into her palm.

"What is it?"

"Trust me, it will make the four-hour bike ride a
whole lot more comfortable." She held it out and
waited for my mouth to open.

I opened, and she stuck the pill on the center of
my tongue. She did the same to herself, which made
me feel a little better.

"Now," she stepped back and examined my
outfit, "leather pants are perfect. I love the skull top,
just change out of heels to boots. Your heels will go
numb from the vibration." She was right. I
remembered I had that problem on the last long
drive to the desert.

Threading my arms through my leather jacket, I
fixed my hair and held up my arms. "Well?"

"I'd do you."

"Good to know." I winked, happy Minnie got me
out of my funk, if only for a moment.

With my suitcase in hand, I followed her out to the van where Jace was loading our luggage.

"Jesus." He smirked at me. "Whoa, sexy outfit."

"Leaves nothing to the imagination, and that's the point." Minnie grinned at me and slammed her suitcase in the van. She grabbed my hand and pulled me close as we walked over to the guys standing by their bikes. "If it becomes too much, there's a few rest stops."

"If what becomes too much? Minnie…" I tried to grab her hand, but she veered off toward Brick. "I thought it was just an edible, as in pot."

"Hello again, leather pants." Rail appeared at my side. "I was wondering when we were going to meet you again."

Trigger rolled up on his bike. He was in a black t-shirt that hugged his biceps and chest, and dark jeans and boots. His cut seemed a bit tight, a sign he had been working out a lot.

He didn't remove his sunglasses, but his stare nearly made me trip as I walked over and took the helmet he handed me.

"You look good," he muttered. "You've been missing for the past week."

"Just dealing with some stuff."

"I don't like it."

"I know." I flipped my hair back and pulled the helmet on. "Me either." I swung my leg over the bike and rested my hands on his hips, and he pulled me so I hugged him. He flicked the engine over and backed us out.

An hour later, we hit a wall of traffic and came to a complete stop. That was when I began to notice the leather cut that wrapped Trigger's midsection was as smooth as lamb skin. As I moved my sensitive fingertips over it, I felt a ball of warmth grow in my belly.

My thighs flexed as Trigger shifted his weight. I didn't mean to ball his shirt in my hands, but fuck me, everything felt amazing.

"You okay?" His raspy voice caught me off guard, and I jolted on the seat, and oh-my-God, it was amazing. "Tess?"

"Please stop moving," was all that shot out of my mouth. He flipped up his visor and turned to look at me. I shook my head and moaned as his ass rubbed my front. My jaw clenched, and I started to grind my teeth.

"Put your visor up."

Oh, shit, don't get alpha on me. I may lose it right here on the freeway.

I quickly shoved it up and stared into his confused eyes.

"What are you on?"

"Nothing." I almost moaned when he moved again.

He stared a beat longer before he snapped his visor down and turned back around.

Ohhh, yes. I wanted to tap his shoulder to get him to do that again, but the traffic started to move.

Sweet, horny Lucifer. I'd broken out in a light layer of sweat, and my thighs burned from the grip on the seat. Three hours on the bike, and its vibrations had built me up to a pleasure-painful level. I'd finish myself off if I weren't surrounded by the crew.

Thankfully, Trigger signaled we were stopping for a break at the next rest stop. We took the exit and rolled up at the light before the small park.

When Trigger kicked his foot out to stabilize us, I grabbed the side of his leg and begged my body to let go.

His hand landed on mine, and I wanted to cry. His touch, his smell, his everything made my world tilt on its axis. I didn't know how much longer I could hold on.

I was either going to kill someone or have the most mind-blowing orgasm known to woman in public.

The bike slowed to a stop, and he proceeded to wiggle around then slid the length of his leg across me. I tossed my helmet, and my palms dug deep into the hot leather. I felt like I was balancing on the loose rocks that lined edge of my orgasm. I had never not-wanted to come so badly in my life.

My mind shifted to images of Trigger touching me.

Oh, no.

Oh, yes.

Oh, please.

"That's one major fuck-me face." Rail burst my steamy moment.

I glared at him, but it did nothing for my problem. "What?"

"Just makin' an observation."

"*Observate* somewhere else."

"Yeah, you probably need to finish that off." He wiggled his fingers and winked.

I closed my eyes and managed to channel my

thoughts back to being underneath Trigger. His hands on my skin, his lips on my neck, his…

A shadow crossed my face and blocked my warmth. "What did you take?"

A deep jolt tore through me as my mind decided if it he was real or not.

"Please," I nearly panted. "Don't talk." I rubbed my hands down my pants. The leather was warm and sent goosebumps through me.

"What?"

"I'm not entirely sure, as this is the first time I ever took ecstasy, but I *think* I took ecstasy."

He blinked "Where did you get E?"

"A fr—"

"What the hell were you thinkin', taking drugs before you got on the bike?"

I reached out and wrapped my fingers around his arm to get him to pull back from the angry path he was about to go down.

Once my sense of touch got hold of what I was doing, I got a head rush. A strange prickle shot through my arms, up my chest, wrapped around my neck, and burst through my mind.

Trigger's warm hand landed just above my elbow and tugged me toward him.

"Look at me." His jaw flexed as my eyes climbed. "Tell me what you're feeling."

When I tried to break eye contact, his finger lifted my chin back in place.

I unlocked the doors to my mind and let the words flow out.

"I'm wishing we weren't standing in a parking lot because I've discovered ecstasy and a vibrating bike is the way for a woman to experience blue balls."

He ran his fingers down to the center of my collarbone with a little chuckle. *Kill me now!*

"Tell me what else is going through you head."

My mouth opened, and more words flew out. "It scares me that my mother will come looking for Clark. So much, in fact, I've had nightmares the last few nights."

His eyes burned into mine before he leaned down to brush his lips across my temple. "And?"

"And if you don't—" His fingers danced along my cleavage, and he palmed my breast. "Trigger." I couldn't think straight…his touch, his hot breath, his raspy voice.

"How ya doing, Tess?" Minnie shouted from Brick's bike as they pulled up next to us.

"Thanks for the heads up." I referenced the bike and the last three hours of pleasure-pain.

She laughed. "Where would the fun be in that?" She glanced at Trigger. "Wanna join in?"

"No! No way," Langley snapped from beside me. Christ, he was like a damn ninja. He made no noise; he just appeared. "And none of that." He pointed at me. "Not until after."

"What?" I nearly choked. "Don't make me go elsewhere."

Where the hell was my filter?

"Tess, don't give Trigger a stroke." Cray shook his head. "We need him focused."

"What the hell did I do?" How did I get sucked into this shit? And why did his arm feel like butter? My mind momentary slipped.

"You and your *fuck-me face*."

"Thank you!" Rail fist bumped Cray.

"It's written all over you." Cray circled his face with his hands.

"Unbelievable."

"Go on ahead." Trigger waved the guys off, and I was thankful to go back to what I was doing. He pulled my hair back and rolled his fist to the root.

"Everything feels good, doesn't it?" His knowing smile almost made me mad. He knew he had the upper hand. "Open." Two of his fingers pushed past my lips and stroked my tongue gently.

"Mmhm." I sucked and swirled them around like I would his erection.

He drew in a breath before he pulled them free. His lips smashed into mine as his hand lowered into my pants and broke the slick opening.

I couldn't care less if the entire crew watched. I needed this.

"You're dripping, Tess," he purred.

My toes were on the edge. All I needed was a little push. He was content to hold still, so I unlocked my knees and dropped down a few inches, and all four delicious fingers made their way inside and rubbed all the right spots.

But before I could utilize them, they were gone.

***

Trigger

"Where do you want these?" Jace had our bags.

"Last door at the end of the hall."

"Both?" he asked, and I folded my arms. "Sure thing."

Apparently, even the guys had noticed the distance between me and Tess. The truck stop was the first time in a week I had touched her. Something changed with her after the dinner with Mike, but I'd been so preoccupied with the fight, I let it go.

"Checked the perimeter." Big Joe nursed a beer, and I studied him for a moment. I never got the chance to talk to him about the desert.

"Good." I nodded, still deep in thought.

"Something up?"

"Why didn't you tell me you helped Tess in the desert?"

He looked around then hung his head. Joe had never crossed me, so I was sure this weighed on him. "She was leaving, regardless. I couldn't just leave her there on the side of the road. I should've told you, but she asked me not to."

I didn't say anything more to make my point, but I wasn't happy about it.

"Sorry, man, but you know I watch over that girl. She's family now."

I shook my head and tried to understand. His loyalty should be to me first, but since I knew Tess was all right, I'd let it go this time.

"We've got steaks, we've got sausage, we've got ribs," Cooper yelled as he walked by me with a huge box from Costco. "Who's hungry?"

"Me!" Rail shouted from the doorway.

"What do you want?"

"Sausage!"

"Shocker." Brick punched him in the arm.

"Tess?" I asked.

"Pool, I think." Brick grabbed the beer from Jace and raced off.

Jace cursed as he opened another one. "I hate being the bitch."

"And I hate carrying my own shit." Rail dropped his bags at Jace's feet. "Third room on the right." He snatched Jace's newly opened beer and roamed over my way.

Jace wanted to be a prospect, and this was all part of it. The faster he got that, the better.

"So," Rail glanced around, "this was where you stayed when you fought?"

My face scrunched with disgust. "No, that was a Motel 6."

"Oh, so why the huge house?"

"I don't like people."

He huffed. "Of course." He downed the neck of his beer. "Heads up, Tess is like a cat in heat. You can smell her mile away. You might want to go piss on her, you know, mark your territory. We have a lot of company." He nodded to the Vegas and Arizona crews. A hot blonde walked by in a towel, and Rail beamed at me. "That's my cue."

Most of the guys were huddled by the barbecue when I came out. Some were in the heated pool, and others were drinking by the fire pits. The property the house was on was massive. It belonged to a friend I made a deal with many years ago. He had made some fast cash, and in return, I got to use this place whenever I wanted.

The less attention I had in this town, the better.

"Trigger," Gus huddled over to me, "I know I've said it before, but I have a bad feeling about this fight. Something still feels off."

"We've been over this already, Gus."

"I know, but something just isn't sitting right in my gut."

I rubbed my beard. Gus never liked me fighting, always said it fucked with my head. It was true. I did get sucked into it, but I always found my way out.

"You know I don't have a choice here, Gus. Gotta play it through. I'm feelin' good."

He closed his eyes for a moment, "Where's Tess? I've been wanting to talk to her all day."

"Not sure," I lied. "Did Vib end up coming?"

He nodded. "Free booze, coke, and cock. She wouldn't miss it. Denton is with his aunt, and Fin is around here somewhere. Little shit ran off earlier, talkin' about your new fightin' ring."

I couldn't help but smile. That kid really did have the fighting gene.

Waving off Gus, I headed down the hill to the hot tub built into the side of a cliff. It had private rooms with streamed music to help drown out nearby noise.

I nodded my thanks to Cooper as he pointed out the room Tess went into. I stepped into the hot water and ditched my t-shirt. My trunks stuck to me in the freezing cold air.

I dove in and stayed under the water until I swam up to the turn in the walkway. Flipping my hair out of my face, I blinked my eyes dry and spotted Tess on the ledge.

Her arms skimmed the surface of the water before she brought them up and let the water run down her skin. I moved closer until she sensed me.

"How are you feeling?" I came closer.

"Better now." She glared. "Nothing my vibrator couldn't fix."

The way she broke eye contact led me to believe she was lying.

I didn't break stride as I came up to her, and she backed up to the rock wall.

"What are you doing?" Her hot chest pressed into mine, and her hands landed on my arms. She might be coming down from her high, but the drug was still very much in her system.

"Fucking you."

"You think so?" Her head tilted, and I ripped her scrap of bikini bottoms off. She yelped but couldn't hold back a moan. Everything in her body was heightened, and I wasn't about to miss an opportunity to make her feel amazing.

"Yeah." I bent down and hiked her up on the rock ledge. "You've been pissed at me, and I'm not sure why, but right now I am going to fuck you senseless."

"You really don't know why?" she started, and I pushed her legs open, and my mouth landed on her swollen mound. Her head dropped back with a moan. I licked, sucked, groaned—I did everything I could to bring her to the edge before I pulled back. She tried to hold my head in place, but I grabbed her hands and held them down as I dove deeper. Her hips bucked, and her chest heaved.

"Trigger, I hate you! Make me come, or I'll—"

"What?" I teased as I came up for air. "What will you do at this very moment, Tess?"

"Something." She covered her face. "If you care about me at all, you'll make me come a million times—Oh!"

I took that moment she had her face covered to sink myself deep into her hot, slick walls. She ate me to the root, and I had to stabilize myself before I could thrust again.

"Yes!" she screamed in bliss. "More!"

I reached around and brought her body to mine. Her legs wrapped around my waist and squeezed.

Slowly, I licked the drops that trickled between her breasts then gently took her nipple between my teeth and tugged. Her forehead landed on my shoulder with a long-annoyed sigh as her nails dug into my back.

I nipped at her neck and massaged her ass. Her body felt amazing against mine. I could literally feel my demons close their cage doors and lie down for the night.

"Hey," she took my head with both hands, "you need to flip your switch, or I will." The look of dark promise nearly kicked me in the gut.

When I didn't react fast enough, she tried to shove me away, but I slammed her to me. I grabbed her neck and bit her skin to show her who was in control.

When she tried to pull away, I swung her around and slammed into her. She fought to hold herself out of the water, so I walked her over to the carved-out seat and laid her front on the smooth stone.

With my hands on her hips, I took her savagely

from behind. Water lapped the walls, and her screams echoed around us. It was like a goddamn fucking porno just for me.

"Trigger," she fought to catch her breath, "harder!"

Fuck me, I loved this chick's sex drive.

I smacked her ass and pumped harder, my fingers entwined in her hair, and I found myself groaning out loud.

"Shit, Tess!" I blurted. "I don't want to come."

"I need more!" She flinched but reached around and grabbed my balls.

Flip.

I didn't remember changing positions, or grabbing her around the throat and kissing her with all I had inside me, but I did remember coming so hard I lost my vision.

She was the only woman I would ever lose control with.

***

After a shower, I joined everyone downstairs. I lost Tess once she returned to the house. Something about Minnie needing her. She was totally out of it when I peeled her off the rock and sat her upright. She had scurried out of the cave the first free moment she had.

"You looked fucked out." Brick laughed as he came to my side with a plate full of ribs. My stomach growled, and I stole one off his plate. "Tess come off her high yet?"

"Think so." The flavor smothered my tongue and

reminded me of where it was just an hour ago. My pants grew tight, and the thought of doing another round with Tess started to overcome my hunger.

Jace walked by, and I snatched his plate from his hands. I needed to fuel up quick.

"Seriously?" he growled but left before I could remind him he shouldn't even be eating yet.

Gus hurried by like he was looking for someone. He had been off lately too. Fin zipped by, nearly knocking him over, and the three slices of pizza he carried almost slid off the plate. I was sure the little shit would go find a quiet spot and eat it all himself. I'd never seen a kid with such an appetite.

"You find out why she's pissed at you?" Brick asked with a rib sticking out of his mouth. "The only time she works out is when she's mad. So, what did you do?"

I shrugged.

"I bet it's over the whole 'she wants more' thing. Women dwell."

Her words, *"I want more!"* suddenly smacked me across the face.

"Trigger!" Langley popped up by the doorway like he appeared out of nowhere. "Time to train."

Brick jumped. "Jesus. Has he always done that?"

"Yeah."

"Langley," he yelled, "feel free to announce yourself instead of fucking jumping out of shadows."

"Maybe you shouldn't be so jumpy, Mr. Brick."

"Man, I've been shot at more times than I can count and been stabbed in the gut. I'm gonna be jumpy."

Langley shrugged. "Maybe you should be more observant so you can see what's coming." He ignored Brick's pissed look and checked his watch. "We are late."

I tossed the rib bone on Brick's plate and rubbed my hands on my jeans.

"Watch the guys."

"Seriously?" Brick snickered at the bone. "Ew."

"You'll live."

"Let's go!" Langley shouted, and Brick dropped his plate, sending hot sauce across the stones. "Heads up, Mr. Brick."

"Shit! That's fucked up, man."

CHAPTER NINETEEN

Tess

Morning broke through the thin curtains of the sunroom where I had fallen asleep the night before with the third book in my hands.

My eyes were still puffy from crying. Thank God no one saw me last night. My heart broke when I got to the part where Keith brought Savannah the fish because she kept pushing people away.

Gawd, I'm a sucker for angsty books!

I ran my hands through my hair and tugged my clothes back into place as I heard voices outside the door.

"Morning." Gus's raspy voice broke through my fog, and I smiled when I saw he had two mugs of coffee in his hands. I stood to take them from him as he struggled to walk without splashing. "Thanks."

"How'd you find me?"

His smile quickly changed into a squint as he dropped into the overstuffed chair across from me. I hated that he was always in so much pain and had two little boys to raise.

"You think Trigger goes to bed without knowing you're okay first?"

"Oh." I almost blushed. I liked how he cared enough to look for me. "I'm shocked he didn't wake me."

"He wanted to." He coughed loudly and fought to catch his breath. "But he thought you probably wanted to be left alone. Do you?"

His blunt question threw me, and when I didn't answer right away, he remained quiet.

"You're different since you came back. Clark's death botherin' you?"

I played with a piece of my hair for something to do and shifted uncomfortably. "I'm not bothered by his death, just by the things he said." I shrugged. I realized I really didn't give a shit. I tried to kill him before, and now it had been done. "I think I struggle with the fact it wasn't my mother lying limp and pathetic on the slaughter room floor."

"Just say the word, sweetheart, and Trigger will make that happen."

"I know. I also know her time will come." I knew Trigger would take her out, but, "I guess it's not time yet. I want her to feel his loss the way I did when she took him away from me. Then I'll make my move."

"There's the fire I love about you."

I nodded. "Trust me, Gus, the fire is right at the surface, but I'm feeling…"

"What?"

"Like I'm a floater, like I'm not really sure what to think about things."

"Things like Trigger?"

"Yeah." I went with the truth. I never thought of Gus as my person to talk to, but he really was the only one who had any insight into Trigger.

"What's he doing?"

I sipped my coffee and nearly moaned at the flavor. It was a strong brew with hazelnut woven through it. "Nothing, really. It's me." My mind spun with the right words.

"I'm confused."

I laughed and set my mug on a triangle-shaped coaster. "Welcome to my head." I crossed my legs and took a deep breath. "Look, Gus, I was always the girl who was in love with someone I couldn't have. Clark strung me along for years, took my innocence, took my choices from me, but even through it all, I did know he truly cared for me. But Trigger…" A lump grew in the center of my throat. "His walls are so high, he won't allow himself to admit how he feels, and when I think I've made progress with him, I'm wrong. I never thought I wanted to fall in love again, but now that I have, I'm not sure how to navigate it…" I trailed off when his face froze.

What?

Oh-my-fresh-hell, what did I just say?

A cold sweat broke out along my neck, and my head started to pound.

"You love my boy?"

"No," I blurted. "My mouth just ran away with

me."

"Oh." His smile showed such unconditional pride for his nephew that it made me want to retract that last comment.

"Even…" I cleared my throat and lowered my voice. "Even if I did, that's not what he wants. He's made that very clear…and so have I. Gus, I didn't mean to fall for him. Truly, I didn't. We had an understanding, but before the whole church thing happened, we had a few days there where I saw behind his walls, and I hate that I fell. Hard." I stood abruptly, unable to stay still, so I paced the room. "I thought about dating someone else just to prove these feelings aren't real. I mean, this isn't me. I never wanted this. I'm the ice queen. But…" I held my head, feeling dizzy. "Help, help me fix this! I can't run and leave Brick again. I owe him the world."

"Tess." Gus stopped my madness. "Sit."

I did as he said but still felt like I was on a hamster wheel with no end in sight.

"Trigger has had women fall at his feet his entire life, but never once have they been able to touch him, sleep in the same bed with him, none of them was kept around this long. And this is a big one— never, ever would he have gone after them. He's shit at communicating his feelings, but let me tell you, he feels something for you. And I know you know that."

"I do, but anytime I let him know I can see he cares about me, he shuts down. It's not like I want marriage." I shuddered at the thought. "But I need to hear from him that I matter."

Gus leaned back, his lips pressed together in thought. I took the moment to down some more coffee. "I came in here to talk to you about something else, but now I'm wondering if I can use your confession as a tool to help me."

"I don't know what you mean."

"Hear me out." He rubbed his face then leaned forward, resting his arms on his thighs. One shoulder rose higher than the other. His body was in such bad shape.

"Look, Tess," he massaged his knee, yet another sign how much his body hurt, "you have Trigger's ear more than anyone right now, and that's sayin' a lot. I need you to do something for me."

"I'm listening."

"I need you to convince Trigger not to fight."

"Why?" The conversation had taken a strange turn.

My senses went on overdrive. I knew something was up, something more than just Trigger going back into the ring. Gus looked straight at me, and his jaw bulged as if he was gritting his teeth.

"You think you've seen Trigger at his worst in the slaughter room. Well, you haven't. The ring is what makes Trigger go into beast mode. It messes up his head, and it takes him over. They talk about how he has a switch, but you really haven't seen his switch fully flipped until you've seen him after that bell has rung."

"So what? He flips it, fights, wins, and we're done."

"No," he shook his head, "it's not that simple. He'll probably win, yes. Allen is sixty-something, but it's the after that scares me. He might go back to the old Trigger. I'm afraid he'll get lost in his hell again, and he won't want to get back out. I've seen it before, firsthand, and I don't ever want to again."

"I'm not sure what I'm supposed to do, Gus. We all know Trigger does what he wants, when he wants to."

He nodded then rolled my arm over and pushed up the sleeve of my cashmere sweater. The corners of his mouth went up and he chuckled quietly.

"What?"

"Nothing."

I glanced at the black and gray tattoo key that was hidden in the thick ivy of ink. I loved how my scar was now hidden so well. The only way you'd know it was there was if you touched it.

His hand fell on top of mine, and I looked over. He seemed to be struggling with words.

"Spit it out, Gus."

"Tess, promise me you'll try anything you can to keep him out of that ring." He swallowed hard before he looked deep in my eyes. "Give him a reason not to."

His words echoed around my head, and then it hit me.

"You want me to ask him not to fight if he truly does love me?" I felt sick. What a way to ask someone to prove they love you. With a threat.

"I get how this sounds, Tess, but there's more to it than Trigger getting lost back in his own hell." He shifted and hesitated. "I have a shitty feeling there's a lot more going on with this fight."

"Like what?"

"I don't know, but Allen hates his son more than anything, and he never does anything without a damn good reason, and he always has a backup plan."

And his backup plan could be death…

***

My shoes pounded the pavement, my arms pumped at my sides, and the cool, crisp air lined my lungs with a thin layer of frost. Light mist hung in the morning air, and dark rain clouds promised another wet afternoon.

I missed my usual running companion who left me alone with my thoughts. Instead, I had a wheezy Rail who had stopped twice now for a smoke break. Jace disappeared this morning to run an errand for Big Joe. Really, I thought he'd offered himself up so he could avoid running with me.

I glanced over my shoulder to see Rail heaved over, hands on his knees. A guy in tight shorts and a headband ran by him in perfect form and slowed.

"Slap my ass and call me jazzed. Beautiful morning for a run, hey, man?"

I fought my laughter at Rail being hit on.

"Yeah, we get it." Rail snickered as he drew closer to him. "You work out, and we're all *so* impressed."

"What?" The cute guy looked confused but kept moving.

"You about done?" I folded my arms once again, annoyed I wasn't able to go out for a run on my own.

"I just need—" He coughed and pulled out another smoke, lit the tip, and closed his eyes as the poison smothered his insides. "Sweet," he purred. "Tastes like sex in the dirt."

"Oh, for fuck's sake." I covered my face and groaned. "Can we just get this done?"

"Why can't we quit now? What are..." He sucked in another breath, and something crossed his mind and his eyes widened. "What are you running *from,* anyway?"

"I'm not running from anything." We both stopped, and he walked over to a railing. He rolled his head and blew a white cloud at my face.

Sexy.

But was it that noticeable?

"Ugh," I huffed and flopped down next to him on the railing. My muscles screamed for a break, and I could really use some food. "Myself. Trigger. I don't know."

"Wow, I was just grasping for an excuse, here. I didn't know there really was something going on," he joked, but when he caught my unimpressed expression, he tried to get serious. "Okay, let me get in the headspace." He squeezed his eyes shut and chanted. "Chick talk, chick talk, chick talk. Ass, tits, scissoring, and wet bits. Okay," he sighed dramatically, "I'm ready."

"Aren't I lucky?" I rolled my eyes at his views on women. "I've been asked to do something, and I don't know where to begin."

"Ah," he nodded, "Gus got to you about Trigger and the fight."

"How did—" I stopped myself. I wasn't sure

312

how much he really knew.

"Not like we all aren't thinking the same thing. Trigger goes rogue after he fights. I've seen the tail end of it, and it wasn't pretty. Ever since he told Gus, the old man has been stressed out."

"Oh." My mind slapped me around a little. *Gus needed your help and what did you do? You decided to go for a run. Talk about ungrateful.*

"Trigger listens to no one but himself. Of course, there's the whole 'is Allen really the one fighting Trigger, and if not, who is he bringing in' thing."

"Yeah, there's that too." Who would be good enough to fight Trigger?

Rail pushed himself up. I joined him and looked around at the clouds closing in. It suddenly felt like it was a race to tell Trigger before the storm hit.

"Gus thinks you might have an in."

"Do I?"

"Don't you?" he countered.

"Fuck me."

"That's the spirit." He slapped my shoulder. "Now, are we done here, or do I have to choke on this fresh fucking air some more?"

"No, let's go."

"Good." He raised his hand. "Taxi!"

After we returned to the house, Rail went directly to the bar and yelled for a beer while he dramatically clutched his chest as if in pain.

I showered and headed downstairs for something to eat. I was almost lightheaded with hunger.

Just as I rounded the corner, I heard voices and slowed my pace. Trigger and Brick were at the island discussing something, and the way they were hunched over and speaking in low voices, I assumed it wasn't something they wanted me to hear.

"You kill him?" Brick quickly switched topics and kissed my cheek.

"Yeah, about that." I rested my hands on my hips. "Why the hell would you send Smokey Joe to run with me when he has the lung capacity of a five-year-old?"

"Jace was busy." Brick shrugged.

"That so?" Trigger checked his phone. "I just saw him."

"He's avoiding the workout." I hoped Trigger was in a chatty mood.

"Won't hurt Rail." Trigger grunted as he texted someone. "Next time, take Cooper."

"Or *you* could run with me."

Brick laughed as he left the room, and Trigger looked up at me. "You couldn't keep up."

"Wanna bet?" I bit into an apple.

The corners of his mouth went up into that oh-so-sexy look he gave me when the promise of sex was in the air.

"And when I win?" He set his phone down and stood like a panther, excited at the challenge.

"Me, anywhere you want." I lifted my head as he came closer. "And if I win," I held my ground, "I want to speak to you about something without you shutting down on me."

His brows drew together, and I could see he was interested. His curiosity would get the best of him.

"What's wrong?"

Seriously? Here?

"Can we talk alone?"

"No." Rail leaned over the back of the couch. When did he get here? "If you leave, I can't eavesdrop."

"Fuck off, Rail." Trigger took my hand and pulled me outside. He led me to a pathway partially covered with palm trees so we could have some privacy. He didn't seem to mind the cold weather, whereas I held onto his arm with both hands to steal his warmth.

"So," Trigger glanced down at me, "we're alone now."

I tucked a piece of hair behind my ear and thought about my words. I wanted to make sure I made my point without scaring the hell out of him. "Promise you won't shut down."

"Okay."

"Okay." I mirrored his tone. "Who am I to you?"

I felt him hesitate, but he shook it off. "We've been down this road, Tess."

Okay...

Here comes a classic female moment.

"Am I your girlfriend?"

His expression changed, and he turned to block my path. "What is this all about?"

My face heated, and I wanted to break eye contact, but I also wanted to hold my ground. "Why did you come back for me?"

"I like having you around."

"Is that the only reason?"

"Tess," he rubbed his head like I stressed him out, "you know I don't do this stuff well. Either say what you want to, or don't."

315

"Okay. Never once have you asked *me* why I let you take me back to the club."

He shook his head as if he never thought about it that way. "Okay. Why, then?"

"I asked you first."

"And I answered you."

"Did you?" I wanted some answers, and I was going to get them if I was going to put myself out there.

"Fuck! I..." He paused. "I have never wanted to have a woman around me. No one gets me. I used the chicks around the club for a release, but that's it. Until you..."

Holy shit, we're making progress.

"Like I've said before, you turn off the shit inside me. You bring me silence, and you flip my switch during sex, and that's never happened before."

I nodded but was nervous to speak. I didn't want him to close up. When he seemed like he was, I tried a different angle. "What if I told you I met someone else?"

His face dropped, and his jaw twitched. "Who?" The tone sent a shiver through me. "Is that what you're doing here, telling me you're interested in someone else?"

"If I was?"

"I'd murder him."

"Why?"

"'Cause you're my woman."

"But I'm not your girlfriend," I reminded him.

"Tess," he warned, and I got pissed.

"Trigger, I get it. We always said we wanted

nothing more than to just be fuck buddies, but I—" My mouth slammed shut.

He stepped closer and slid his warm hand around the back of my neck. My eyes fluttered, and I was once again consumed by his simple touch. "You, what?" he whispered as he leaned down and licked my lobe. "Tell me."

"I've fallen in love with you."

His muscles locked, and his head drew back slightly to read my face. "I'm unlovable, Tess. It's just lust."

I saw red.

I wiggled out of his hold and jammed my finger in his face. "Don't you ever tell me how I feel," I hissed. "I don't want to be—I don't want to be feeling this way when the other person doesn't. I've been here my whole life!" Raw, empty feelings started to surface, feelings I'd buried deep down inside, and anchored themselves to my soul.

"Hey!" he snapped and reached for my arm, but I was too fast and jumped out of his way.

"Jesus Christ!" I covered my forehead with my hands as I thought about what I just admitted. "Fucking Gus and Rail all inside my head."

"Gus?" he asked, clearly confused what I was rambling about. "What the fuck does Gus have to do with this?"

"Nothing. Just forget all of this." I turned to walk away when he hooked my waist and pushed me up against the trunk of a palm tree.

"Stop running. Just give me a fucking second to process this."

"There's nothing to process. One of your dumb

chicks opened her mouth."

"Don't *ever* compare yourself to those women," he barked. "No one has ever told me they loved me and meant it for the right reasons."

"I have no desire for your money, Trigger. There's no hidden motive here."

He shot me a look like he knew that already.

I figured since I was doing a stellar job of fucking this moment up, I might as well say it all.

"If you have any feelings for me whatsoever, please hear me when I say this. Please don't fight your father."

He cocked his head, confused. "So, Gus has been talking to you."

"Yes."

"Fucking Gus."

"It's not just Gus, Trigger. Your whole club is worried. I'm worried."

His body seemed to relax, and he closed his eyes as he thought. I reached up and ran my fingertips along his cheek.

"You and I are a lot alike, Trigger. I never meant to mess up what we had. I was content with it, but there was a point where it hit me. When Clark kissed me, everything inside suddenly became clear, and I knew. When I saw you in the house, dressed in a suit and tie, I almost died. You did that for me, and I thought maybe, just maybe, you felt it too, but—"

"What does it feel like?" He towered over me, and I couldn't help but slide my hands up his arms. He was stunning in a dark way that made my mouth water. He was everything Clark wasn't, and that called to me.

"I'm dizzy around you," I murmured as the first few drops of the storm fell. "My body heats and reacts when you enter or leave a room." His throat contracted, and his eyes looked hungry. "I think about you all the time, and I get..." I stopped, feeling exposed, "jealous when you're around other women."

"Jealousy can be a bitch." He smiled, and I felt the lust burst through me, like a bubble deep down in my belly that picked up speed as it rose. "I feel that way with you."

His confession caught me off guard, and I matched his smile.

"Go on." He kissed the corners of my mouth.

"Your touch," I nearly moaned, "calls my body to attention. It's not just pure lust, but pure need."

"Mmm." His breath shot across my collarbone. "Why do you think I spend so much time here," he kissed his way up my neck, "and here?" He sucked at his spot. "I can't get enough of your body."

He pressed his massive erection into my stomach, so I reached down and wrapped my hand around it and gave a good tug.

"Jesus, Tess!" His head dove into my neck as he panted. "I need to be inside of you." He grabbed my waist and held me over his shoulder.

"What the hell?"

"Shh." He slapped my ass and hurried to the garage. Once inside, he sat me down on the lawnmower then left to lock the door. I noticed he looked around first.

"You see something?"

"Don't need Langley interrupting."

"You're not allowed to have sex, are you?"

He grabbed my jeans and hauled them down, and his hand was between my legs before I could even think.

"I love that you're so wet for me."

"Should we be doing this?" I wasn't about to stop, but I didn't want to fuck up his fight if I couldn't convince him not to go through with it.

"Come here." He lifted me onto the workbench, which had a fairly smooth surface, and undid his pants. His gorgeous erection bowed under its weight and leaked from anticipation.

He lined up and pushed just the tip in before he held my head in his hands and stared into my eyes.

"You came into my life and showed me that I am worthy of something, maybe even love. Countless times you have proven you're loyal. Any man who can't see what you are is a fool."

I am speechless.

"I'm not good at this, but I will try for *you*. I might struggle with the words, but I can always show you my feelings." He nudged further in.

My head spun, and my heart opened wide.

"You can't miss something you've never known before." He held my gaze. "But, shit, when you left, it felt like my insides were bein' ripped out. I couldn't think straight and couldn't do anything but kill. Never do I want to go through that again."

When I tried to speak, he shook his head like he didn't want me to break in on his train of thought.

"You're so fucking pretty, Tess."

Tears fought their way to the surface, and I

rubbed the back of his neck while I let his words sink in. It was the most he ever said to me at once about anything so personal.

"Thank you," flew out of my mouth. The corners of his mouth rose, and I saw a real, genuine smile.

Jesus.

His hands slowly descended my back and curled around my ass. He pulled me to him and dove deep inside of me.

I jolted, and he nuzzled my hair. "I laid out all my feelings for you, but I will never change the way I fuck you."

Good!

***

Trigger

"He's been sitting like that since he won the fight." Langley eyed me from behind the asshole who lost his bet and was now trying to get his money back. *"What's wrong with you?"*

"He's fine." My father smacked my shoulder hard, but even that couldn't shake me from the alternate world I was caught in. I hated it there, but it was the only way I could handle the demons that ran free whenever I fought. It was as if I needed to be still and stay quiet so they'd retreat to their cages.

I could feel their nails. They seemed to click against my bones and drag me back to each swing, each blood spray, each moment I punched my opponent. The reaper loomed a little closer, and his cold, dark presence cloaked my world as I had fought like hell through their heavy shadow to get back. Sometimes I wondered what it would be like to stay there and just give in to the madness.

"Hey, boy!" The loser kicked my leg. "Show some respect when I'm talking to you." He went to kick me again, but I latched onto his wrist, yanked him down, and smashed his face into my knee, and the blood sprayed. Next, I rammed the heel of my boot into his mouth, and his teeth broke off and fell from his tongue as he screamed. I covered his lips and watched as he struggled to breathe and not swallow little chips of bone.

My father caught my attention, and he smiled and shook his head at someone who was about to intervene. He held up a hand to stop him.

"The boy's a natural killer. Let him finish."

A chill pricked at my skin. He was here, ready to take my next offering. I leaned back and gave him some room.

"Again," Langley shouted from the corner of the ring. "Arms up!"

The boxing opponent Langley had brought in had a hard time standing, and I could see he had a concussion. Five hours in a ring and multiple blows to the temple would do that.

"Tap out or fight," I spat and waited. He blinked, but he wasn't there.

He stepped forward but collapsed, nearly taking my shoulder off in the process.

"Jace!" Langley pointed at him, and Rich, my newest prospect, grabbed both arms and pulled him out of the ring.

Another man took his place and got into position.

Once the word was out I was in town, there were lots of men willing to help me train. There was a time when the underground world was my life. I ate, slept, and breathed the ring. Everyone knew my name and placed their bets in my favor.

The excitement sent a feverish rush through my veins, and I twisted and sent a kick straight into his neck. His eyes bulged, and when he went to grab his neck, I punched his shoulder, knocking it out of its socket.

He yelped but stayed standing. I smirked, happy with his decision.

"Name?"

"Hugo."

I nodded and waited for Langley to reset his shoulder, then we started back up again.

Back and forth we went. No helmets, no gloves, just skin to skin, bones to bones.

Every punch I took made my demons scream. Their nails clawed the floor, and their teeth gnawed at the bars. They wanted out, they wanted to be free, but it wasn't time yet. Tomorrow they could feed.

Hugo's gaze flicked over my shoulder, and I saw a change in his face. I didn't need to see who it was. I felt her.

Rail looked uneasy as he dropped the screwdriver and headed over. I tried to stay focused. I didn't need Langley up my ass with Tess. Three more punches and a few more glances from Hugo, and I finally called a break.

"Like what you see?"

His eyes took another detour to Tess, then snapped back to mine, and he shook his head. "No."

Tess caught the attention of both males and females. She held herself with confidence, and dressed fucking hot. Having her in the same room as guys like Hugo made me want to take on every one of them.

I knew I'd kill anyone who went near her if I wasn't careful.

"Where's your head, Trig?" Langley's voice broke through my murderous thoughts.

I jumped and kicked Hugo in the chest, and he flew back into the ropes. His knees hit the floor first, then his hands.

He didn't speak as he peeled himself off the mat and stood on shaky legs.

"Take a break," Langley shouted and tossed me a cold Gatorade.

"Hey." She hopped up and stood on the other side of the ropes. Her breasts were squeezed into a black tank, and her ass was in a pair of tight jeans.

I leaned over and kissed her and grabbed a large handful of her ass, giving it a grope. She started to protest but soon gave in. Her body sagged into mine. She didn't seem to care I was covered in sweat.

"Territorial much?" She rolled her eyes, but she couldn't hide the fact she was horny.

"Get used to it."

She looked over at Langley then smiled and nodded at the ring.

"Can I try?"

A sudden flash went off in my head, and it nearly froze me. Tess crossing over into my past scared the shit out of me.

"No."

She completely ignored me and ducked under the ropes.

"Hey," she waved at Hugo, "I'm Tess."

"Hi, Tess." He stepped to the side of the ring with Langley, who shot me an unimpressed glare. He muttered something and handed Hugo a bottle of water.

"So, like this?" She put her hands up like she wanted to fight.

A cold rush broke over me, and I almost felt sick. She needed to get out of here now.

"Tess, get out."

"Why?" She moved around the ring with a wink. "Think you can't handle me?"

I shook my head and fought my switch. I wanted to yell and tear a strip off her, but I also didn't want to hurt her. I had done that enough already.

Instead, I lunged at her, wrapped myself around her arms, and pinned her back to my front.

My mouth rested above her ear, and I tried to speak very calmly. Each word came out slow. "I need you *out* of the ring."

"Why?"

She wiggled her ass, and I wanted to fuck her into submission.

Calm yourself.

"Tess."

She turned and looked up at me. "Okay." Gently, she pulled away, but when she started to duck back

325

under the ropes, I caught her worried face.

"Hey." I grabbed her arm to turn her around. "What?"

Her eyebrow rose, and she shrugged. "Have you thought about what your father really has in store for you? Or are you overshadowed by the need to fight again?"

"I have."

"And?"

"And nothing. We're prepared for everything."

She let out a long sigh. "I heard a saying once. Just because you can't see evil, doesn't mean it can't see you."

"Oh, trust me, sweetheart, I can see evil." *By looking in the damn mirror.*

She played with the necklace that hung between her breasts, and my hungry gazed followed her fingertips as they descended into her cleavage.

"If you won't listen to me in the ring, maybe you will in bed tonight?" Her sexy mouth curved up, and her gaze dropped to my lips. "Or will you be too tired?"

"Never too tired for that." I hooked her waist and slammed her tight little body to mine.

I shook my head, and as I was about to devour her mouth, I heard a voice.

"Tess, you need to leave." Langley appeared at my side. "You're a distraction."

She tried to hide her smile as she ducked under the ropes.

"We wouldn't want that."

"Your timing is flawless." I snickered at my coach.

"Your mind is elsewhere."

True.

***

I didn't stop training until nine o'clock that night. Everything burned and started to feel stiff. I had a massage and a cortisone shot to help with my back. It was acting up, and Langley thought it was necessary. I disagreed, but I trusted his opinion. He had never steered me wrong.

I set the whiskey bottle on the night table and flopped into bed. Took me a moment to realize the smell that drifted from the bathroom.

"You're interrupting my date." Tess came into view with a thick joint between her slim fingers. She took a drag as I took in her outfit. Heels, purple silk nightgown, matching robe, and her hair was curled.

"Am I?"

"Mmhm," she purred before she sat on the couch across from the bed.

"Who do I need to kill?" I shifted the pillow under me so I could see her better.

"You're hurt."

"Sore," I corrected.

"You fight tomorrow. You think it was wise to train that much on the day before?"

"Are you questioning my methods?"

She blew out a long trail of smoke while she thought. She fished around in her purse and pulled out her lipstick vibrator.

My brows rose, and so did my erection.

J.L. DRAKE

Slowly, her legs spread, and one hand inched its way to her opening. I licked my lips, hungry to see more. Her eyes fluttered closed, and she shifted down the couch a little. Her movements were mesmerizing, and the way her fingers eased in and out in the slick coating had me unzipping my pants.

The click of the vibrator made my stomach knot and my head swim.

She set the joint on the rim of her wine glass and pushed the tip of the lipstick into her mouth to moisten it.

I groaned with primal need. Everything inside of me ached and begged to be released. Heat burned its way to the surface to the point of pain.

She slipped the vibrator between her folds, and her head flopped back with a huff. Her free hand pulled at her nipple, and her chest rose and fell heavily.

"Mmm," she moaned, and I joined her with a few pumps to my erection.

"Come here," I ordered, but even my voice seemed strained.

She ignored me and kept going. She pushed, twisted, and pumped that little shit into her hole, and I started to get frustrated. She wasn't listening, and I needed her to.

"Tess," I warned when she got dangerously close to coming.

A layer of sweat glistened on her forehead, her cheeks were pink, and her breathing told me she was close.

"So close," she hissed.

"Fuck that!" I jumped out of bed and grabbed her

328

waist and tossed her on the mattress face down. I crawled over top of her ass and hiked up her nightgown. Holding her down with my body weight, I spread her legs and thrust.

She was so tight, so ready that she took me to the root. She was flat on the bed, and when she turned her head to the side to gasp for air, I saw the need in her eyes. Sex was our drug, one that we shared. She consumed me in every way, and that scared the shit out of me. But I was addicted and willing to fight to the end to keep her.

Grabbing both hands, I pulled them forward and held them as I molded to her curves. We were both slick, and I slid around easily to change direction.

I used my free hand to hold some of my weight. Using only my hips, I fucked her hard. Occasionally, I slowed and ran my fingers down the curve of her spine. Her skin heated under my touch, and she wiggled when I hit a sweet spot.

I allowed myself to smile, feel, and be raw in these moments. When we were together, nothing mattered.

"Trigger," her knuckles were white as the anticipation built, "please."

With my knees on either side of her hips and my hands on the headboard, I flicked my hips upward, and she jolted forward with a sexy cry.

She clawed helplessly at the tangled sheets. Her lungs fought for air. Her eyes squeezed shut.

My favorite part was when she first let go. Her insides clamped around me, and her back bowed as her orgasm ripped through her center and slingshotted me into mine.

I dropped down, and my head hit her back. I wrapped my arms around her midsection as I hung on. It was the only moment I was completely defenseless. Completely at her mercy.

***

Allen

"What, exactly, do you mean?" His forehead had broken out in a heavy sweat, and he squinted as he absorbed my words.

"I mean it's time."

"I don't think I can do this."

I slapped my hands together and smirked. "I don't recall asking you."

"He'll kill me."

"Him or me. Really, I think you're getting the better end of the deal if he does." I glanced back at my hungry weasels. "I'm done with you now."

He slowly rose and looked out the window at the other guys.

"Time to go." Zay popped his head in the door, holding my bag. He turned to my visitor. "You better not fuck this up."

"Don't have a choice, do I?"

"No," we said in unison.

He muttered as he went for the door. Zay stepped in his path momentarily before he let him go.

"She's pretty." Zay turned his phone around so I could see. Tess was at the market looking through the wine section. Her hair was long, and her ass was stuck in the air.

"Yes, she'll be a fine match for you."

I tapped on my laptop and checked in. "Shall we?"

Zay hopped to his feet with my bag in hand. "You worried?"

"Scared of my own son? No."

"Of him." He nodded out the door.

"He knows what will come if he doesn't do his part."

CHAPTER TWENTY

Tess

"Thanks." I nodded at the doorman who handed me an all-access pass to hang around my neck. Trigger, Langley, Brick, and Rail all came to the event before the rest of us.

I was told to wait for the all-clear back at the house with Gus. He seemed to hover around me the entire morning. *I have never seen him this way.* He kept asking if I needed anything or if I wanted a drink. It didn't take me long to see he was the one who needed one.

Even on the car ride there, he checked his phone a million times, and his fucked-up knee bounced out of control.

"Shit, Gus." Big Joe shook his head across the limo from us. "If I didn't know better, I'd think you were the fucking mole."

The entire car went silent.

"Poor taste," Gus muttered as he stared out the window. He was right, though. It wasn't the time to go there. We needed to get through today.

Jace covered his face and sighed. "I don't think I have ever been this nervous over someone else fighting."

"Trigger will win." Cooper poured himself another brandy.

The dude was feeling no pain today. I guessed we all coped differently.

The guys hopped out, but when I reached for the door handle, Gus hauled me back in and locked the doors.

"What the hell?" I whirled around and looked for an exit plan.

Cooper looked panicked and called to the other guys.

"Tess!" He grabbed my hands so I would make eye contact. "I did something. Something bad."

"Gus, if you're the mole, you're about to break my heart. You're like a dad to Trigger and to me." Why on earth I admitted that now was beyond me.

"Are you fucking kidding me? I love Trigger like he's my kid, and you too." He rubbed his face like he was weighing his decision. "I found her." He paused so I could connect the dots.

"Who?"

"His mother."

Oh, shit. I looked over my shoulder at the guys waiting by the door. Cooper was the only one who wouldn't take his eyes off the car. I motioned to him that everything was okay.

"Why were you looking for her?"

"No one can get through to Trigger. She was my last try."

"Gus," I fought for the right words, "do you really think it's smart to bring her in at this time to fuck with his head?"

"What choice do I have? The fight starts in an hour."

I leaned forward and took his hands. "Why are you really so nervous about this fight? What are you not telling me?"

"You wouldn't understand."

"Try me." I squared my shoulders to show I was ready.

"I watched that boy become something big, and never once did he get cocky. He fought, he won, he lived that life. But every punch, every blow, every victory pushed him into a dark place. He fucks with fate, doesn't feel the fear, just rides full speed ahead. He'll look at you differently, Tess, and it will hurt. That something you have between you two will fizzle out. He'll flip off his humanity switch, and you'll grow tired of waiting for him to return. That's what you'll feel."

I could tell by his tone he had more to say.

"What about you? What will you feel?"

"I will lose my nephew, the club will have a ruthless leader, and my sons will lose their father."

My head snapped back at that last statement.

"Come on, Tess." He shrugged one shoulder. "He's been more of a father to my boys than I have. They weren't planned. Vib just needed an anchor to the club, and I'm weak when it comes to her. They need him. I need him, and I cannot believe I found my sister."

"Hold on." I felt twenty different things fire off

at once. "I thought you were Allen's brother?"

"Nope." He raised his head a little higher. "She is my sister. I hung out at the strip joint where she worked."

"Ahh." I couldn't help but be freaked out by that.

"No," he made a disgusted face, "it's not like that at all, but she is only a half-sister."

"Doesn't make it better."

He huffed, but the humor quickly faded. "I watched over her. I knew Allen was shitty from the moment he walked in, but my sister saw what you saw in Trigger. Tall, hot, brooding." He rolled his eyes. "He pursued her until she gave in. He was relentless. I warned her he would fuck and chuck, and that's exactly what happened. She really thought he'd come back after she told him she was pregnant. Instead, he ran, and that's when she started to go down the rabbit hole. She was always on coke, but it was the speed that did her in. She couldn't handle the baby. I was useless when it came to the kid. All I did was worry about her, and one day she came home without him. She packed up her stuff and left. I never saw her again."

His eyes saddened, and he looked down at the floor, lost in his thoughts. "Took me a year to find him. Trigger was about one and half by then. Fucking cute little thing, big dark eyes and a mop of hair to match. Allen didn't want me around at first. Took me a long time to show him I only wanted to be a part of the boy's life. I was in and out of prison for a while, doing stupid shit. But I came back," he whispered more to himself. "I always came back."

I shook my head to try to shake the visions clear.

"I had...wow. How did you find her? I mean, does she even want to see him?"

"Anyone can be found eventually. You just need to know who to ask." He massaged his knee and winced. "She's clean, at least she seems to be. I know I'm playin' with fire here, but this whole thing..." He pointed to the windowless building. "I know it's going to be something bad. Allen's planning something. Nothing is ever what it seems with him."

Fuck. I didn't know what to think. His mother could throw him over the edge. What if Allen saw her? What would he do?

"Where is she?"

"She's inside."

"Does Brick know about this?"

"Brick knows some things about it, but he thinks she's a friend of mine. That's all. I might need you to run interference. Will you help me?"

Fuck!

"Yes."

"Good." He leaned forward, unlocked the door, and motioned for me to get out.

"This way." Gus pointed down the hallway. As we got closer, the sound of the crowd grew louder, and my anxiety kicked in bigtime. It was a cocktail of nerves, fear, excitement, sadness, and, I couldn't deny it, a little hope.

"Hey," Gus stopped me at the door, "if anything happens tonight, please remind Trigger of Mr. Rabbit."

"Huh?"

Gus pushed the door open, and there stood a

woman with long black hair, dark eyes, and prefect teeth. There were signs of drug use, but she was extremely pretty, and she was the spitting image of Trigger.

"Hi." She extended her hand and waited for me to do the same. "I'm Elizabeth Wise."

"Tess." I glanced at Rail, who was devouring a chocolate bar like it was a one-night stand. He stood there completely oblivious to what was happening around him.

Men.

"She's a friend of Gus's," Brick chimed in from across the room. "Guess she was in town or something."

Finally! I knew I could count on my best friend to feel the strangeness of the situation. He gave me a worried look as he pushed off the wall and headed for the door. "Tess, you should see if Trigger needs anything."

"Oh." Elizabeth eyed me a little more closely, and the corners of her mouth raised. "Are you and my son dating?"

Gus flinched bedside me, and Brick nearly tripped into Rail, who was still busy with the wrapper of the bar.

"What the fuck?" Brick blurted. "What the fuck did you guys do?"

"I didn't," I started, but stopped. I didn't want to toss Gus under the bus, not when he was legitimately trying to help.

"Brick," Langley stuck his head in the door, "I need more tape."

"Get some Gatorade," Trigger ordered behind

him.

Oh, shit. It was like a snowball gaining speed as it came toward us. Just as I turned to get the hell out of its path, Trigger walked in, and I froze to the spot.

"Hey." He started to give me his lazy smile but stopped when he felt the mood. His eyes flickered over to his mother, and his brows pinched together. It would be impossible for him to remember her, but not impossible to see they were related. He was looking in a damn mirror, for shit's sake.

"Do you know who I am?" she said softly.

"I do."

"Good." She let out a small breath.

"Is it?" he challenged.

"I get it, you're mad at me—"

"Are you fucking kidding me? Why now? Why here?" She started to speak, but he squeezed my hip and urged me out the door before she could convince him to stay. "I will not feed more to *those*..." he hit the side of his head hard, "savages!"

Once outside, he pulled out his phone and headed in the opposite direction.

"Don't go back in there."

"I won't," I assured him and waited for him to leave before I went to find Brick to see just how bad this shit storm had become.

***

Trigger

The bottle called my name. It dangled from my

fingers, but I knew better. I didn't abuse drugs, but right now I could use a hit of something. I needed my head clear, but my mother showing up threw me off center in a major way.

Shit.

I snatched up my phone and texted Tess.

Trigger: Where are you?

Nothing.

I switched screens and called her.

Nothing.

Fuck.

I tried calling two more times before I turned and caught my cold, dark reflection in the mirror. My tortured soul stared back at me from the glass, and a dark aura hovered around me like a shadow. Was there ever going to be an end to all of this?

With all my might, I swung back and smashed the bottle into the mirror and watched as bits of clear and green glass sprayed into the air like blood.

My temper rose as I lunged at the door. I could not believe my mother was really here right now.

"Where is Tess?" I barked at Langley while he tried desperately to look over my shoulder at the mystery guest who had just flipped my world upside down fifteen minutes before my fucking fight.

Wrong room, Langley.

"Trigger, I didn't mean to—"

I whirled around and jammed a finger in my uncle's face. I wanted to snap his neck for what he did. For the second time in my life, he flinched at my reaction. My arm dropped, and I covered my face to calm myself. The first time was when he saw me covered in bruises after my first fight. I guessed he thought he had failed me as a protector, and to be truthful, he did. I never blamed him. I wasn't his problem. He wasn't the one who gave birth to me then tossed me aside, and he wasn't the one who left the scars on my body. He was an uncle who dropped by to check on me occasionally. He was the one, however, who had become more of a father to me than my own ever had. He was the one who was there when he saw I was heading down an even darker path, and the one, after all, who suggested I kill my father.

"I had to do something," he whispered and stepped back into line with the guys.

"We need to talk. Just give me a second." I couldn't do this here.

"What the hell is going on?" Langley snapped, clearly annoyed. "You disappear minutes before the fight, there's some chick in there with you, and now you'll be going in cold! Are you trying to kill me?"

I turned. "Where's Tess?"

"And now you're thinking about pussy?"

"You mean that blonde with the great rack?" the little shit who carried our stuff chimed in. "She's talking to some guy by your room."

I did a quick sweep of my guys and saw they were all here. Pushing past Rail, I raced down the hallway. People pressed into the wall to get out of my way.

"Trigger, wait," Jace called out, a bunch of girls surrounding him. "These ladies want to meet you."

Turning the corner, I came to a stop and saw her

reading something on her phone. She must have sensed me, because she looked up.

I grabbed her by the waist and hauled her into the empty room, slamming the door in Langley's pissed off face.

"Are you okay?" She touched my face as I stood over her, trapping her against the wall.

I squeezed my eyes tightly shut and fought my way through the darkness, using her scent to guide me.

"You're scaring me a little, here," she whispered. "Speak to me."

I opened my eyes, and for the first time in my life, I felt something other than pain and emptiness.

"I love you, Tess." I shook my head in disbelief that I could finally see it so clearly. "I love you so much that the idea of anyone hurting you, or even flirting with you, makes me want to snap every limb on their body very slowly. I'm sorry I didn't see it before, but I need you to know I'm here now, and I want all of you."

She blinked, and I was sure I threw her off course, but I didn't care.

"You've already had me." She kissed me in the dirty way she did. When we came up for air, I pressed my forehead to hers to catch my breath.

"But," I paused, knowing this would set her back, "I need to fight now."

She tensed, and I pulled back so she could see my face.

"I need you to trust me on this."

"I do trust you, Trigger, but I'm with Gus. Something is not right here. Do you really think he's going to just fight and be done?"

"No, I don't. But I need to do this."

"Tell me," she blurted, and I knew exactly what she was referring to.

I held my arm next to hers, so her key lined up with my skeleton wrapped in chains. The angle allowed the key to fit the padlock.

"You free me."

Her lips parted as her fingers slowly drew over my arm.

"I can't believe I never made the connection."

I held her head in my hands. "Give me tonight, and I'll give you the rest."

I didn't wait for her answer before I peeled away and out the door. If she had said no, I didn't think I could fight.

"Ready?" Langley mouthed through the sea of people shouting behind the main doors.

I nodded but looked back to see Tess standing next to Gus. Both looked very unhappy. Gus leaned over and whispered something to her, and she nodded with her eyes on the ground.

When she looked over, I gave her a wink. Her eyes lit up, but I knew the trouble that still stormed inside her, and it wouldn't take a lot for it to brew to the surface.

I reached out to grab her hand and tugged her to my side once more.

"No," Langley shouted. "Your fans don't want to see her. They want you. Bad marketing move, Trigger."

"Don't care," I grunted and pushed the steel doors open. Cameras flashed from all directions, and fluorescent lights beat down on my shoulders. I felt my shoes squish on the rubber mat, and my hearing tuned in and out of the insane crowd ahead of me. Tess flexed her grip and stepped closer as I urged her forward down the ramp to the ring.

Eighty percent of the crowd were my old fans, and the rest were new. I recognized the black t-shirts my father had made up many years ago when I was at the top.

"Flip your switch" ran across the front in red letters, and "Trigger" was underneath.

The buildup started in the pit of my stomach. The warmth invaded my veins and sent a steroid shot to my system.

I was back.

I pointed to a chair and leaned in next to her ear. "Stay here."

She nodded and took the chair next to Brick, and he wrapped his arm around her for comfort.

She mouthed, "Good luck."

I locked eyes with her once more then broke away. I could feel the fear radiating off her. I was aware of my habit after a fight, that I'd disappear into another dimension, but now I knew I had a reason to come back.

I needed to get my head in this now, one hundred percent, before I stepped up the stairs.

Langley lifted the ropes, and I ducked under and did a turn for the crowd. I was never an attention seeker, nor was I now, but I felt they deserved a little attention considering it had been nearly two decades since I stepped foot in the ring.

The vibrations of the crowd traveled up the

length of my body, powering everything to the max. It was like when you started a carnival ride. The lights flickered on, and you could hear the beast of the engine start with a roar.

I have been awakened.

The announcer spoke, but only his mouth moved. I whirled around, waiting for the devil to show its ugly head.

It was time.

I saw Jace and Rail lean over and say something to Tess. She looked unsure but stood. I didn't have time to think as the crowd went crazy. The energy in the room swirled around like a wild dirt devil, and there he was. The man I feared as a boy, killed as a teenager, and hunted as an adult.

He stood just shy of a foot away from me. He wasn't as built, but he was lean. I never underestimated Allen and what he brought to the table, and I wasn't about to now.

"Son," he greeted me, and I felt the same rush of hate I got when I was younger. Instead of letting it fester into fear, I channeled it into fuel.

He made sure to glance over at the ropes like he always did, when he'd lean over them and wait like the reaper. He was referring to my tattoo. *Death is never far.*

The announcer, dressed in a flashy suit, stepped into the center of the ring, lifted his hand, and waited for the mic to lower from the ceiling.

"Ladies and gentlemen, welcome!" I was momentarily deafened by the roar of the thirsty crowd.

His mouth started to move again, but I had my

eyes on my father, who wore an evil smirk. If I concentrated, I could snap back to twenty years ago when he loomed over me with the same expression.

Suddenly, my father raised his hand and stepped over to the announcer. The man bowed and got out of the way.

"Damn, it's good to be back!" He egged on the crowd, and they went wild for this sideshow act. "Now, let's be honest, here." He did a spin, making sure to show his respect. "This," he waved between us, "isn't a fair fight. I'm sixty-three, and he's thirty-six. That's a twenty-seven-year difference." The crowd booed, but he held his hand up, and a cold feeling washed over me. "So, I thought to myself, who would be wild enough to go up against my son? The boy who killed his own father? Well," he patted himself down, "almost."

I looked around to connect the dots, but I didn't see anyone come in from his door, and no one was waiting around the ring.

"Son?" My father's voice snapped my attention back to him. His arms were stretched out, his hands raised like some kind of prophet.

Just when I thought I couldn't be any more betrayed, I saw my childhood anchor whip off his t-shirt and pants and his raise his fists to start.

"Why?" was all that came out.

"Money can make you do a lot of things, son." Langley shrugged and nodded at my father, who slipped between the ropes and whispered something to the announcer.

"Place your new bets now!" screamed over the mic.

I gave in to the dark hole that opened at my feet. I had been betrayed before, but this cut to the core. Langley was the only one I thought ever cared. He had tried to protect me from my father. What the fuck had changed?

"You gonna fight me or stand there?"

I vaguely noticed the bell ringing, and my arms shot up to block my face.

Langley moved in to throw a punch, but I leaned back, and it fell short. I counterpunched with my right. I moved toward him, but he expected that and threw a kick to my ribcage and followed through with a left. Fuck, he knew all my moves. He was the one who trained me.

I threw a left, a right, an uppercut, and Langley moved back out of the way to the corner. I grabbed him around the chest and held him, throwing my knee toward his stomach. Langley blocked my knee with his arms.

I had to come up with a move he wouldn't expect. I had to slow the fight down to think. I pushed off him and threw my elbow desperately into his face, cutting him above the right eye, then stepped back and turned with a three-hundred-sixty-degree roundhouse swing. Langley anticipated me by ducking and countered with another kick to my ribs, then threw a left, right, left, opening a cut above my eye. He followed that with a kick to my thigh, buckling my knee, and as I fell forward, he kneed me in the face, busting my nose. Blood streamed down my face. Shit, he was all over me. I fell into the ropes, and Langley stepped back, knowing if he grabbed me, I would be able to overpower him. So, he switched up and threw another kick to my thigh. I knew I had to get into the game fast. My head was ringing.

Langley threw a couple of left jabs, followed with a right that rocked me backward, and sent a kick to my ribs, but this time I grabbed his leg and knocked him off balance to the canvas. I jumped on him and threw a couple of punches. He grabbed me and pulled himself up close to my chest, so I couldn't get a swing at him. I dropped an elbow hard into his already bloody face.

Suddenly, I heard hands slamming against the canvas and Brick roaring, "Trigger, end this shit. They got Tess!"

"What the fuck?" Langley escaped from the hold when I lost my concentration to scan the crowd for Tess. Her seat was empty. Langley threw a kick at my face, spraying blood over the spectators.

Punch, punch, punch. I turned into a robot. Kick, kick, kick.

One of my punches hit air, and I shook my head, confused. The darkness faded into grays, and I saw Langley on the ground, unconscious.

The announcer raced over and checked his neck while I searched the ring's perimeter for my father.

He was gone, but what caught my eye was Zay. He was climbing the steps to go outside. What the fuck was he doing here?

I felt a stab to the gut and whirled as Brick's words hit me like a wall. Tess was gone. I vaguely heard the results. "Our victor! Trigger!"

CHAPTER TWENTY-ONE

Tess

Fifteen minutes earlier…

"Okay, okay!" Jace wiggled his way through the seats and repeated our order to himself.

"Don't fuck it up, prospect, or the next round is on you."

"Hysterical." He flipped Rail the finger, and I shifted at the nerves eating away at my core. Trigger was on the bench in a zone, while Langley yelled a bunch of things that couldn't be heard over the roaring crowd.

"Oh." Jace's hand landed on the back of my seat. His eyes closed, and he looked almost sick by the way he swayed on his feet.

"You good, Jace?"

"Yeah." He took a deep breath through his nose then started up the ramp we came down. The doorman glanced at his ID badge and let him out. The door swung wider as someone came in with a cart, and I saw Jace double over on the floor.

"Oh, my God!" I leaped from my seat and raced out the door before it closed. My knees hit the floor hard as I pushed someone out of the way.

"Jace!" I shook his shoulders. "You okay?"

His eyes fluttered open, and he looked at me strangely. "Oh," his hand landed on his head, "I feel like shit."

"Well, you look like it, so that would make sense," I joked, but I looked around for a place to prop him up. I scrambled to my feet and tried to help him up. I wasn't strong enough, and he fell back down.

"Shit, let me grab Brick."

"No." He grabbed my hand again and tried to rise, and just as his legs began to give out, someone caught him under the arms.

"Damn, dude, what'd you drink?"

"Nothing yet," I replied for Jace. "I think he may have eaten something."

Jace shook the man's hands off him and glanced around. "I just need the noise to stop." He grabbed my shoulders and sagged into me. "Help to the manager's office. He knows me. He'll let me crash for a second."

"Okay." I tried to smile at the man. "Thank you."

"Yup." He stepped away and shook his head like he was annoyed.

He's not drunk, dude.

I pushed the door open and found a room littered with trophies and medals, a rusty desk, no windows, a small door in the far wall with pictures framing it, and a leather couch. I nearly dropped Jace onto it and rolled my shoulder to relieve the muscle strain from his weight.

"Fuck, that's better." He rolled to his side and pulled his knees up to his chest. "What the hell was in that burrito?"

"If you insist on eating street meat, you get what you deserve."

"Stop parenting me."

I chuckled. "Stop acting like a child, and I wouldn't have to."

He rolled his head to look at me but didn't move his body. "This won't count for much later, but thank you."

"Why won't it count later?" That was a strange comment, but I couldn't focus on Jace anymore. The noise of the crowd told me the fight had started, and I needed to get back to the arena.

"I'm sorry, Tess."

"You're losing it, Jace." I stood and gave a little wave. "I'm going to grab Brick, okay?"

"Tess…"

Just as he said my name, I turned to find Zay standing in the doorway.

Huh? No!

I mentally kicked myself for believing the piece of shit in front of me knew my family. He was that prickle up my spine sometimes when I was out in public. He was the one who watched me from across the street or at the pier. How did I not remember his face? *Stay calm, Tess*.

"Jace, go get Trigger."

"I can't. I'm sorry." His tone made my heart drop into my stomach as it all clicked together.

"No, not you, Jace?" I wanted to cry. Not my friend, not the mole. Please, no.

"Now," Zay pulled on a pair of leather gloves, and I almost laughed out of pure fear, "we need to leave before they arrive."

"Who?" I jumped when Jace grabbed my arm, looking much better than before, and pulled me toward the door. I couldn't look at him, I was so hurt. I had been there for Jace after Ty was killed. We had formed a bond, and this was where it got me. "Don't fucking touch me!"

"She runs," Zay checked his gun clip, "shoot her."

"Shut up, Tess," Jace warned as I tried to wiggle out of his hold, but he latched on tighter and pushed me out the exit door to the outside. "Just do as they say."

Fucking cliché line, Jace.

"Help!" I screamed at the top of my lungs. "Someone help me!" Zay flipped around and slammed the butt of his gun into my stomach and knocked the wind right out of me. Before I could think, I was shoved into a limo, and as the door shut, I heard Gus's voice. I scrambled to my knees and tried the doors and windows.

"Take me too." He waved his arms. "Two for one. We are all he cares about, Zay. You know that. Why not hit him where it hurts most? Family."

Holy shit, what was he doing?

"Gus! No!" I hardly recognized my tone, it was laced with such terror. He wouldn't be able to

351

handle this.

A thick dose of panic rippled through me like an earthquake. What were they going to do?

"Just fucking grab him, man!" Jace screamed. He seemed amped up, unlike the Jace I knew and became friends with.

Zay put a radio up to his ear and looked all around. I went for the handle of the door when it clicked open, but Jace beat me to it. He shoved me back hard as he sat next to me.

"Don't make me hurt you, Tess, please." He covered his face and whispered, "Shit, this is so fucked up."

"Jace," I reached over, but he jumped at my touch, "please, please don't do this."

"You think I want this? You think I had a choice?" he nearly screamed. "I'm a goddamn prospect. I do as I'm fucking told."

"Wait." I tried to understand. "Trigger asked you to take me?"

"No!" He shook his head. "Him." He nodded, and for the third time in my life, I had the devil in my sights. Trigger's father.

Zay pointed his gun at Gus, and I snapped back to what was happening. I screamed and clawed at the window for him to stop. Not Gus, not someone as sweet and harmless as Gus. The boys popped into my head, and I wanted to cry and take his place. No kid should go through life without parents. They needed him. Shit, I needed him. He filled a void I hadn't even known I had.

"If that's her reaction, imagine Trigger's." Zay snickered. "Get in, old man." He grabbed Gus by the shirt and tossed him inside.

"Jesus Christ, be careful," I snapped at Zay. He tried to elbow me in the throat, but I ducked out of the way. He slammed the door, and I helped Gus to the seat and held his hand.

"You okay?"

"Yeah." He squinted and held his knee. "You?"

"Why would you make them take you? What about the boys?"

He rolled his head to face me. "I'm your only hope of getting through this." He lowered his voice. "And that ain't saying much."

He snapped his gaze over to Jace, who looked to have lost three shades of color. They exchanged some kind of look, almost an understanding that we were royally fucked.

My phone vibrated against my leg, and I shifted to pull it free.

Oh, my God!

Gus bumped my knee to get my attention and mouthed, "One, two, three."

"Savi!" I screamed in a desperate plea, and Jace's head whipped around in confusion. "Savi! Allen took us. Gus and I are in—"

Jace lunged for the phone, but Gus tossed his body weight at him.

"Tess! Where are you right now?"

"Vegas! Outside the fight. Trigger is still inside!"

"You stupid bitch!" Jace grabbed my leg and tried to pull himself upright. "Give me that!"

"Savi, you need to tell Trigger that Jace is the mole and—"

"Listen to me," she said to stop my mad chatter. "Where are they taking you? Did they say?"

Just as I was about to answer, Jace knocked the phone from my hands and scooped it up.

Gus huffed with his arm wrapped around his stomach and struggled to get back into the seat.

"You're fucking insane, Tess!" Jace quickly turned it off, but I noticed he didn't toss it away. He just tucked it in his pocket. "You're going to get me into trouble."

"Yes, and we wouldn't want that." My voice dripped with sarcasm as my heart dropped into my stomach again. Did I fuck everything up by showing I had my phone? Did I just lose our one lifeline? Gus was still holding his side. One eye opened, and I saw him peel back his fingers to show me he had his phone on, and it was on a map.

Sneaky old man.

Jace was staring out the window, and when he suddenly sat up straight, I knew things were about to get a whole lot worse.

He rolled down the window. "They're here."

Blue and red flashing lights filled the inside of the limo and flooded the main parking lot.

Zay waited as a blue car rolled up, and out stepped an officer I hadn't seen before. I squinted to read his patches. Why wasn't I surprised to find a Santa Monica cop here? A flashlight skimmed his name tag, and I caught the first few letters. DOY.

"Who's that?" I whispered to Gus, who looked like he'd seen a ghost. The engine started, and we peeled out of the driveway and onto the street. I turned to see the lights of the building slowly trickle away like so many fireflies.

Gus shook his head at Jace. "What the fuck did you guys do?"

***

Trigger

"Where is she?" I screamed over the crowd as people tried to grab at me from every direction.

I was wild and drunk for his kill. I needed to smell his blood, to watch as it drained from his body and circled my feet. I wanted to remove his eyes, teeth, and burn off his fingerprints so he didn't exist anymore. I wanted so much more, but he was gone, like so much fucking smoke and mirrors.

I tore myself away from the darkness, but it felt like I had left a layer of my skin behind.

Focus.

"Find him," I barked at Rail, who had fought his way over to me.

"On it." He ducked under the sea of people and disappeared.

I had my father inches from the reaper's grip. He was there in the flesh, ready to be taken out, but I lost my focus, once again trapped by betrayal. I yanked the door back and screamed with frustration.

"Where is she?" I boomed at Cray, and he put his hands up so I wouldn't hit him. I heard my men come up behind me, but nothing mattered.

"Hang on!" He tried to stop me, but I was five strides ahead. "Trigger, before you flip out, you need to hear this!"

I ignored him and tore open my door and saw the room was empty. I went on to the next, and the next, and every empty room elevated my anger.

"Nolan!" my mother squealed. "I saw what happened."

That stopped me.

"I saw them take—"

My hands snapped around her neck and pushed her into the wall. Brick appeared on one side of me and started to shout, but nothing made it through the demons' cries for more. They were savages and slowly taking over.

Cray and Cooper came up with their weapons drawn, ready to do what was necessary.

Her fingers clawed at my arms while her face turned bright red.

"Allen. He took...her."

My grip tightened as I fought to stay in the present, but Nolan was fading fast, and so was Tess.

No. This wasn't happening.

"His fucking assholes jumped me!" Rail held his broken nose and limped as he came into view. "I'm sorry, man. Allen's gone."

What the hell?

"You did this, didn't you? You played me! You know I love her, and you took her from me!"

If I couldn't kill my father, my mother was the next best thing.

"No." Tears streamed down her terrified face. "I don't even know her. But I can help you find her."

"Trigger!" The familiar voice cut through my rage, and a small body slammed into mine. I didn't move. I was stone, but I broke the hold on my mother, my fist still raised, about to pound.

"Listen to me!" Fin's face was bright red, and tears pooled around his cape Tess had helped him make to support the fight. So much terror was held in such a tiny face. "Stop fighting and find her!" He started to sob, and I broke. I scooped him up and buried my face in his neck. He shook as he sobbed and held onto me tight. I knew that fear. It was that of a boy who just lost his mother.

A feeling I knew and held onto for many years.

"I'm sorry," I whispered. "We'll get her back, I promise."

"Oh, my God." Brick covered his face as he turned around, looking about ready to puke. I reached out and grabbed his shoulder. Anchor to anchor.

"Where's Gus?" I barely heard Cray ask.

I glanced at Minnie and handed Fin to her. I started to scan the hallway. He was slower than the rest of us.

"Watch her." I jammed a finger at my mother but directed my words to Minnie. "She moves, shoot her."

"Yeah, okay." I noticed Brick as he tucked a gun into the waist of her pants, careful not to show Fin.

"Trigger?" Morgan nearly ran into me and turned his phone to face me.

Mike: Jace is your mole! Get Trigger to call me now!

What? That sucked the breath right out of me.
"Jace." He shook his head, the betrayal

357

deepening the creases around his eyes. "He took her. He's the goddamn mole!"

Motherfucker! I clenched my fist, and my muscles quivered with the need to kill something. I should have known. Jace and Tess became close quickly. He burrowed his way into her trust, only to rip it away.

He betrayed me—no, us—his fucking family that fed and housed him.

I am done.

My head tried to keep ahead of the demons. I wanted so much to give in and let them take over, so I could get through this without the terrible ache that held my body prisoner.

"Trigger!" Big Joe burst around the corner. His face was broken out in a sweat. "You need to see this."

"Joe, if this has something to do with Tess, you need to—" Brick couldn't finish the sentence, and I didn't want him to.

"No." Big Joe motioned for us to follow him. We raced down two hallways, through the lobby, and down another hall. He held open the door, and we rushed in and our boots were covered in…blood?

"Holy shit." Brick glanced around at the five twisted bodies. One's neck had been snapped, an ear looked like it had been ripped off another, and the smell of bleach almost took our breath away. "Who?"

"Stripe Backs." I pointed to the lime green eyes staring back at me as the rest of the guys joined us. Minnie covered Fin's eyes and hurried back out with my mother on her heels. "Trigger." Brick turned with a haunted look, and I nodded. It looked like one of my kills.

"Get Rich to call Sam," I quickly instructed Rail. I had a sinking feeling we'd need our lawyer. He went to pull out his phone but stopped when we felt someone come in.

"You mean your prospect?" One of the men who carried our bags in before the fight suddenly appeared next to Cooper. "Yeah, man, he left, like, ten minutes ago with that girl Trigger had on his arm."

What the fuck?

"With who?"

"Shit!" Big Joe jumped back, and a team of police held their weapons on me.

"Oh, my God!" My mother snagged my attention as she stared at her phone, not the police.

"Everyone freeze!" one cop shouted, clearly taken over by fear.

I raised my arms, ready to fight. The sound of their weapons filled the room as most of the guns pointed in my direction.

"Stop." My mother stepped forward, almost as if to shield me. "Let me say goodbye to my son."

I couldn't help but feel a strange ripple run through me at the word *son*. Before anyone could say anything, she wrapped her arms around me and whispered, "They have Gus. He has his tracker on." She slipped the phone into my hand. She stepped back and blocked the SWAT team's view of the phone. I watched as the little blue dot moved farther and farther away from me. I couldn't believe it.

"Nolan Vineyard, Matthew Montgomery, and…" Officer Doyle stepped into the room with a rag over his nose, and my blood went wild. He turned to Rail. "Silas Hunter, you're under arrest."

No.

Morgan sidestepped behind me and pulled the phone from my grip as Doyle went on.

"For the mass murder at the Final Temptations Strip Club in Santa Barbara four years ago, and," he paused, and I saw him smile behind the rag, "the murder of these five Stripe Backs."

My blood ran cold as I made the connection that I had indeed been played by one of my own. But it wasn't only Jace who'd betrayed me. I slowly shifted and locked eyes with my second mole.

Nolan disappeared into dust as the cold steel clamped down around my wrists.

The End

Too strong to run,
Too proud to hide.
For this I'll pay…
For this I'll die.

My soul is black,
The demons are worse.

Pain was spread,
Love has burst.
Won't move forward,
Can't go back.

The reaper is circling,
Can't fight back.
The world has gone black.

She is gone,
Time will pass.
Evil has spread,
Will we last?

DEVIL'S REACH, BOOK THREE

The yard was mainly hard-packed dirt. The few little sprigs of grass that tried desperately to survive were slowly being choked to death under the boots of hundreds of inmates. It seemed like random groups at first glance, but each cluster was in a specific spot divided by race.

I glanced at Rail as he rolled a cigarette like it was the fifties, and Brick was eyeing the Koreans who felt we didn't belong here.

A guard with shiny black boots stepped into the yard and walked the inside perimeter. He didn't carry a gun or a baton, and his unmarked hands were a dead giveaway that he wasn't a fighter. Once he completed his rounds, he eased down onto a bucket and started to drum a song. It was Otis Redding's "Sittin' on the Dock of the Bay". I noticed the leaders of each gang tuned into him and stopped what they were doing.

A dark chill filled the yard, the scruffy hair on the backs of the wild beasts inside me stood to attention, and started to hiss.

A big Hispanic man cast a shadow over my face

and cracked his knuckles like he was about to fight.

"Heard you take out some of my man." His English was broken, but I understood enough.

I nodded and blew a puff of smoke toward him.

He snapped his fingers, and the rest of his gang joined him.

"You die now."

Flip.

Acknowledgements

My mother and stepfather, thank you for stepping outside your comfort zones and providing me with endless feedback and support along the way. What would I do without you two?

My husband, who encourages me to write every day, knowing what it does for my soul.

To my beloved friends, Jaci Wheeler, Ariana McWilliams, and Thayra Rothweiler, thank you for listening to my many plot twists and murders.

My betas, Ariana McWilliams, Jaci Wheeler, Ceej Chargualaf, Kathy West, Tanyia Pfennighausen, Allison Cheshire, and Joe Rossi, thank you for taking time out of your busy days to read my chicken scratch and give me your take on it all.

To my editor Lori Whitwam, here's to book number ten. Cheers!

To Sgt. Steve Chamness and his lovely wife Jill Chamness for saving me on a few key points in this book. I greatly appreciate your time and hope to work with you again in the near future.

To Matt Neve, president of the Clueless motorcycle club for all your help with this story. Your kindness and time will not be forgotten.

To one of my all-time favorite bands, Radiohead, for allowing me to see scenes in a different way. Thank you for opening another door inside my head.

And a huge thank you to my readers, who inspired me and waited patiently while I dealt with a pretty emotional year, both physically and mentally. Your support means the world.

About the Author

J. L. Drake was born and raised in Nova Scotia, Canada, later moving to Southern California where she now lives with her husband and two children.

When she is not writing she loves to spend time with her family, travelling or just enjoying a night at home. One thing you might notice in her books is her love of the four seasons. Growing up on the east coast of Canada the change in the seasons is in her blood and is often mentioned in her writing.

An avid reader of James Patterson, J.L. Drake has often found herself inspired by his many stories of mystery and intrigue. She hopes you will enjoy her books as much as she has enjoyed writing them.

Facebook:
https://www.facebook.com/JLDrakeauthor

Twitter:
https://twitter.com/jodildrake_j

Website:
http://www.authorjldrake.com/

Goodreads:
http://www.goodreads.com/author/show/8300313.J
L_Drake